D1548572

HERO'S INSTINCT

CERBERUS TACTICAL K9 TEAM BRAVO

CERBERUS TACTICAL K9
BOOK 3

FIONA QUINN

HERO'S INSTINCT

Cerberus Tactical K9

Team Bravo
FIONA QUINN

THE WORLD OF INIQUUS

Ubicumque, Quoties. Quidquid

Iniquus - /i'ni/kwus/ our strength is unequalled, our tactics unfair – we stretch the law to its breaking point. We do whatever is necessary to bring the enemy down.

THE LYNX SERIES

Weakest Lynx

Missing Lynx

Chain Lynx

Cuff Lynx

Gulf Lynx

Hyper Lynx

STRIKE FORCE

In Too DEEP

JACK Be Quick

InstiGATOR

UNCOMMON ENEMIES

Wasp

Relic

Deadlock

Thorn

FBI JOINT TASK FORCE

Open Secret

Cold Red

Even Odds

KATE HAMILTON MYSTERIES

Mine

Yours

Ours

CERBERUS TACTICAL K9 TEAM ALPHA

Survival Instinct

Protective Instinct

Defender's Instinct

DELTA FORCE ECHO

Danger Signs

Danger Zone

Danger Close

CERBERUS TACTICAL K9 TEAM BRAVO

Warrior's Instinct

Rescue Instinct

Hero's Instinct

For an up-to-date list, please visit FionaQuinnBooks.com

If you prefer to read the Iniquus World in chronological order you will find a full list

at the end of this book.

The Players

CIA

McKayla Pickard — officer
Johnna White — handler
Misha Popyrin — unwitting asset (Pronounced: MEE-sha POP-y-rin)

Cerberus Tactical K9 Team Bravo

Asher (Ash) Gideon and Hoover
Ares and Judge
Mace and Diesel
Bear
Juan Ortega
Goose — veterinarian

Strike Force

Lexi (Lynx) Sobado
Commander Gavin (Striker) Rheas
Blaze
Jack
Gator
Deep
Dr. Jeffers — Iniquus doctor

McKayla's London-based Security Team

Rupert
John
Jeremy

HOW IT STARTED

August of LAST YEAR
Richmond, England

1

McKAYLA PICKARD

Last August, Chesterton House, Richmond, England

CLICKETY CLACKING across the marble hall in her hot pink stilettos, McKayla would choose combat boots any day of the year.

The ridiculousness of squeezing a woman's toes and having her balance on the balls of her feet for hours on end was sadistic. High heels, in McKayla's estimation, were merely a vehicle for torture and a means to keep a woman from successfully running away.

Or maybe a high heel's purpose was to weed out the complainers early on. If a woman couldn't handle the agony of toe cramps, they might not be willing to put up with her lover's crap for long.

Yeah, that mindset made sense to McKayla—a means to test a woman's capacity for stoicism in the face of pain.

She looked up at the grandeur of the sweeping, red-carpeted staircase that would take her to the ballroom in Chesterton House, an eighteenth-century stone mansion nestled along the Thames just outside of London.

A stunning show of affluence.

Even if it felt farcical that lil' ol' McKayla Anne Pickard, of Bentwood, PA, was here with her name hand calligraphed on the invitation in her purse, this was indeed the twisted turn that her life had taken.

She could do this.

Penance, that was how McKayla viewed her new career with the CIA.

Lifting her chin, McKayla moved elegantly up the stairs as her etiquette coach, Mrs. Peabody-Strumpkins, had taught her to do. Face soft, lips lightly bowed into a gentle inviting smile, eyes warm, McKayla gathered her skirt near her thigh.

The hand sweeps back and tucks just to the side of one's bottom, so the fabric doesn't tangle the feet, and... Up we go.

Picture perfect, she made the ascent.

While Langley had offered McKayla an escort for the evening, she thought that would be too clunky. McKayla wanted to go where she wanted to go, move where she wanted to move, and not be tied to anyone or any baggage they might drag along.

Simple and clean.

No sidekick for this superhero.

McKayla tipped her head down as a smile curled her lips and a puff of laughter escaped.

Though, it wasn't a completely absurd thought.

When McKayla had approached the CIA, in her mind's

eye, this kind of assignment was exactly what she'd envisioned. Sort of like turning herself into a modern-day female Bruce Wayne.

McKayla grimaced at that image.

It wasn't the right metaphor. But McKayla couldn't find a better one. She would be using her name, notoriety, and financial status to give her cred and entrée into elite spaces that Langley would have difficulty maneuvering into.

She was a key that could unlock the doors to royals, political leaders, and financial supernovas.

Yes, this evening's charity dinner with the nobility and the glitterati was *exactly* the type of assignment McKayla had envisioned when she'd approached the CIA and asked for a job.

It was the best way McKayla could figure to both help her country and scrub some of the scum off her karma.

McKayla rounded into the perfumed garden of bejeweled women and the knots of tuxedoed, highball-clenching men.

Her internal monologue announced McKayla: Arriving on the red carpet, we have our rags-to-riches Cinderella making the magical transformation sans Prince Charming. Financial world crypto disruptor. The world's newest *female* billionaire. While everyone else relaxed back to enjoy the music of the soon-to-be-drowned orchestra, this is the lady who slipped onto a water jet and peeled away from the Titanic just shy of the iceberg. Yes! Ladies and gentlemen, I present McKayla Pickard!

Ooo! Ahhh!

Now that she was here and could see the setup, she needed a good tactic.

Her mark?

Misha Popyrin, a Russian oligarch's son.

Misha was a means to an end. No one thought Misha did anything wrong.

He just went to the parties and hung out with the people that might give a better picture of what was up on the world stage.

Really what the CIA needed was to keep a finger on the pulse.

That was, after all, the CIA's mandate. They had nothing to do with investigating crimes. That was the FBI, among other alphabets.

Nope, the CIA was mainly about schmooze and gossip.

Whom do you know?

What do *they* know?

The job was keeping an eye on everything and reporting in.

That cloak and dagger crap? Yeah, mainly for TV.

Not to say that the CIA didn't do dangerous things. Of course, they did.

Just not her.

Not for today, anyway.

Standing in the shadows, McKayla rested her hands on the boning that compacted her ribs and tried to take a deep breath. She was used to belly breathing on a tactical cadence. No wonder the highbrow crowd had a bunch of females who just stood around like store mannequins. The poor women didn't have enough oxygen in their systems to do anything else.

Here we go! Game face.

Stress—she'd learned back in her Army days—got picked up by people's danger antennae. Out on assignment in Afghanistan, the women she was supposed to interrogate would shy from conversations and slip from the rooms when McKayla felt tense.

Release it. Loosen up.

There really didn't seem to be much to tonight's gig. The goal was a handshake, and that was it. "Easy day," she muttered under her breath.

McKayla had figured that bumping into Misha and trying to involve him in a random conversation would seem odd.

The French-styled nine-course meal, McKayla figured, would be her best opportunity to make an impression.

When the gong sounded to assemble the guests in the dining hall, there wasn't going to be a run on the best seats to join in the "it" crowd of one's choosing.

No, oh no, this had been plotted in advance.

The criterion was known only to the curators of discourse, or whatever their title was.

This was what Mrs. Peabody-Strumpkins explained about seating arrangements: Apparently formal events no longer did things old school. There were no more tables with seating cards lined in alphabetical order standing outside of the dining hall. Mrs. Peabody-Strumpkins described how the usher at the door would check for McKayla's name on their tablet and escort her to the correct seat.

And the CIA had no way to affect McKayla's seating placement at this event.

McKayla was on her own to get the job done. She headed to the dining hall.

"Excuse me," she said with a pleasant smile. "I'm looking for the head usher, please."

"Is there a problem, madam?" A server in an immaculate uniform looked ready to jump forward and fulfill any task.

"I just wanted to check on my seating assignment. As there is no air conditioning, and the windows are open... allergies." She offered a little shrug.

"Of course, madam, if you'll wait but a moment," he said without a return of McKayla's smile. She wondered if they all went to stick-up-the-rump school or if it was the consequence of too many baked beans from their "full-English" breakfasts that made them clench that way.

McKayla turned to stare into the immense bosom of some long-ago regal ancestor. Pretending to appreciate the composition of the neo-classical styled painting, McKayla pulled out and counted ten fifty-pound notes, then folded them neatly, positioning them between her thumb and the back of her handbag.

"Madam?"

McKayla spun toward the voice.

A thin man dressed in tails, like a penguin, stood with his chest puffed out and his chin tucked in. "I understand there is a concern."

This guy was greasy in a way that McKayla had not expected. She saw the glint in his eye and thought that she was not the first person to slip into the shadow and ask a small favor. "I would like to check on my dinner seating assignment," McKayla said, stepping back behind a column.

The head usher followed along. "Your name, madam?"

"McKayla Pickard."

Ah, that name meant something to him. Yes, well she had been in all the papers. Just not as a blonde.

"And you have a concern about the windows is my understanding?"

"Yes, I have terrible allergies. And I'm afraid that the only place I can find relief is if I were to sit, for example, at the same table as Irene Bellini."

Their gazes met and held.

"Is Irene on your list?" McKayla flipped her hand over to expose the wad of cash.

The move dropped the usher's gaze. He seemed to be mentally calculating how much she might have there.

It hadn't been McKayla's intention to have an entire wad, but it seemed that England's largest bank note was a fifty. McKayla dropped her hand to her side.

"I see." The head usher scrolled. "I don't seem to have that name on my list."

Of course, he didn't. McKayla had made up the name out of thin air. But she thought going right for Misha would be a mistake. That information sent into the wrong ear could out her.

"Mmm, well she was coming with Misha. Let's see, that would be…" McKayla pretended to search her memory. "I believe it's Popyrin Mikhail Victorovich. He's Russian." She shrugged. "That would be the way he'd formally write it." She made a grimace that said, sorry, I'm trying. "No idea. Maybe he doesn't do that here in London.

He might have changed it to the western style? Mikhail Popyrin? Irene just calls him Misha. It could be on your list like that, too."

This was the first mission where McKayla had no anonymity.

In the Army she'd been called "Dealer." In boot, her fellow recruits thought they were being clever with her last name. Pickard became Pick-a-card, which then became "Dealer."

Trying to get them to change her call sign, she told them that it was a magician that said, "pick a card." But it was too late. Until she left the Army, she was only some-times called Captain Pickard. She was mostly just "Hey, Dealer!"

It sounded like she sold drugs on the side. Maybe it headed a sniffer dog toward her locker and made her pee tests more frequent than for the others. She'd always seen that name as hazing, but there had been nothing she could do about it.

With your Army name, you kind of got what you got and dealt with it.

Dealt with it, Dealer? Ah, I see what you did there.

McKayla's inner dialogue was interrupted when the usher said, "Popyrin Mikhail Victorovich is seated at Table Five along with his plus one."

"Irene." McKayla smiled with satisfaction. In truth, McKayla was thrilled that there wasn't a woman's name, and it was a plus one. It made this a smoother transaction. "Is there a way that I could address my allergies without creating a disturbance?"

"Yes, of course, madam. It will be my honor to help

you remain comfortable this evening. Your name card shall be placed on Table Five. I am updating the seating arrangements in my system." He tapped silently for a moment, then looked up to catch her gaze. He turned the tablet to show her that she would be seated across the rectangular table from "Popyrin guest."

McKayla slid the wad under the tablet and into the usher's hand.

"I will go and move your place card now. If there is anything else you would need this evening, madame," he offered a slight bow, "please do not hesitate to elicit my aid."

At the ridiculousness of that bow, McKayla wanted to offer a sarcastic curtsy. Her foot moved into place just the way Mrs. Peabody-Strumpkins had taught her, lest McKayla somehow come within the environs of the king. McKayla caught herself just in time. And offered a smile and a, "You are most kind, thank you."

And so, her first spy effort was a success. Could she keep that going?

2

McKayla Pickard

Last August, Chesterton House, Richmond, England

As it turned out, the Misha-plus-one chick's name was Simona Fiorini, an haute couture model who, in her heels and poofed hair, towered over Misha.

The whole table was a suck-joy. Nobody spoke throughout dinner.

Misha never looked directly at McKayla—or anyone else for that matter. He seemed to have developed a way of looking around with enough vacancy in his gaze that everyone knew he was physically there, but mentally he was off somewhere else. And from the curl of derision on his lips, McKayla would surmise he wasn't planning his next vacation.

She'd read his file, and he sounded kind of useless as far as her needs went.

Work. Home. Charitable events. There wasn't even

rhyme or reason to what charities Misha supported. It all seemed random and half-hearted.

Unless, of course, they weren't random at all, and Misha was showing up to whisper the right thing into the necessary ear.

Whether it was Misha or someone in his social circle who had an interesting snippet of information, McKayla needed to develop the kind of intimacy that would open the doors to those rooms and where she could become privy to the secret whispers.

McKayla wanted to become the proverbial fly on the wall. One that no one would notice. And hopefully, not the kind of fly that brought a swatter into play.

Access was gold.

The *only* kind of gold McKayla needed.

But since Misha had, evidently, decided to pretend to be a ghost, McKayla was left to contemplate the Amazonian flower who had graced Misha's arm this evening.

Simona was in a mood.

She pushed her *hors d'oeuvres* around her plate.

She merely skimmed her spoon through the soup at the first course.

McKayla, on the other hand, had to stop herself from lifting the plates and licking them clean. She was famished, and the serving sizes had been Lilliputian. McKayla would have pre-fed herself except there was no room in her bodice for such things.

After watching the fish come and go without Simona taking a single bite, then the sorbet, and now the same with the main course, McKayla was fairly sure that Simona's anger was caused by hypoglycemia.

Or it could be the woman, sitting two seats down from McKayla, who expressed condescension and animosity.

From the way they kept flinging darts at each other with their eyes, they knew each other from before tonight.

"Monique" was the only name on that woman's place card McKayla could see from her position.

Monique, like Simona, was a silent stew of vitriol.

Was theirs a rivalry about work? Competition for Misha's affections?

After all, he wasn't a half-bad-looking guy. And his millions could make up nicely for what he lacked. Possibly the only drawback would be the threat of brewed plutonium being served with their biscuits at high tea, or of being in the way should Misha trip and fall out of a fourth-story window, which seemed to be a fairly common hazard for Russian nationals in the past few years.

Suddenly, Simona pushed her chair back as she slapped her napkin down onto the table like it was a gloved invitation to a duel—a no-no according to Mrs. Peabody-Strumpkins.

As she rose, Simona glared at Monique.

Misha must be used to tantrums, McKayla surmised, when he showed no curiosity at all about the anger that swirled with the fabric of his date's ball gown. He didn't even turn to watch as Simona stormed out of the room.

After Monique rose and followed, McKayla thought that—since she wasn't getting any conversation and friendship-building out of her five-hundred-pound bribe—at least this might be a bit of entertainment.

And of course, it might be that McKayla could gather some piece of intelligence to better approach Misha.

Entering an echoing corridor lined with busts resting on carved marble pedestals and 18th-century canvases of tables laden with rustic foods, McKayla glanced around. She had assumed the women would head to the privacy of the ladies' room to work through their issues.

McKayla stood there confused. The women were nowhere to be seen.

Secret passage? Wouldn't that be fun!

Catching the eye of the usher, whom she'd bribed earlier, McKayla canted her head.

He held up two fingers and a questioning brow.

When McKayla gave a subtle nod, he pointed toward a set of stairs that led back outside and far away from the dining hall.

With her skirts hitched up in the front, in a way that would make Mrs. Peabody-Strumpkins recoil in horror, McKayla did her best to hustle jog in the stilettos down to the stairs.

She slowed as she approached the exit, dropping her skirts and patting them into place. If the women were hissing at each other on the other side of this door, no need to look like McKayla was chasing them down instead of just needing a breath of fresh air.

McKayla's adjustments allowed the doorman time to bow and pull the door wide.

It had to be fifteen feet tall and made of four inches of solid wood. McKayla wasn't sure she could have mastered it on her own with so much dress fabric to contend with.

Outside, McKayla stopped on a dime.

The women were standing on the porch, almost as McKayla had imagined, spit yelling in French with very emphatic arm gestures.

McKayla reached for her phone. Her French was pretty much basic conversation and food ordering. What the two women were engaged in seemed to be punctuated with a lot of curse-sounding words that McKayla hadn't learned, yet.

Hovering in the shadow, McKayla tapped "record" on her phone just as Simona's hand reached up and grabbed Monique's face, pushing the poor woman into a backbend.

Monique, being shorter by about four inches, was teetering on the edge of the porch, windmilling her arms, trying to catch her balance.

With the grass below only about two feet away, McKayla wasn't sure Monique would be able to stand back up. Monque's dress was tight enough that McKayla thought she'd probably end up lying there like a turtle balanced on its shell.

Desperately trying to stay upright, Monique swung her arms upward, sinking her claws into Simona's hair as a handle, trying to stay upright and on the porch.

Simona staggered forward, and of course, that did it. Both women went over.

McKayla was horror fascinated. This was nothing like what Mrs. Peabody-Strumpkins had described to her about tonight's soirée.

When McKayla watched women fighting—heck, when she had been in fights herself—it was either about training or the stakes were life and death.

McKayla had never seen a catfight before.

Running forward to capture the video and to record what the rivals were screaming at each other, McKayla hoped it was juicy gossip that the agency could use somehow.

The linguists at Langley could translate.

It was crazy as all get out what they were doing.

Clearly, Monique was at a severe disadvantage. Wrapped up in that sausage casing of a dress of hers—that McKayla had predicted would be a problem—she was flopping like a fish trying to get herself onto her stomach.

Bad move, girlfriend! *Never* get on your stomach in a fight. Use your abs. Scoop like an ice cream and roll up—but of course, Monique couldn't hear McKayla silently offering advice.

She had no idea what Simona was doing gathering her skirt up like she had to squat and pee. Her heels had sunk deep into the garden soil making her look like she was wearing flats.

McKayla's inner announcer was calling this like it was a prize fight:

And Monique is showing off her years of yoga practice, pushing her weight into her hands. Piking her hips, Monique is now using her arm strength to walk her body into a downward facing dog posture, leaving her wildly open to further attack.

Is this a bluff? Will Simona fall for it? Or will Monique navigate herself to standing and come face to face with Simona once more?

Oooof.

It's bad news for Monique. Salmonella—no sorry. Simona...Simona finally got her legs free from her miles of tulle and has pulled one foot out of her stiletto. She push-kicked Monique square on the rump.

Monique has come out of her shoes as she flies forward.

Faceplant!

We'll have to check with the judges, but that looked like a "ten" to me.

Yes, ladies and gentlemen, that was a rip that you heard, and the sausage is freed of its casing.

Just in time, Monique is flipping onto her back. She curls up, protecting her vital organs as Simona is launching herself on top.

Oooo! Wow. That last-second hike of Monique's knee hit squarely into Simona's stomach. Simona is hunkered over Monique, retching. Lucky for Monique, Simona probably hasn't eaten anything this year, so no spew should come out.

At this point, the fight degenerated into flailing dress parts, slaps, and hissing shit-talk.

Oh, if she wasn't here for the CIA, how McKayla would love to post this to social media to read the comments from her Army buddies.

Face's obscured, of course. McKayla wasn't a bitch.

But she was crouched, pressing her knees together to keep herself from pee-laughing.

Surely, this wasn't how the women at these events conducted themselves or when Monique and Simona huffed from the hall, all the men would have given chase to watch and lay bets like it was a cock fight. Hen fight...

Oh man, McKayla grimaced, that was a strip of hair extensions that went flying. And from Simona's howl, that must have been excruciating as Monique tore it from Simona's head.

Now, the extensions lay in a tangled snarl to the side looking like a dead squirrel.

McKayla checked to make sure her phone was recording.

Yup. All was good. Up here, it was anyway.

Down there in the mulch, not so much.

Two red-coated men rushed out of the door, jumped into the flower bed, and pulled the women apart.

Yeah, that last Monique screech was high-pitched and kinda hard to ignore.

Both women lay flat on their backs on the grass, gasping for air.

It looked like they'd just completed the throes of passion. Time for a cigarette.

Holy shit!

The ushers were asking both women for their driver's phone numbers so they could come around and collect them away from the dinner guests' curious eyes.

McKayla quietly slid back into the hall. Maneuvering through that massive door hadn't been a problem after all.

Once McKayla had forwarded the video to her handler, McKayla slipped the phone into her purse and headed on to find the ladies' room.

Welp, McKayla thought with a smile, looked like Misha was single this evening.

Could McKayla exploit that?

3

McKayla Pickard
Last August, Chesterton House, Richmond, England

McKayla had *not* been prepared for the bathroom attendant to go into the handicap-sized stall with her to assist with the volume of her dress when McKayla went to relieve herself.

It was like pictures McKayla had seen of maids of honor holding up the bride's skirts—which seemed okay for a bestie.

Less so for a stranger.

When in Rome…

The woman actually did the flushing, then brushed McKayla's voluminous bell skirt, fluffing the hem until it laid just so.

There were, apparently, jobs much worse than McKayla's.

When McKayla signed her CIA contract, she had

trusted that, out in the field, she'd be handed assignments she could sink her teeth into. Something dangerous and exciting. Something that required skill and cunning and maybe a bit of *sangfroid* to go along with actual cold-bloodedness.

McKayla rolled her eyes at that thought.

She wasn't a killer. Ten years in the Army, playing in foreign lands with the special ops boys—through gun fights, explosions, and mayhem—she'd never even come close to killing someone.

Though, when McKayla left the service, she had a uniform covered in chest candy that told anyone who knew what the ribbons and medals meant that she'd done some badassery in her time overseas.

Even so, maybe she'd failed to impress her superiors.

Maybe that was why Langley thought her skills lined up with *this* assignment.

Overwatch on a catfight?

Hmph.

McKayla checked her appearance in the mirror as she washed her hands. Her long blonde hair in its fancy updo remained sleek. The makeup looked airbrushed and flaw-less thanks to her stylist.

McKayla dried her hands, then curled her fingers into the embroidered cobalt satin and heaved her strapless bodice up into place, jostling the fabric to make sure her boobs weren't lost in the shuffle. *Come on girls, I'm depending on you to do your job, front and center, standing at attention.*

McKayla left a tip in the basket before she maneuvered herself through the door.

Back to the Misha trenches.

The blisters along her bunions felt like they were starting to bleed.

This gig was so antithetical to McKayla's comfort zone. And it was a very far cry from the kind of mission she'd valued in her stint as a captain in the Army, working on the cultural support team with the special forces community.

But even McKayla would agree that with her level of international fame (or infamy, depending on who was weighing in), it would be a stretch for Langley to let her parachute out of a heli on the Syrian border.

There were no go-backs.

Nope. Not after she'd disrupted shit.

This evening's reparations to the free world were fashioned from the boning in her corset. And the pinch of her fuchsia pink, feet-destroying, pizza-wedge stilettos.

In the dining hall, an usher trailed behind McKayla to her place across from the gap where Simona would not return. He pulled out her chair, gently pressing it against the back of McKayla's knees as she took her seat.

She arranged her skirts and drew her napkin across her lap.

The sweets course had arrived.

Mrs. Peabody-Strumpkins said "sweets" was a synonym for dessert. Tonight, they were having a chocolate cake of some kind. And they still had the fruit and cheese course to go on this nine-course event.

McKayla now understood the tiny portions.

Without Simona at the table next to him, Misha was less vacant and more willing to communicate. Though, the only person Misha addressed was the man sitting across from him.

McKayla wondered who the heck he was. Long friendship if not kin, she would guess from the way they let subjects drop mid-sentence.

She considered trying to get a surreptitious photo—since he was sitting directly to her left—but thought better of it. She'd try to get one later.

Both men tapped impatient fingers on the white linen. Their gazes roamed the room, never finding anything of interest on which to perch.

Not once did Misha or his buddy even turn their head so McKayla could catch an eye and introduce herself. She wouldn't be memorable unless she spilled her wine or choked on a piece of ice.

McKayla considered both.

But now she'd missed that chance. Dinner was done.

There was a general bustle as people rose to leave the hall and wander in the garden until they were called to this evening's auction.

Shadowing Misha, McKayla hoped for an opportunity to bump into him, literally if necessary.

Mmm, she'd see if something else popped into her head.

She'd hate to report back to her handler that she'd not even introduced herself.

And she wasn't excited about a future fishing expedition in another pair of stiletto heels.

Mission fail wasn't on her dance card tonight.

Out on the lawn, Misha's buddy—the one who had sat to McKayla's left at dinner—dragged two cigars from his breast pocket and offered one to Misha. After the lighting ceremony, the buddy pointed to a bench near the topiary out where they wouldn't be heard.

Oh-ho-ho, what are you two chatting about?

McKayla walked along the patio to the far stairs where she stepped out onto the lawn. There, her heels instantly sank. Bending, she yanked her shoes off to feel the sweet relief of the cool nighttime grass massaging her feet.

She hustled forward until she was parallel to the bush, then headed straight in to sit on the bench on the opposite side. *"Who me? Eavesdrop? Why no, I simply was hiding over here so I could get some foot relief."* Yes, if caught, that was what she'd say.

"—is a bitch. Did you pay her to be here?" That was the buddy.

"No." There was a long pause where McKayla imagined Misha was inhaling from his cigar. "We thought we might try dating. I think everyone can agree that's not going to work out."

"Her complaint?" The two spoke in polished Russian. This made their accents easier for McKayla to understand.

"Normal," Misha said. "She didn't like that I can't get my cock hard."

"You explained your medical history? Your medication?"

"Of course not."

The man snort-laughed. "You blamed it on her, didn't you? I can see a beautiful woman like that being horrified that she couldn't get a rise out of you, so she'd stick around and try and try."

"I told her it was okay, that I enjoyed her personality." There was a smile in his tone.

"What did she do?"

"She slapped me." It was an off-hand comment, like he got slapped a lot, and so did his buddy.

"Tonight, this happened? That's why she was so sour?" Misha must have made some gesture.

"I'm sorry for all of this," Buddy's tone suddenly changed. McKayla had to strain as he dropped his voice. "And I'm going to add salt to your wound. Your reputation is in a dangerous place."

"Oh?"

"These women, they talk behind your back. It travels around the circles. Your claiming headaches and never bedding the women, no matter how beautiful, it hurts their egos as with the woman tonight."

"And so, they're saying…"

"That you are a closet homosexual. While this is a non-issue for the people of western-Europe, it is deadly serious in Russia. The women are saying that you escort them out, making them an unwitting conspirator to your subterfuge."

There was a long pause in which McKayla could imagine Misha painting a hand down his face.

Was it true? There was nothing about that in his file…

McKayla had had no interest in seducing the man, but this opened up possibilities that didn't exist before. Her mind raced forward, creating a strategy.

"The headaches are often real. And Ivan, you know it's my medication that makes it impossible for me to get hard. This is something that I can easily prove should someone confront me."

"There are no alternatives? No other choices?"

"Yes, of course, but not good ones. The doctor says it would be dangerous for me to orgasm. I'm not willing to risk another heart attack on humping. It's just not that desperate a need for me."

"I understand. But you will need to find a way to manage this. No one would confront you, allowing you the opportunity to offer the name of your pills or your diagnosis. You don't wish to inform your father?"

"No, for many reasons."

"But if Moscow believes you to be gay—I will warn you, this is a dangerous game. Powers would much prefer you have an accident than that they condone or even *seem* to condone buggery."

Again, Misha answered with silence.

"Look, I'm anxious to be sitting with you this long. I don't want to be caught up in this. I don't need anyone's speculation extending to me. Think on it. Find a solution. I would be very sad to have to distance myself from you. You have been my family here in London."

A few moments later, McKayla watched the buddy—"Ivan" Misha had called him—climb the stairs to the porch and wander toward the bar.

McKayla stood and walked around the topiary to sit on the bench next to Misha.

He stared down his nose at her. "I know you," he said in an interesting accent that was a stew of British English and Russian.

"Do you?"

"I don't know you. I know *of* you, McKayla Pickard."

She sighed. "Okay, I know this conversation all too

well. Let me skip to the chase. No, I'm not a crypto pirate. I didn't know in advance of the crash. I'm not a rat with a sixth sense jumping ship."

"Then why did you cash in?"

McKayla pulled in as much air as her bodice would allow as she looked out over the lawn. "I had a long conversation with the FBI."

"They suggested you were breaking a law?"

"Not at all, they were bringing something to my attention is all. While I thought I was giving power to disadvantaged communities, in actuality I was giving power to very bad people."

"Yes, well, when you deal in money at the rate that you or I would. You, in particular, as I am merely the recipient of my family's generosity," he put his hand on his chest and gave a deprecating bow, "this would be the expectation."

He had his charm. And also had a lot to drink. It didn't seem like too much, though. He'd probably remember this conversation tomorrow.

"Misha Popyrin." He held out his hand.

McKayla placed hers in his for a shake, but he turned her hand and bowed to kiss it.

"I sat across from you all night." McKayla pulled her hand back. "Simona, if you don't mind my asking, does she ever eat?"

"She's up for a big contract, and she's concerned that she might gain a gram. That and the woman who is also up for the contract was sitting across the table."

"Monique."

"Yes." He tipped his head. "They didn't return to dinner."

"They got in a bit of a scrum behind the boxwoods. I think they both needed to visit their hairstylists to replace their hair extensions and repair some broken nails."

"That violent?"

"Body blows. Nothing to any place that would show bruising. Their makeup was still immaculate." She tipped her chin up and pursed her lips for a beat. "I'm just going to cut to the chase here," McKayla said. "You have a problem, and I'm your solution." *Just go in guns a blazing, why don't you, McKayla?* When she was with the special forces teams, it was hesitate and die. This wasn't the time for nuance and finger-crossing. She felt like Misha would trust someone who didn't play games.

Misha's gaze slid down her outfit and rested on her bare feet.

"My feet are killing me. I hate high heels."

Misha's face softened as some of the stress dropped away.

"I'm glad you're sitting here alone, though."

Misha canted his head. "Oh?"

"I'm not going to be coy." She made her body and tone as relaxed and non-confrontational as she could. She'd decided to take the bull by the horns, this might well be her one and only shot at roping Misha Popyrin. "I overheard your conversation just now."

Misha's whole body became rigid. Eyes unblinking. He took the blow then melted his reaction so that he too looked relaxed. "Oh?"

4

McKayla Pickard

Last August, Chesterton House, Richmond, England

"You speak my mother tongue?" Misha asked in Russian.

McKayla responded with a fairly convincing Muscovite accent, "I know a bunch of languages."

He switched to English. "Russian? That's improbable. Americans usually learn French or Spanish in school."

"I speak Farsi, too. A bit of French. Well, enough that I know not to order the escargot." She smiled.

He stretched his legs out in front of him, crossed his ankles, and puffed at his cigar. "Odd languages for a female."

"Aren't they? Yeah. I had to learn them in my first real job."

"Oh?"

"Before I was an entrepreneur," she qualified.

"Disruptor, you mean."

McKayla raised a single brow. "That sounds pejorative, don't you think?"

"I don't know," he said. "Possibly, you're right. What was this first job?"

"U.S. Army."

Their gazes caught and held.

"This conversation will be a no from me, thank you." He waggled his fingers in the air. "Hobble along. And let me enjoy my cigar in peace."

She sent him an "I've got a juicy secret" smile. "Don't you want to know what I did?"

"I have no interest." He turned his head to focus on a group that was gathering just out of listening range on the porch.

"I felt women up." McKayla laughed.

Misha turned back to her with an odd look of confusion and humor on his face. "That's a job in your army?"

"It is. In certain countries, a man can't search a woman. I got that joy."

"Like a TSA agent in the United States?" He paused before his cigar made it between his lips.

"Very similar, only without the state-of-the-art body scanners. My chances of blowing myself up were exponentially higher."

He pulled his chin back as he assessed her. "That took bravery."

"I signed on the dotted line." McKayla shrugged. "You do what your dad tells you to do, right? I did what Uncle Sam told me to. Would I have preferred ordering shoelaces as a job? No. Did I love going outside the wire?" She paused. "Also, no."

"Okay." He clenched the cigar between his teeth.

"Okay, what?"

"We can continue our talk. Why did you join the army? Armies are men's business."

McKayla enjoyed the rich spicy scent of Misha's cigar smoke. "I guess what I like is to see new things. I would have been a pioneer, heading out into the wilds to see things that I had never seen before. In the future, I'd be one of the first to colonize outer space."

"Outside of the army, have you done anything like that?"

"Like what?" She lifted up to smooth her skirt underneath her, repositioning on the garden bench.

"Climbed Everest, for example?"

McKayla folded her hands gracefully *à la* Mrs. Peabody-Strumpkins. "Everest is a known. It's on too many people's bucket lists, almost a cliché." She offered a Mona Lisa smile. "And I don't like the cold. I'm looking for the new."

"Becoming an industry crypto disruptor seems exotic," Misha said. "Few people understand how that works. Are you going to do it again? Is this an investment pitch?"

"No." She shook her head. "I have some ideas that I'm sure would work. But I've done that. Boring."

"What's next on your list, then? World domination?" He swirled his cigar through the air as he spoke.

He sounded genuinely curious. Would he take her bait? Even if she didn't get any further than a polite conversation, that would be progress.

McKayla laughed, warming to the banter. "Now, what would I possibly do with the entire world? Then, for sure, I'd have bored out of my mind." She held her feet out in front of her, then dropped them back to the ground. "Next? I would like to expand my imagination and that leads to my conversation with you."

"Listening."

McKayla leaned in, closing the distance between them, and lowering her voice. "You have family ties and a lot of money."

"You, too, have a lot of money."

"More than I can spend in a lifetime. What I don't have are your connections."

"To do what exactly?" He leaned away from her, wrapping his arms over his chest.

McKayla looked across the lawn to give him some psychological space. "Oh, to go places and see things that aren't written about. The things that are hidden away when the journalists for glossy magazines pull up in the drive to take the pictures." She turned to catch Misha's gaze and popped her brows. "The forbidden."

"Sounds criminally minded."

"I'm going to admit to you that I considered that." She smiled conspiratorially. "Becoming the great cat burglar that defies logic and physics to get to the most guarded items in the world sounds like a good challenge."

"But?"

"There's the thought of prison. Confined would be my death."

"I see," Misha took a long drag on the cigar and sent out a luxurious exhale of smoke rings. "And you think, somehow, I could or would take you to these secret places?"

"Yes." She smiled; her whole body radiated excitement.

Misha's eyes brightened with laughter. "You're like a child that I just told we are going to the circus."

"Exploitation of animals, no thanks. Going to meet the king, perhaps."

"I don't know him. Your expectations of me are too high."

"Maybe not the king. But I've seen you in pictures with certain princes and other royal types. And I've seen you in pictures of private islands that are spoken of and described but visited only with permission."

"Ha! Well, yes, in my younger days."

"Days before your diagnosis and medication regime, I assume."

"You do seem to understand Russian very well. Please, that is not something to be discussed, especially in such a public place."

"Look, Misha, my mom was a mail clerk, and my dad was a line cook. I hit on an idea that made me a quick fortune, sure. Rich." She offered up jazz hands. "But I sold my company. Money isn't prestige. Money doesn't make me interesting. I have no familial ties to power. Sure, I can go to the far reaches of the world, eat the finest foods, and see the tourist sights. But isn't that boring? What I'm interested in is what's *not* available to me. The forbidden fruit, if you will."

He rubbed his chin. "You wish to go with me to the private world of the rich and famous. And in return?"

"You would be relieved of innuendo and speculation."

"I'm beginning to see the picture. Is this a fair exchange?" Misha asked.

"I have no idea. I guess that's something for you to decide." McKayla brushed her hand through the air to indicate the other partygoers. "You see how the men here surround themselves with flitting butterfly women? One woman is interchangeable with the next. Few, very few here look—even if married—like they are in a loving, lasting relationship."

"They're in—"

"A show."

"I see." He hadn't followed her gesture. He was looking at her with very keen eyes, his mind focused and thinking hard. "I believe I understand this metaphor. You aren't a butterfly. You're solid relationship material." He tapped a finger on his lip as he looked McKayla over like a man considering an object at an auction. "You might be on to something. A butterfly, as you call them…" He raised his eyebrows.

She nodded.

"Has a short lifespan. That is not what I need to convey to get people to turn their speculation and gossip elsewhere. I don't need a show horse. I need a plow horse." He opened his hand toward McKayla.

"Now, you're being insulting."

He bunched his fist and drew it toward his chest. "I need a horse that has stamina and is dependable. Are you dependable? How long would you anticipate this relationship going on?"

"Forever if it works for us. For another five minutes if you call me a plow horse again."

He laughed. "I like you."

She furrowed her brow. "That's helpful in this scenario."

"What is this scenario exactly?" He rested a hand on her shoulder as if he were trying the sensation on for size.

"Besides learning languages working for the military, one thing I learned when I was working in certain countries is that the bias against homosexuality can be life-threatening."

"Are you a lesbian?"

"Asexual," she lied. "No one does anything for my libido, including me. Sexual stimulation isn't appealing to me."

"Mmm." His gaze took her in from head to toe and back again. "As you pointed out, the men in my sphere have models on their arms. How would this work? You are far from being a supermodel. You're too short. What, five feet four, in American measurements?"

"Five-five."

"You do too many squats. I've seen your photographs in the newspapers. Your thighs are like a man's. Your ass is much too round."

"You say 'ass' to a woman you don't know? You were scrutinizing my bottom in my pictures? Why?"

"I'm a man, of course I look."

"And judge. Okay, I think we can agree that I'm not supermodel material."

"You have that wonky nose." He flicked a finger toward her face.

McKayla felt along the sides of her nose. "Wonky?" she whispered.

"Your eyes are too big for the length of your nose," he explained.

"Wow, when you analyze—"

"I don't like the color of your hair. It should be brown. Sable brown. Of the things that I listed, that can be corrected."

"My hair? I—"

"Then there are your nails. They are short."

McKayla felt defensive. Tonight's presentation—not even counting the price of her dress—had cost her a grand. *And* she'd passed muster with both Mrs. Peabody-Strumpkins and the dress designer. "Manicured though. They have to be short, I'm on the computer keyboard much of my day."

"Yes, you look like a worker, not, how they say, 'arm candy'."

McKayla rolled her eyes. "Do you really want candy on your arm? I'd imagine, in heated situations, that would be sticky."

"And you are pale."

"That would be my DNA." McKayla changed her tone to irritation. "Look, forget I broached the subject. I thought we could help each other. But clearly, this isn't a solution."

"Don't be so fragile." Misha's voice, too, dropped its previous warmth.

"Me?" McKayla lifted both brows toward her hairline. "I can look at you and pull you apart too. You look like you haven't exercised in years—though I understand there's probably a medical reason for that. But it can't be removed from the equation any more than my DNA can be removed from mine. You have a pot belly and skinny legs. There are hairs growing out of your ears, and a receding hairline. The red birthmark on the side of your neck is shaped like a chicken leg. Your skin has a gray cast, and you spit when you make the s sound. But would I say such things to you?" She touched her hand to her chest and drooped her lips, making herself look hurt that someone would think such a thing of her. "No. I would not. Why would I not? Because I'm not kissing you or screwing you. I'm playing a role with you. So, I don't need to take pleasure in the way you look."

"To others, I look like a catch," Misha said softly.

"Your money looks like a catch," McKayla clarified. "Your connections look like a catch. You?" She pulled her shoulder toward her ear in a one-sided shrug. "Not so much. Take away the money and connections—given to you freely simply because your dad was the childhood bestie of Russia's president—and all you would be is a middle-aged tired guy at a bar, drowning your sorrows, and heading home to your cat."

Misha laughed richly. "Touché."

"And the problem with the rich connected man with the supermodel on his arm is you can't follow through." She tipped her head. "What I hear you say is that my physicality doesn't match your idea of beauty."

"No, I'm saying that in this sphere of men, people might wonder why I would choose you when I can choose beauty queens half your age."

"Half my age would get you a ticket to jail," she deadpanned.

Misha nodded. "In their twenties, then."

"*Sex* follows those rules. Love doesn't follow those rules. Love loves beyond reason. You met me, I made you laugh. We have honest conversations. It seems to me that we're companionable. These things are visible to others. They would see our rapport and think, 'Oh, Misha has met someone he really cares for'."

Misha tapped his chin.

"I'm not after your money—I have my own. That makes me trustworthy."

"I'm beginning to see your point. However, I will not risk being cuckolded behind my back and further decline my reputation."

"Honestly, I will never understand why anyone cares about anyone else's sexual drive or proclivities."

"Scandalous is fun," Misha said. "What else are we going to talk about? We all drink too much and have access to the same fast cars and toys. What's left other than scandal and manipulation?"

"I don't know. It's as interesting to me as finding out about someone's bowel movements and pee patterns."

"Unless they're part of the salacious gossip because that's someone's kink." Misha popped his brow.

McKayla held up a hand. "Now, I'm nauseated. Going back to address the cuckold thing, let me make sure you understand that I'm not interested in sex. Not even a little bit. Not from a terrible experience. It's just not me."

Okay, here it is, McKayla, go big or go home!

"I don't enjoy men, or women, for that matter, hitting on me. It's boring and inconvenient. I don't like managing people. If they thought I was in a committed relationship—"

"You think that would stop people from approaching you?" Misha asked.

"I think I could cut the number at least in half with an engagement ring on my finger."

"Ah, so now I understand your scheme." He took a puff from his cigar. "Asexual." He pronounced the word slowly as if that was a completely foreign concept.

"I was born a square peg in the round holes of society," McKayla said then gave an internal wince at her choice of words.

"Sounds painful, sexually speaking."

"In most ways speaking," McKayla said. "And then there's you with your dick issues."

Misha chuckled. "All right. I'm growing more comfortable with this idea. How do you see this playing out, McKayla Pickard?"

HOW IT'S GOING

July, PRESENT DAY

5

ASHER GIDEON

His Condo, Washington, D.C.

ASH THREW an elbow over his face to protect himself from the dog breath and inevitable drool that was Ash's every morning wake-up call. He had no need for an alarm clock when his German shepherd, Hoover, enjoyed the job.

And just like every morning when Ash didn't leap from under the covers, Hoover's snooze alarm was a tongue bath and high-pitched whines that sounded to Ash's ears like "I love you. Now get up!"

Chuckling, Ash scrubbed his fingers over Hoover's head, focusing on the spot low down at the back of his ears that turned the whines into moans. Ash checked the clock. "Hey, remember? We talked about this. I was working until one. We were going to sleep later than usual today. I had another fifteen minutes, buddy. And I was having an amazing dream. Fifteen more minutes would have been appreciated." He swung his legs out from under the sheet. "Seriously appreciated."

He'd been dreaming of Dealer. Still. After all these years…Afghanistan. Dealer had turned a very sucky outpost into Nirvana for nine weeks, and then the mission ended.

Ash would have thought that Dealer would fade from his memory. But she never had.

He didn't have time for a cold shower this morning.

Man, he remembered every inch of her body. The smile on her lips. Her gentle way of doing hard business under the worst of circumstances when they were outside the wire.

In the bathroom, it was minimal. Relieve the bladder, brush the teeth, pull on a pair of running shorts and training shoes.

Even so, Hoover was stomping his foot—Ready to go, Dad!

Hoover got his name because of three specific puppy traits.

One, he seemed to have a power cord that was always plugged in, so he was always ready to go.

Two, he had a very distinct off-and-on switch. "Off," Hoover went through life with a laid-back, happy-go-lucky family pet demeanor, a domestic pooch. It would fool anyone into thinking he was a sweet angel. Flip the "on" switch with the right command or situation, and Hoover was a badass professional. Trustworthy. Smart. And lethally athletic.

The third, and probably the real reason for his name,

was that Hoover could suck up his food in the blink of an eye. And everyone else's if they weren't paying attention.

Hoover was an eating machine.

But his guts didn't like for him to eat and run.

Hungry Hoover ran their morning ten with enthusiasm knowing that when he slid through the kitchen door, he'd have a bowl ready for him.

As Ash pulled the back door open to head out, his cell rang with the tone he set for Cerberus Command. "Sir."

"Ash, heads up." It was Juan Ortega, the chief of Cerberus Bravo's Tactical Operations. "We need you in for a brief, ASAP."

"Sir." Ash swiped the screen to end the conversation, looking down at Hoover. "No run this morning, Dude." Ash pulled the door shut, and Hoover sat, waiting for his next command. "I'll make it up to you when I can. Looks like something's spinning up."

Hoover swept his tail back and forth over the tile floor.

"Your lucky day, Hoove." Ash pulled the prepped meal of chicken, rice, and veggies from the fridge. "You're starting the day with your bowl."

Hoover scrambled over and sat politely at Ash's feet.

Ash laid the bowl on the ground, and before he could stand back up, Hoover was licking the bowl clean, making it spin and clang against the ceramic tiles.

Ash chuckled as he went in for a shower and a shave.

Looked like the day was going to take an unexpected turn.

6

JOHNNA WHITE
    Washington, D.C., Iniquus Headquarters

"I'M TELLING YOU, WHITE," McKayla said breathlessly over video chat, her face pink from exertion, her hair pulled back into a sweaty ponytail that swung rhythmically with each strike of her foot as she jogged the tree-lined path, "something has shifted. The dynamic is off. It feels... mmm, I can't find a more precise word for this—it feels *ominous.*"

"Does this have to do with vengeful people still threatening you?" White sat in her car outside Iniquus Headquarters.

It was a beautiful white building that looked more like an upscale golf club or perhaps an antebellum southern mansion with its wrap-around veranda and regal columns. It looked *nothing* like what one might expect from the top national security firm that signed contracts with the famous and the wealthy, universities and corporations to keep Americans safe on the front end or save them from the worst situations should they come to pass.

With their high-level security clearances, it was safe for the U.S. government to sign contracts with Iniquus when a more direct route—using the government alphabets —might put treaties and relationships at risk.

After she got McKayla's report, White was sure that she was making the right decision getting Iniquus involved.

McKayla had shared a lot of interesting and valuable information over the last year. She'd never said anything close to "ominous".

"A lot of people were hurt when the crypto-currency imploded." McKayla's phone wobbled around as she moved through her run. "Even if I was no longer involved, they blame me. Fair. The financial disruptor was my brain-child. The threat to my security is a whack-a-mole game that my security team will continue to play, I'm sure." McKayla took a breath. "This isn't about me. It has to do with Misha and his friends."

"Okay. Let me get on the same page. What friends? When did this shift begin? Misha's friend, Nadir al Attiya, came in from Qatar on Thursday. Him and Rajja al-Saidi." McKayla paused, assessing White. "You know those names already."

"I do."

"Care to give me context?" McKayla asked.

"No. It's just interesting that this particular group is reaching out to Misha at a globally sensitive time. Karl Davidson didn't happen to be there, did he?"

"Karl, no. As per my report, I met Karl in Saudi Arabi, he is staying with Rajja, so I know who he is. Rajja did mention that Karl was planning to be in the Seychelles."

"Okay." White nodded. "Thank you."

"Is this particular group putting Misha in danger? And I guess, by extension, putting me in danger? I'll need to let the head of my security—well, hell. Rupert and his motorcycle accident slipped my mind for a moment. You were going to—"

"Get a U.S. team in place." White watched an Iniquus SUV curl into a parking space across from her. "I called to let you know the plan is a go."

"Okay good. I've already apprised my team that this was going to happen."

"Were they at all suspicious?" White asked.

"They understood my reasoning for wanting a cohesive team that practiced and trusted each other instead of trying to slide someone new into their dynamic. They're all glad to have the paid time off, I'm sure."

White balanced the phone against the steering wheel so she could scoop her long black hair out of the way. "Back to the shift in dynamic from the visitors."

"It started the other night at our dinner party," McKayla said. "The whole thing was weird."

"That's what I wanted you to explain to me. You mentioned in your message... You didn't include specifics."

"I have none to give. No data points and facts, anyway." McKayla's gaze turned left and right, then she rounded under a tree and continued down the path. "They had halting conversations like their words were all for show. It felt heavy and forced. Misha is a convivial guy. Vodka and booming laughter. That night Misha didn't drink. He sat stiffly in his chair. He sang no songs, told no jokes. One of them, Nadir, is an old friend, so I expected the typical 'back in the day' kinds of stories. But none came up. There was no warmth there. Let me revise that. No *real* warmth. It all felt like a show."

"The others? It was just the three men?" White asked. "No one brought a date to distract you?"

"Right, Misha and the two friends. Their security who were told to stay outside on perimeter. We already had my protection officers and Misha's. We didn't need twenty men with weapons. That was the main thing, I think. Misha didn't want anyone around him that he didn't personally hire. Guns being illegal doesn't mean that guns don't exist in England."

"Misha, understandably, has always been a little bit paranoid about his security," White pointed out. "He told you as much at the beginning of your arrangement when he asked you to fire your security team and hire people he'd vetted."

"His suspicious streak runs deep. It wasn't only for his own safety that he wanted to choose my team. He wanted to keep tabs on me. He's terrified of the indignity of being cuckolded."

"Cuckolded." White pronounced slowly. "Do people use that word nowadays?"

"He does."

"Okay, the guests that evening. What did you observe?"

"They kept eyeing me then they'd slide into silence

like they wished I would get the heck out of there, and they could say what they'd come to say."

"How did Misha respond to that?" White asked.

"He was nervous," McKayla panted as she ran. "He compressed his body tightly and kept licking his lips. Sweaty. I was worried about his heart. But later he said he felt tired from not sleeping well the last few days. During the evening, though, he kept touching me, holding my hand. At first, I thought it was to make a bigger statement for his friends' sake—about his being in a relationship with me. Looking back, it felt more like he was trying to anchor me in place like he didn't want me to leave his side."

White pinched her lower lip, thinking. "Atypical for Misha."

"The night was winding down. I was looking at my watch to give them the hint that it was time for the guests to go. That's when Nadir brought up the gathering in the Seychelles this next week. Rajja al-Saiddi extended an invitation to come. And by invitation, it sounded more like a command appearance. Nadir mentioned that Misha's Uncle Niko—that's not a biological uncle, it's an old family friend—was already en route with his yacht."

"Not an oligarch, though? There's a search for those yachts. Western governments are snatching them up as part of the sanctions package."

"Not an oligarch, but insanely wealthy. Chupov Nikodim Tarasovich is his full name."

"Niko Chupov is going to be there?" White's heart caught. Chupov's business was shipping. Since international sanctions had stopped the flow of goods in and out of Russia, what could they be brewing?

Whatever it was, it would have a global impact, White had no doubt.

"When Misha found out Uncle Niko would join the gathering in the Seychelles, Misha didn't look happy about it at all. He tried to find an excuse to say no. At that point, I decided that they wouldn't speak freely until I left. I excused myself to go to the bathroom, thinking I had the listening devices in place. But they were using a scrambler. All I got from the whole night was the impression that something ominous was going on and a case of indigestion."

"I don't think I've ever had a friendly dinner where my guests brought along scramblers. You couldn't get Misha to explain?"

"When I pressed," McKayla came to a halt under a tree, "he pulled out his heart monitor and was sending data to the cardiologist. He said he needed to get some sleep and that was that. He won't speak of it other than to let me know he assumes I'm going."

"Of course, you're going. We need to know what these people are up to." White focused on Iniquus Headquarters as she drummed her fingers on the steering wheel. She wanted the space and time to think this through. "Okay. It's a good start. We know more than we did twenty-four hours ago."

It seemed serendipitous to White that Strike Force was the team that Iniquus had chosen for this assignment.

Did it matter that this team had tangled with these same players in the past?

White's gut said that their familiarity would be an asset.

"What was that spark I just saw cross your face?" McKayla lifted the neckline of her T-shirt to wipe sweat from her mouth as she walked along to cool down.

"I had speculated that it was Victor Popyrin that was sending a message to his son without worrying about phone taps. Perhaps, it's the other way around, maybe the son was communicating information to his father. I'll have to think about that." When White noticed the time on her clock, she undid her seatbelt and reached for her bag. "All right, I'm here at Iniquus now. I'll be reading Strike Force in on the situation. They'll be providing your security. Langley has already signed the contracts. Your new team will be wheels up at midnight, landing at Heathrow. It's a seven-ish hour flight."

"Okay."

"It'll be a four-man close protection team and the rest of their force will be providing support from here in D.C. This will replace the same number of executive protection officers that you already have guarding you. We don't want it to look like you've upped the ante on your security." She opened the door and felt a wave of sweltering heat hit her full in the face.

Humidity in D.C. was ninety percent today. If White could make it from her car to the front door without looking as sweaty as McKayla, that would be a miracle. She pulled her foot back into the car and shut the door again. "It shouldn't look like you're concerned or interested in the antics of Misha's friends. You're just looking for a new experience. Something fun."

"Understood." McKayla looked around then focused

back on White. "I have to get home and get ready. We have high tea with some of his friends at the club."

"Nadir and Rajja?"

"They left. This is a friend from Russia. Ivan and his English wife Rachel."

"All right. Tomorrow around noon, expect a knock at your door. It'll be someone from Iniquus."

McKayla looked up the path. Her brows pulled together. "Thanks, White," she said distractedly, and the screen went blank.

7

___

ASHER GIDEON

Barkshire Hotel, Washington, D.C.

A CLOSE PROTECTION contract was signed early this morning and assigned to Cerberus Tactical K9 Team Bravo.

It was a little unusual to pick up a last-minute gig like this.

At the Training Center, the team was briefed on today's assignment.

A family was traveling in from Vegas, where a man, Vito Napoli, had received a threat to his family's safety. Napoli thought that getting out of town was a clever idea while his business partner tried to cool the situation.

The Napolis flew to D.C. with the excuse of attending a family party. At seventeen hundred hours, they needed to be at the airport to fly to Italy where they'd stay with Napoli's grandparents.

It turned out Washington, D.C. wasn't far enough.

This morning, Napoli got a message from a friend that "they" knew he was staying at the Barkshire, and Vito needed to watch his back.

On the recommendation of Napoli's partner, Napoli called Iniquus at six that morning to hire close protection until he could get everyone on the plane.

Napoli told Iniquus that he didn't know who was making the threats.

That was taken with a grain of salt.

It was probably true that Napoli didn't know the exact person who was threatening his family. But he knew why.

He just wasn't saying.

The really odd piece was that Napoli insisted that his security use K9s.

The contract stipulated a three-man, two-K9 team today.

Bear, Ares with his dog Judge, and Ash with Hoover got tapped for the assignment.

They hadn't had a lot of lead time to get the team briefed and plans in place.

When maintaining a client's safety, it took the three Ps: planning, preparation, and practice.

The team had to understand the choke points, the traffic patterns. They had to know how to get to nearest exits as well as exits that were tucked away and off the public's radar. They needed medical histories of their clients, and fastest routes to the hospital. Safe house addresses, which could be anything really, even a police station, as long as it was a protected place to regroup.

Last-minute contracts could be accommodated, especially in D.C. where Iniquus had prep plans already in place.

It just wasn't preferred.

Luckily, all the locations on today's agenda—the hotel, the botanical garden, and the airport—were well-known to the team.

There were some ominous clouds in the sky, but the weather report suggested only a forty percent chance of rain. With ninety-five-degree temperatures and ninety percent humidity, this weather along with being out in the mid-day sun was going to be hard on Hoover and Ares's K9, Judge.

The transportation was an Iniquus limo and a follow car that had more maneuverability.

The plan was to rotate the K9s every forty minutes. One would be in the car, to cool down in the air conditioning. The other would be with their principals. The operators would use the crossover time to walk the perimeter.

The botanical garden was a tricky place to secure.

Why anyone would have an outdoor party in July in D.C. was beyond Ash's comprehension. But he was from Alaska, and most everywhere was hot to him.

When he was in Coronado going through Hell Week and Buds training, Ash had felt sorry for his brothers raised in southern states. The cold bit them extra hard. They in turn, felt bad for Ash when he got assigned to SEAL Team Three that worked exclusively in Iraq and Afghanistan, a bit up in Syria. Ash never could acclimate to the heat.

Ash was a bit jealous that Bear would be doing the K9

babysitting in the follow car, Bear didn't have a tactical K9. Bear's dog, Truffles, was strictly search and rescue.

If they ended up needing Truffles, it meant this mission —protecting Vito and Marge Napoli and their four-year-old, Joey—was FUBAR.

The bellhop trailed behind Bear to put the Napolis' luggage in the trunk of the follow car.

Ares, with Judge sitting politely by his side, caught Ash's gaze.

It was ten-thirty in the morning, and even at this distance, the men could smell the scotch on Mrs. Napoli's breath as she joined her husband in the lobby.

She seethed as she came to a stop beside her husband.

Dragging her son forward, Mrs. Napoli clung to Joey's shoulders, presenting him as both a shield and support as she hyperventilated.

Her gaze moved from Judge to Hoover. Back and forth. With each shift of her head, her face incrementally heated until she was blazing red. Eyes wide and bloodshot, she turned on her husband. "No!" she yelled. Her finger came out, and she was thrusting her sharp red nail at her husband's face like it was a knife, just shy of where Ash would have needed to intervene. "You did this on purpose." Her other hand was a vice on the child's shoulder.

This had to be a common experience for Joey, he looked unphased. With his fat pink cheeks and head full of black curls, he was smiling at Hoover, holding out his purple sucker as an invitation to come and get a free pet.

Hoover sat at attention. He knew when it was time to work and when it was time to play. Hoover scanned the room, gathering information. His relaxed posture told Ash that other than the storm brewing in front of them, everything here was fine.

"You want me to get in the car with *that*?" She pointed first at Judge then at Hoover. "I will not. No." She crossed her arms over her chest and tapped her toe.

"The family would take your absence as an insult," Vito tried to reason. "And now, more than ever, we need calm in the family. *Capice*?"

Mrs. Napoli burped without covering her mouth. "*Capice*?" she asked.

Her husband rolled his eyes. "Not a problem, Marge." He turned to Ares. Spreading his arms wide, he gave a shrug. "You have two cars."

Ares and Ash would listen to the man's solution, but Team Bravo was duty-bound to keep this family safe, and they'd ultimately make the decisions.

"So, we sit in one car and the dogs sit in the other."

"We can accommodate that," Ares said. He tapped the comms button under his dress shirt and apprised Bear of the new plan.

Today—despite the weather—the client had requested their security detail wear dark suits for the luncheon in the park.

Vito, too, was in a suit. Coming from Vegas, he might understand heat, but he might not understand the effects of humidity.

The temperature was going to make for short fuses.

And angry people made for a bad day.

After a quiet consultation, Ares took Judge and Hoover's leashes and walked the K9s out to Bear who would load them into the follow car. Then, Ares positioned himself beside the passenger door of the limo while Ash prepared to transfer the family from the relative safety of the hotel into the vehicle.

Loading and unloading transportation was always a tricky maneuver. There were so many ways that things could go sideways—the choke point of the doorway, the pedestrians on the sidewalk, the sudden appearance of a car that blocked their vehicles in.

Bravo trained to make this transition smooth.

Ash was waiting for Ares to signal that he'd visually cleared the area, and it was safe to bring the clients out.

Joey had pulled himself away from his mom and was stomping his feet to the lobby music. His little fists tucked under his armpits, he twitched this way and that with his eyes closed, enjoying the beat.

When Ares keyed the radio, it was time to move the family.

"Ma'am," Ash caught Mrs. Napoli's attention, "if you will take your son's hand as we exit." Ash opened his hand toward the door. "You will be getting into the car first. If you don't mind helping your son into the car seat facing you, then sliding to the far side of the vehicle, and buckling your safety belt."

"Far side. You want me to slide? No. Why?"

"This limits your exposure to any threat, ma'am," Ash explained. "I'm sure your husband would like you to enter first, for your safety's sake."

She sent a suspicious glance toward her husband. "I'll walk around. I'm not getting wrinkles in my skirt by sliding." The dress she was wearing had bright red poppies splashed over light blue fabric. It reminded Ash of the women in Afghanistan in their blood-stained burkas, lying dead in the street, peppered by a strafe of gunfire.

Ash blinked to clear the pictures. "No, ma'am. You will always enter and exit the vehicle by the door closest to the building."

"We're going to a garden." She glared. "There are no buildings."

"Ma'am, this is our protocol." Ash's voice was even and unperturbed.

"Fine." She snatched at her child's hand and faltered as she made her way to the front door, followed by her husband.

Ash walked a step behind and just to the left, to protect Napoli's back, ready to grab his collar and belt and propel Napoli into the car should trouble present itself.

As Mrs. Napoli climbed in, she turned and hissed. "You wanted to torment me. You know I'm terrified of dogs. You got them on purpose."

Mr. Napoli shrugged. "Sure, I did, sweetheart." He raised his voice enough that he knew that both Ares and Ash could hear. "If the guys've got dogs by their sides, you're a lot less likely to screw the security." He smacked her hard on the rear, and she flopped her way in.

Ares and Ash caught each other's gaze.

Today was going to have its challenges.

8

JOHNNA WHITE

Iniquus Headquarters, Washington, D.C.

WHITE STOOD at the front of Strike Force War Room.

She was a tiny woman with a powerful job. Standing just over five feet, White weighed about a hundred pounds. Though her father was French, White was the spitting image of her Japanese mother. When she used her real name in the everyday world, Lula LaRoe, White enjoyed the confusion that would cross people's faces.

Here though, in a room of men who were all well over six feet tall with broad shoulders and powerful arms, White was well aware that her own strength came from her intellect and job title.

When push came to shove, physical strength could easily trump all other forms of authority. Those with physical power acceded to allow the weaker person to have any kind of sovereignty.

And while White got that dynamic, she ignored it.

Here in the war room, wooden conference tables were arrayed in such a way that when the automatic screens were lowered, everyone had a clear view. The atmosphere was professional but comfortable as the team and the outside support people involved in a mission came together to share information and strategize.

Much like the SEALs, Iniquus put together tactical forces to be lean mean fighting machines. Led by Striker Rheas, there were six ex-special forces operators in the room. His number two, Jack, along with Blaze, Randy, Gator, and their computer guru, Deep.

The Iniquus Puzzler, Lynx, was also here.

Lynx didn't fit into these macho hard-edged surroundings and that always amused White.

Where all of Iniquus dressed in black and gray, Lynx alone wore pinks and corals. The force operators wore tactical pants and compression shirts that showcased amazing bodies, and Lynx wore form-fitting bodices and wide skirts.

Very sweet. Very feminine. Very much a landmine hidden beneath the flower garden.

Lynx—though she was in her mid-twenties and had a movie-version of girl-next-door looks—was one of Iniquus's most formidable tools.

Iniquus Command knew they'd hit the jackpot with Lynx.

So did White and many of the upper levels at CIA.

But Lynx and the CIA had an adversarial relationship.

The CIA had a history of crapping on the woman.

White didn't think that Lynx would do anything that

would jeopardize her team, or anyone who was innocently involved in a mission. But White had been watching the water in the pot rising to a boil for a while now.

An angry Lynx could easily and thoroughly shred them.

White honestly wondered why she hadn't already.

Lynx caught White's eye, and White knew without a single word of exchange that Lynx knew what White was thinking and agreed.

White felt the color drain from her face.

Yeah, she'd keep a suspicious filter in place until the CIA did right by Lynx.

With a breath, White signaled to Deep. He brought up White's presentation on the screen.

"Hello." White smiled at the men sitting in front of her. "It's good to be working with Strike Force, again," White said, avoiding Lynx's gaze. "This is a last-minute assignment to provide security for our undercover officer. I can't tell you how happy I am that the timing on this is near perfection. As I'm sure Command let you know, last night things took an interesting turn. Since this is moving past personal protection, the contract now extends to your support members—Deep and Lynx—to help us navigate the changes." She gave Deep a nod of welcome. And rolled her lips in as she turned to Lynx. "I thought that the first thing I would do today is to introduce the players that we know about. Some of them are familiar to you."

White pressed the button and pulled up a picture. "McKayla Pickard. No doubt you recognize her from the news."

"Disruptive economies, cyber-dollars," Deep said. "She made hand over fist when she sold the company."

"Lucky for us." White nodded. "McKayla joined the CIA as an undercover officer. She's a playing piece we needed on the board. And she's your principal." White used the close protection term for the main subject of the contract.

Blaze leaned forward. "Pick a card, any card." He turned to Striker with a pop of his brow.

Striker's slow smile spread across his face. "Yup, that's Dealer, all right. I never put it together before."

"Fancy magazines airbrush the personality right off of folks' faces," Blaze said with just the mildest seasoning of the west in his accent and just a glint of mischief in his cornflower-blue eyes.

White leaned her hips into the table and let her fingers tap on either side of her. Okay, she knew it was a possibility. "Yes, in fact, Dealer was McKayla's military call sign. You knew her overseas? And if so, what are your thoughts about her?"

"Long time ago," Blaze said. "We ran some missions where she was our cultural support team member."

"She had a way of relaxing the women around her, even with a rifle in her hand." Striker added.

"Yeah, well that evolved," Blaze said. "Remember the first time she went out with us, Striker? She hadn't quite gotten the feel for what her assignment was about. She tried to act like special forces."

"In essence, she was," White said.

"Of course, she was." Striker laced his fingers and pressed his steepled thumbs together. "She did the job without the same training opportunities or the same level of—"

"Respect?" White lifted a single brow. "Star power? Glory? Adulation?"

"You've got the gist," Striker said.

White circled a hand in the air to draw out more information. "So, she went out trying to look like a SEAL and fit in with the team."

"But her job was to work with the women," Blaze said. "And that 'I'm as good as any man' attitude—no matter how correct, didn't go over in the cultures we were working."

"So, what happened?" White asked.

"Dealer very quickly adapted." Striker crossed his arms over his chest and leaned back in his chair. "She pulled her own weight along with my team. She also softened her eyes and her posture, took the bark out of her voice. Dealer learned how to do things—cook, what have you."

"Cook?" White asked.

"She'd join in and do the chores next to the women," Blaze explained. "Dealer said that conversations flowed easier when she was kneading bread dough, less confrontational. She was thrown in with her training, and like anyone who survives and thrives in demanding situations, Dealer proved that she could quickly adapt, think on her feet."

White mimicked Striker's posture and looked him in the eye. "You like her."

"She was a good teammate," he said. "She was professional and kept us at an arm's distance."

"Single female out in the desert with a bunch of men who hadn't seen their girlfriends in a while?" White said. "I bet she did keep her distance."

"True story. The women over there had to contend with a lot of harassment." Blaze put his hand to his chest. "I don't think she experienced that with our team." He looked around at Jack.

"I never saw anyone harass her. And if I did, I'd have shown them what I thought about that." At six foot five, build like an action hero, Jack could put the fear of God into anyone just by standing there. "Besides, she was an officer, and we were all enlisted."

White had been to enough posts overseas. She'd seen what the women had to put up with. "Officers are only about twelve percent of the sexual assault cases. So, it didn't pop onto my radar. Besides, we screen our officers for everything in their background, sexual or otherwise." White swept her focus from Jack to Blaze to Striker.

White pressed the button for the next slide, bringing up photos of Misha Popyrin. White ran through the basics of McKayla's assignment. "To us, Misha Popyrin's a vehicle for McKayla to get into the right places and learn more about the personal habits, perhaps the right pressure points for various players. The information that she's produced over the last year has been incredibly valuable, especially as we've been briefing policymakers concerning Russia's war."

"We understand the circumstances of her team taking time off," Striker said. "What changed last night that you brought on our whole team, including Lynx?"

White looked up and caught Lynx's gaze then turned

her attention to Striker. "McKayla says there's a gathering of prominent bad guys forming in *République des Seychelles*." Her French pronunciation had an American accent. "It looks like you'll need to brush off your French language skills."

She clicked to bring up a map of the hundred and fifteen island archipelagos in the Indian Ocean off the coast of East Africa about three hundred nautical miles from Kenya.

"This party will probably include some faces that you're familiar with. Now, before I bring up their images," White looked directly at Gator, "let me say that I've weighed this, and I've concluded that your familiarity will be a positive. I'll depend on Striker to manage the situation. If things become heated, or Striker believes it will serve the mission best, we can switch to Tidal Force. Command says that's doable. They're doing a training exercise in Madagascar trying to build rapport with their government."

"So, what's the issue?" Jack asked.

"This meeting has some very interesting people going," White said. "Movers and shakers, king makers."

Lynx shifted in her seat. "That could be a song lyric."

"Who are we talking about here?" Gator asked.

White rolled her lips in and rubbed them together before she caught herself. Lynx was a master of body language, she'd know, and tell her gang, that this dynamic was making White nervous.

And it was.

White could be blowing it here. She turned to Gator.

"It's your brother-in-law, Karl Davidson and his buddies Nadir al Attiya and Rajja al-Saidi.

Gator let out a long low whistle.

"Yeah," White said. "I know."

Gator raked his hands through his short blond hair and leaned his head back until he was staring at the ceiling.

"If it's too close to home, I understand."

Gator sat back up. "No, ma'am. I appreciate the opportunity. I hope this case finds a way to bring Karl to justice. He's a threat to too many people while he's on the run."

"I thought you'd say that." White nodded. She pressed the button for the next slide. And pointed at the map that came up. "Why the Seychelles? You're asking yourselves."

White stood up and walked around to the other side of the table so she could pace as she talked.

"There was a meeting a couple of years ago with the Omega Security's founder, Dillon Cartwright. The CIA and our sibling alphabets took great interest in it. We still do. We think that Cartwright used Saudi Arabia to facilitate a meeting between certain United States politicians and the Kremlin. That was our mutual friend Rajja al-Saidi. We think he knows the island and feels safe from scrutiny there."

White turned to look up at the map.

"In Seychelles, we expect Nadir and Rajja to be there with Karl. Though, we don't know that for certain. So, what do we know?" White asked, turning back to the team. "We know that these three people were involved in developing an international helium crisis for fun and profit that brought a lot of industries to their knees. And guess what was just discovered offshore in the Seychelles?"

"Hydrocarbons," the team murmured.

"Excuse me, ma'am," Gator said. "But the Seychelles, the U.S. does have an extradition treaty with them, right? They could take Karl Davidson into custody?"

White smiled. "I knew you'd ask that. The paperwork is prepared. Our diplomats are working with theirs." She pressed her lips into a grimace. "Once Karl Davidson lands, we are asking them to prevent his leaving but to not take him into custody right away."

"And they've agreed to that?" Striker asked.

"They have. We can't get to Nadir or Rajja. We simply don't have the authority. Their crimes, unlike Karl's, were perpetrated on foreign soil. And they all seem to like to do their 'criming,' if you will, on international waters. But if we can get Karl to America, we can take him off the world stage." White licked her lips. "You all want to know why he won't be arrested upon landing. The answer is, he is a cog in a machine. We need to know what the machine can do. If we pull him out, if they know we have access to their friends, they may dive too deep for us to find them."

"Understood," the team said.

It made sense to White that Karl, Rajja, and Nadir would want to get involved in that offshore discovery. Hydrocarbons produced not only natural gas for energy but also helium as a byproduct.

But these were people who didn't need money. They needed stimulation. Excitement.

Helium was *so* last year.

White put her knuckles down on the table and leaned

forward. "And one might think that's the play, the hydrocarbons, especially now. There's money to be had for sure. Russia is a major producer of helium. With the war going on, that revenue falls under international sanctions. But that isn't what I think is going on here." She filled her lungs. "While the world's helium is still at risk, we have an even bigger international crisis at hand."

"Oil?" Jack asked.

"Food." White clicked the button to show fly covered babies with bloated bellies. "It's very possible that there's a plot afoot to bring the world to its knees through starvation."

9

ASHER GIDEON

Barksdale Hotel, Washington, D.C.

WITH THE NAPOLI family safely tucked into the limo, and Bravo having a better assessment of the personalities involved, Ash and Ares stood on the sidewalk, finetuning their action plan.

"I'm going to let you take point with Hoover to get going," Ares said. "Maybe Mrs. Napoli will see that Hoover and Judge are professional dogs and under our control. Maybe she can relax a bit." He flicked his hand into Ash's chest. "Let's ease her into the day. No offense, but Hoover just doesn't come off as killer material."

Ash smiled. "Silent but deadly."

"Usually refers to their gas. But yeah, Hoover's a sweet soul with a dependable bite." Ares cast his focus up and down the street as he spoke. "Okay, just like we planned, we'll do this in forty-minute rotations. When we get there, Judge and I will take a tour and get a feel for this party. I'll see if Judge shows interest in anyone. Then, I'll take him to the follow car to sit with Bear and come to cover with you. At the forty-minute mark, I'll go back and pick up Judge, bring him straight to the family, and you can repeat the process with Hoover."

"Napoli is going to ditch his family first chance," Ash said.

"We're going to dissuade that as much as possible. But I think you're right." Ares rested his hand on the limo door. "If that happens, the dog stays with whoever has the kid."

"Mrs. Napoli will have Joey, whether she likes that scenario or not," Ash said. "And Mrs. Napoli's got a phobia."

"Nothing we can do about that. Two clients get two security units especially since we were told no weapons are allowed at this event."

Ash smiled. "Good thing they didn't put teeth on the prohibited object list."

With one last check of their environs, the men moved into position.

Ares drove the limo, while Ash sat in back with the family, in case the parents came to blows, and he needed to intervene.

In the car on the way to the party, Mrs. Napoli was drinking booze—scotch from the smell of it—from a sippy cup she pulled from her kid's backpack.

Joey kept reaching for it, and his mother kept telling him, "It's mommy's sippy."

Finally, Ash pulled a bottle of water from his backpack

and asked Napoli if it would be all right to offer it to Joey. With the heat and humidity what it was, they were going to have to watch their protectees for dehydration and heat sickness.

Joey was at high risk because of his size.

Mr. Napoli was at risk because of his high blood pressure.

Mrs. Napoli was at risk because of the booze.

Napoli waved his hand by way of permission, and Ash unscrewed the top for the boy.

As Joey slugged it down, Mrs. Napoli looked put out. "Now, he's gonna have to pee."

It was a tense thirty-minute drive to the gardens.

Arriving, they pulled up to the road where an Iniquus support worker had coned off a section of street parking.

Seeing them inching through traffic, he moved the cones to the sidewalk and waved the limo into position on the corner. Bear parked the follow car to the rear of the limo. Where possible, they always parked their vehicles on the corner. This would allow Bear to maneuver onto the road with ease.

If they had to, they would park between cars, but the safety of the client was paramount. In dire circumstances, that typically meant tactically disengaging, slamming into any car to their rear, to push it back enough that the tactical car could steer out into the road and be gone as fast as possible. The damage would be covered by Iniquus.

The corner was better.

If there were enough protection operators covering the party, it was protocol that a car had a driver and was running at all times. In an emergency, trying to rally the troops, dig the keys out of a pocket and start the engine, could all be the seconds that added up to disaster.

No matter how hard special ops trained, fine motor skills vanished in high-adrenaline circumstances. When the heart was pounding, from hormones or physical exertion, it was better to avoid the need for finger dexterity as much as possible.

Ares waited in the driver's seat with the Napolis in the air conditioning, while Ash went back to get the dogs suited up.

As the Iniquus support guy climbed onto his motorcycle to leave, Ash raised a thank-you salute. It would be Bravo's task to collect the cones before they drove to their third location.

Bear was at the back of the car retrieving the dogs' tactical cooling vests for Judge and Hoover to help keep them safe. Ash pressed his sternal comms button so Ares could hear the conversation.

"Ash. With this heat and humidity, none of our clients have hats to block the sun's rays. I don't think they're going to last very long. We need to develop a contingency location for keeping them safe and comfortable until they need to be at the airport."

"Bear. I can work on that with Headquarters while I'm on dog-sitting duty." He handed off the vests and Ash snapped them into place across the front of the K9s' chests and under their bellies.

These vests had a wrap of stab-resistant material on the outside but wouldn't stop a bullet. The operators had to choose, based on their task, what posed the most danger to the dogs and then try to mitigate it.

Cooling vests were antithetical to ballistic vests, which were hot as Hades.

When Ash was working with SEAL Team Three in the desert, there were days when wearing his protective plates became unbearable. The choice: going down with heat stroke or going down from a bullet wound.

Today, gunfire was a much lower probability.

Once the dogs were set, Bear pulled seven slender gel packs from the freezer.

Ash put three of them into an insulated pocket inside his backpack, there in case they needed them to mitigate heat illness for the Napolis.

Two went into Ash's suit coat pocket to hand to Ares.

And two, Ash slid inside his suit jacket in the underarm pockets designed for the men to carry the gel packs. With large blood vessels lying close to the skin surface under their arms, the cool gel helped to lower the risk of the operators becoming incapacitated by the heat.

When they changed out the K9s at the forty-minute mark, they'd also change out their gel packs.

As requested, today, the team wore Iniquus-gray suits. While the suits looked like office wear, these specialized bespoke garments were developed specifically for Iniquus operators to wear in public while performing close protection duties.

The tactical summer suits were constructed with Merino wool, which was lighter weight.

Shoulder gussets, elastane in the material, reinforced bands stitched into the waistband to help support their duty pistols (when they were allowed) meant their movement wouldn't be constrained.

Their pristine white shirts were made of antimicrobial space age cooling materials that wouldn't show sweat and wouldn't stink no matter how long the operators were out melting under the sun. These, too, were cut for ease of movement.

The operators wouldn't get bound up in cotton if they needed to go hand to hand.

Mirrored sunglasses completed their look. With the operators' height, the breadth of their shoulders, and the overall "I didn't come to play" cut of their uniforms, they exuded "lethal" by design. It was meant to dissuade would-be aggressors from even thinking about approaching the Iniquus client.

The best defense was not needing a defense.

With the dogs at his heels, Ash made his way to the car and signaled to Ares that the area was clear.

Ares exited, and rounded the front, while Ash watched for anything concerning. Typically, there was only a minute or two of exposure, and they had their clients inside. Today, no such luck.

Ares accepted the gel packs and slid them in the interior pocket systems, then took Judge's lead from Ash.

Ash had first watch. He turned to Mrs. Napoli. "Fears about dogs are real. I'm sorry you're feeling anxious."

She glowered at him, then at her husband.

"This is Hoover," Ash continued. "As you can see, he's a long-haired German shepherd. They call his coloring a 'black and red'." Ash sent her an affable smile. "He's the same age as Joey. But a lot more mature —dog years." Ash petted a hand over Hoover's neck, hoping that giving Mrs. Napoli a bit of information might calm her even a bit. "Hoover's a laid-back kind of doggo. Very well trained in his manners." Her braced stance hadn't changed. "I'll give you as much distance as is allowed." Ash made his voice as calm and pleasant as he could.

Normally, security wasn't chatty or friendly. But Mrs. Napoli was wound tight. And based on her wobbly stance, seemed pretty tipsy. If she kept drinking to deal with her nerves, there were no good outcomes. Vomiting, and passing out, drunks could draw attention from external threats and focus the operators on managing their client.

And too, Ash thought, if she seemed inebriated, the airline might just refuse to let her board.

Then what?

And that was when everything turned on a dime.

"I gotta hit the can," Mr. Napoli said.

"All right." Ares bladed his hand toward the entrance. "It's through the gates, we can escort you all there."

"Not 'we'. 'Me'. *I* need to go to the can. And it will take as much time in there as I want." He locked eyes with his wife, and she turned red in the face again. Her lip quivered as she held back whatever it was that she was thinking in that moment.

Ash decided that if they came to blows that he'd scoop up Joey and get him into the limo and let Ares separate the adults.

"And when I'm done in the can, I'm going to the bar with the boys."

"Sir," Ares started.

Napoli turned hard eyes on Ares. "I'm paying the tab on the three of you. Three. One in the car, one with me, one with the whiners. Capice?" His hand swung through the air.

Judge and Hoover were intense as they watched the move. They were trained to reposition in order to keep an eye on the hands of a threat.

And more importantly to get between the threat and the client.

Hoover circled around positioning himself between the adults. He sat at attention right in front of Mrs. Napoli.

She dropped her gaze to him, then brought it up to her husband and back down to Hoover, again. In her inebriated brain, she was still able to figure it out. Hoover was taking her side, saw Napoli as a threat, and was warning the husband to back down.

Ash always trusted his dog. *Always.*

Mr. Napoli simply turned and walked away.

Ares shot Ash a look that clearly said, *No plan survives first contact with the enemy.*

They'd have to figure this out on the fly.

10

MCKAYLA PICKARD

The Cumberland Greens, Richmond, England

THEIR AFTERNOON TEA had been a strained affair, McKayla thought to herself and then smiled. She amused herself to no end. But if she'd said that aloud, the rest of their group would look at her blankly. Over the last year, McKayla had learned to keep her jokes to herself.

Taking a sip of tea, McKayla listened to the conversation. So far, there hadn't been a single interesting thing to take back to her handler, Johnna White. Today was a waste.

"In Paris," Rachel said. "It could be worse."

"Food, music," the other woman agreed with enthusiastic nods, "walks down the rain shimmered streets." The feathers of her fascinator danced in the current from the 1920s styled fans that hung from the coffered walnut ceilings.

McKayla, too, had a kind of hat-like confection balanced on her updo like some extra frothy pink icing on a cupcake.

And she felt absurd. Like a caricature. Like a five-year-old at a teddy bear tea party.

When in Rome…

Fascinators were serious business in Misha's set. They were discussed ad nauseum by the women.

"Fun fact," Mrs. Peabody-Strumpkins, had told McKayla when she was having her lesson on when, where, and how to wear this particular piece of frippery. "Fascinators were so named by the original designer mostly because it had to be fastened to the side of one's head. And fastened and fascinator sounded similar."

"Fascinating." McKayla had batted her eyelashes at Mrs. P., prying the ghost of a smile out of her etiquette coach. McKayla had been immensely proud of that shadow of amusement.

McKayla was thinking about Mrs. Peabody-Strumpkins at that moment because of a very clever piece of advice that she'd offered McKayla on how to stay present for very boring conversations. "One must pretend that it is France in the 1940s. You are communicating with a member of the Resistance, and they are hiding coded messages in the most boring conversation possible in order to thwart the Nazis."

Sometimes it worked.

Today, it had worked for the first hour and then no one really had anything to say, so it had degenerated down to this conversation of Paris grass is greener than London grass.

White always said that the CIA wasn't movie material. It was 99.9% "bored to tears" and with only a possibility of .1% being "all of humanity depends on my success!"

A year in, McKayla had experienced the 99.9% banality of the job. Though, she knew that the salacious information that she'd gleaned in private homes gave the CIA leverage to develop important new assets.

"Yes, my dear, I would far rather be with you in Paris," Ivan was saying. His accent was still very thick despite having lived in England for years. Probably because the Russian ex-pat community in London was vast, and he preferred the ease of familiarity. As one does.

McKayla realized she'd tuned out long enough that she was no longer following this conversation.

Bad spy craft.

"Since we're heading right over to the concert, Ivan," Rachel gathered her handbag and rose, "I'm just going to go freshen up." Her friend stood, too.

Rachel looked around at McKayla to include her. Girl trips to the loo was a thing here just like it was in the States, but McKayla had quickly snagged her phone and pretended to be engrossed in a text message, missing the implied invitation.

McKayla had discovered that, on this assignment, men rarely said anything of import when a woman was around. Over the last year, she'd honed her ability to become a piece of furniture and be overlooked, much like the tribal women had done in Afghanistan.

The posture of being a fixture rather than a sentient being meant that the women were able to absorb a wealth of intelligence. Despite their intellect, the men had seen the Afghan women as being of little value, and often forgot they were in the room while sensitive information was discussed. Grateful for the medical care and gifts that McKayla brought them, the women were willing to talk about some of the things that concerned them. The things that might make their compound a target.

Ah, if only a bottle of pain reliever and a solar lamp could bring McKayla the answers she needed in *this* situation.

While in Afghanistan, McKayla, too, had learned to blend into the women's spaces, to silently absorb as much as possible about moods and concerns as she could before she opened her mouth with questions that might help Uncle Sam.

She applied those on-the-job lessons to her present situation.

When the women walked away, McKayla said, "I don't mean to be rude, but would you excuse me for a minute?" Without waiting for a response, she popped her earphones into her ears and turned on her app that allowed her to look like she was in the cone of silence but sent the ambient conversations to Langley to analyze and store while McKayla listened in real time.

Ivan leaned into Misha and said under his breath, "I hear things from inside Russia. Is very bad."

Misha said nothing.

"The oligarch class is *kaput*. We are now an endangered species, worse than pariah. We cannot do business. We cannot travel. Treated as lepers everywhere we go. A contagion. I have received many threats." He pressed the outsides of his fingers together and brought them to his chest. "I am not the son of oligarch, I merely do business for one and *yet," He stabbed a finger into the air,* "threats come. I am threatened in London for ties to Russia. I am threatened from Russia for not showing enough loyalty. And newly," he leaned forward and lowered his voice even more, "I am threatened by Iran because I am not able to find a route to get them what they're asking from me." His voice wavered with emotion.

And then, ladies and gentlemen, in an act of great courage, it seems that Ivan the Great just might show the Cumberland Greens clubbing world that real men do cry. None of this "stiff upper lip" business. None of this "Keep Calm and Carry On" silliness. McKayla immediately stopped her inner announcer's voice when Ivan gripped Misha's elbow and asked, "Are they coming for you, too? How do you cope?"

Misha grew up between Russia and England, and McKayla was fairly sure that the discomfiture that she read in Misha's posture was about the cultural prohibitions on Ivan's display of vulnerability and not the discussion of threats.

As far as McKayla knew, their security risk profile hadn't changed since she'd moved to London last August when she and Misha agreed to their relationship.

"I've always kept my head down," Misha said. "I go to as many varied charitable events as I can to spread good-will for me personally."

Ah, *that* was the strategy of the strange array of chari-table events. McKayla had never been able to figure that out. And when she'd asked, Misha had shrugged and said that he liked to meet new people. That was sarcasm; Misha *hated* to meet new people.

"As to threats from within Russia? I never go above the second floor. This protects me from tripping down the stairs or accidentally tumbling from a high window." He smiled to show that was a joke. But looking up under her eyelashes, McKayla could see stress crinkling the skin under his eyes. "My security takes care of the threats," Misha concluded. "And I have the added protection of McKayla's security, since we are most often together."

"You've moved your wealth to places that cannot be touched?"

"Of course." Misha leaned forward, rattling his teacup on its saucer as he placed them on the table.

McKayla knew it was the effects of his meds. She wondered if Ivan would read it as nerves.

"As soon as there was a rumbling about freezing accounts," Misha continued as he sat back up. "Belize is very good for such things."

Ivan dropped his hands between his knees and rubbed them together. "I must consider what is to be done. I cannot live like this. I need to either hire a security staff, like you, or move to where people won't know me until things calm. This Belize you speak of, perhaps."

"Not enough infrastructure for your comfort there. Perhaps Abu Dhabi or Qatar." Misha paused. "When do you think that will be, that things calm?" Misha asked.

"No idea. Years? Decades? I haven't told Rachel about what's going on with the threats. I appreciate your caution when you speak to her. I can worry for the both of us."

And there it is, the protection of Rachel, fragile creature that she is.

Like many of the Afghans, with the Russians that McKayla had met, gender stereotypes were alive and well.

It was Gone with the Wind with Vodka. *"Oh, you needn't worry your pretty little head with that. That's for men to take care of."*

McKayla thought that Rachel's needs for safety would be low down on Ivan's concern list. He'd prioritize his social standing and sexual needs over Rachel's survival. Rachel really should know if she was hanging out with a guy that was being threatened by Russia *and* Iran.

But McKayla shouldn't know, so McKayla couldn't say anything.

"And truly," Ivan continued, "what would Rachel do? Other than divorce me, that is. I suppose there is a scale where my wealth keeps me in her good graces. At what point does this scale tip, and she feels more fear of being associated with me than pleasure in my wealth? That, I do not know."

Misha didn't answer.

"She speaks of Paris because many friends—*most* of her friends—are turning cold shoulder because I am Russian. It will only grow worse, I fear."

Misha still said nothing.

Ivan shot a glance toward McKayla. "And her?"

"What about *her*?"

McKayla was surprised that there was a bite to that question, as if Misha was being protective. Of her? Of their arrangement? Hard to say.

Ivan shifted his attention. "The ladies have returned."

The men stood, and McKayla pulled out her earbuds. No point in that subterfuge now.

They all started out of the tearoom and toward the back door where Ivan had parked.

"What were you boys talking about while we were gone?" Rachel asked, taking Ivan's arm.

"Oh, boring things. I was telling Misha that my family wishes me home this week. My mother."

"You want to go home, though?" McKayla asked, glancing at Misha who was texting as they walked.

Ivan looked uncomfortable. "I have some business things to attend." He reached across his barrel of a chest to scratch behind his ear.

The party followed along behind Ivan.

"Did you text our driver to bring the car?" McKayla asked.

"No. Just some business," Misha said tightly.

"I'll tell him. I have things I need to get to." McKayla pulled out her phone and sent the message.

Misha looked at her with hard eyes. She could see him clenching and unclenching his jaw. He pushed her back a step. "Wait here in the shade." His voice was a command. He went down to the sidewalk, taking the final step then turning to see if she'd obeyed.

Was her taking control a bad look in front of Ivan? Probably. Oh well. What was done was done. She wouldn't make a scene. Sometimes he got like this when he wasn't feeling well.

"Where are you parked?" Misha asked Ivan.

Ivan pointed off to the middle of the parking lot.

Misha said, "The women are in heels, that's a long way

for them. Why don't you get the car? And I'll stay here with them while my man pulls round."

Ivan turned and sent him a scowl, then pulled his fob from his pocket.

Rachel turned to her friend with an eyeroll as Ivan sauntered away.

"What's going on in Russia?" her friend asked as they stepped on the walkway waiting for Ivan's return.

"The embargo mess," Rachel said. "Ivan's not able to follow through with his contracts. People want their money back. There's a lot of heated anger. He doesn't want to go back to Moscow right now to try to straighten it out, but he's going, day after next. I'm not sure when he'll get back to London."

"I really don't see how I can do this much longer. At least with Ivan out of the country, I won't have to put up with his *bullsheet* attitude." Rachel turned to smile at McKayla, looking pleased with herself for saying that last sentence with a caricature Texan accent.

"Bullsheet," McKayla repeated, watching Ivan approach his car, the fob extended.

The car chirped as it unlocked.

Out of her left eye, McKayla saw a flash of light.

Her amygdala—the threat assessment part of her brain —recognized, then acted.

Her arms stretched above her head like a swimmer.

Bending her legs, she twisted and dove back through the open door into the club.

With her momentum, McKayla slid along the cold marble.

Glass shards tinkled over her.

With a bright biting sensation, like a winter ice storm, McKayla pulled her knees to her chest, tucked her chin in tight, protecting her face with her bent arm.

Her head was a siren.

Her limbic system froze her in place.

In McKayla's mind, she was back in Afghanistan in that far away restaurant. It was the day of the car bomb.

Car bomb!

11

MᴄKᴀʏʟᴀ Pɪᴄᴋᴀʀᴅ

The Cumberland Greens, Richmond, England

Lʏɪɴɢ ᴛʜᴇʀᴇ, with ringing ears, McKayla's mind flew to a decade ago.

She just needed to stay very still and Giddy would come and scoop her into his arms.

Any second now, he'd be there patting her body, looking for breaks or bleeds, brushing the glass from her hair, and telling her with his actions that she was going to be all right, just hang on. "Stay with me." Unable to hear, she'd read his lips.

They'd needed a helicopter for an evacuation. Giddy had handed her to one of the PJs, then climbed onto the heli deck with her. Sprawled between Giddy's legs, the medic stuck an IV in her vein and a high-powered antibiotic in her mouth.

Giddy got her to the field hospital where he bullied the medics into moving McKayla to the front of the line.

Those images were spinning through her mind—the assessment, being released to return to her tent while she healed—the only woman in the only woman's tent at their forward operating base.

She remembered how Giddy made sure that she rested, ate, and took her meds at precisely the right time.

And how all the passion that they'd found in each other's arms before the car bomb had true depth and substance.

Giddy, I want you here. I've wanted you here. Shit. Where the hell are you?

The moment passed.

That whole scene that played out in her head was a hell of a surprise.

It was as if the blast had shaken down the structure that had held those thoughts and emotions back. And she needed them to be back since Giddy hadn't been part of her life since his mission ended and his team rotated home. McKayla was assigned to another unit, and they were off-grid, poof, gone from the horizon.

They'd both moved forward, and life continued to unfold.

Since I'm thinking the word move, that might be the thing to do here...

McKayla slowly pushed herself upright.

Process! McKayla commanded herself.

Letting her tears clear her eyes of debris, she took in the room.

Now, McKayla could separate the two events.

Her mind was no longer in Khandud, Afghanistan, a soldier with teammates.

This was London, England at the Cumberland Greens. She was a CIA officer, working alone.

She had a duty to her mission.

McKayla spread her hand on the marble, feeling the glass splinters piercing her skin as she pressed her weight down, struggling past vertigo to stand.

Halfway up, her body wobbled, and she crumpled back to the ground.

Stop! Her military training was taking over while her brain stuttered.

She thought back to Giddy—follow his lead: step one, step two, step three.

First step: Suck it up, buttercup. Work the problem.

Looking for wounds that adrenaline would mask, McKayla patted her hands over her body and looked at her palms trying to see blood.

She was bleeding, but nothing was gushing.

There were no projectiles sticking out of her body.

Her limbs were still straight lines, not heading off at odd angles.

She thought that because of quick reflexes and muscle memory, she had made her dive into the building in that whisper thin time between the explosion and the shock wave.

The compressed air that travels at supersonic velocities following the detonation could easily kill where the initial blast had not.

Looking at the people around her, McKayla saw jaws dropped, lips pulled back to expose teeth. She knew that people were screaming, she couldn't hear anything past the siren in her head.

Sirens...surely someone would call for help and there would be real sirens soon.

Not able to manage standing, McKayla crawled out the door to find Misha.

Outside, the parking lot was filled with burning cars, their lights flashing and surely their alarm horns blaring.

She could hear none of it. Burst ear drums? Permanent hearing damage?

The air was filled with thick black smoke, acrid and sticky as she breathed it in.

McKayla snagged a finger into a hole in her dress up by the shoulder. After ripping her sleeve free, McKayla tugged at the cuff until the button popped. Wrapping the stretchy fabric around her mouth and nose and tying it in a knot behind her head, this would have to do as a gas mask.

Inching forward on hands and knees, she vibrated with fear.

Misha and the two women lay unconscious.

Ivan was nowhere to be seen.

With a shaking hand, she reached out to press her fingers against Misha's carotid.

She felt nothing.

McKayla licked the back of her hand and held it over his nose. There was a wisp of cold that told McKayla he had exhaled. Her cheek to his chest told her that his heartbeat was faint but existed.

The air was thick with burning plastic that singed her nostril hairs.

He'd choke out here in the chemical-filled air.

McKayla rolled Misha onto his side and then scuttled underneath him.

She lifted his lifeless arms one at a time and shoved his fingers into the front of his pants so his belt would keep the arms from dragging.

The weight of his torso rested at her hips; his head lolled against her chest. She couldn't think of a remedy for that.

Reaching under his arm and across his chest, her hand grasped into his belt to keep him in place. McKayla pressed her free hand into the pavement, squeezed her thighs into either side of his abdomen, and pressed into her heels as if she were at the gym on the rowing machine using her legs to propel them mere inches. Her ass scraped along the bricks. Her skirt caught underneath her and pulled the dress tight around her neck as she moved.

Rocking side to side, McKayla was able to inch her skirt up to her hips and out of the way, tying the excess fabric into a quick knot.

Again, she pressed her heels into the bricks.

Her panties slid down her thighs as she scooted toward the stairs. The rough cold texture abraded her skin.

Ass rash, she thought as she pressed a third time, bumping up against the step.

One step at a time, leaning forward, power pressing as she leaned back, McKayla made ungainly gains. *It's only three stairs.* She tried to rally herself to the task.

Once on the patio, things were easier. She got a rhythm to her tuck and push, like rowing a boat.

One last extra effort got them over the threshold.

McKayla and Misha were back inside the building, safe from falling debris and the worst of the acrid fumes.

Here on the slick, white marble floor, McKayla could crawl, then drag Misha by the collar to a place where the air was cleaner.

She yanked her panties up over her blood-covered ass and untied her skirt.

McKayla was quite sure that there was no more Ivan.

Just like in the sandbox, you can be talking to someone one minute, and the next, they'd transform into a fine pink mist.

Rachel and her friend were lying unconscious in the parking lot, McKayla processed. No one went to help those outside.

McKayla's training said to focus on one victim at a time, stabilize as best as possible, and then move forward.

But McKayla knew that she'd expended her adrenaline on Misha. Exhaustion was wrapping around her, and all she wanted to do was close her eyes and sleep.

Unless McKayla could stand, she wouldn't be able to move the women inside.

Hopefully, that initial blast would be the only one. There would be no further harm.

This was England *not* Afghanistan.

In Afghanistan, it was often a series of two. The blast that killed the citizens, followed by the blast that killed those who ran to their aid.

England, and there had been a car bombing.

McKayla thought that she was done with that in her life.

Had hoped she was done with that in her life.

And there was the memory of Giddy with his thick brown hair and warm eyes, looking at her with such intensity of purpose. With her ears still ringing from the blast and unable to hear, Giddy had scribbled a message onto his notepad: *I'll be gone only for a minute, Dealer. I need to find the person doing triage. I don't want them to overlook you. It's swamped. I'll be back.*

McKayla pictured the field hospital when she was unloaded from the heli. They had people on stretchers lined up outside the hospital tent in row after row. Soldiers from that base were scrambling to throw up tarps to protect the injured from the glare of the noon sun. It had done little to give the injured relief from the hundred-and-twelve-degree day.

The moans and screams, it hurt to remember.

There was a phrase for that image though. Rupert, her head of security here in London, had said it when he was going over his protection plans with her—upside-down triage. It was the idea that the least injured would arrive at the hospital first, taking up space and attention because they could stand up, walk to their cars, and drive there on their own. The worst injured would be held up by EMS travel time to the event, triage, stabilizing, packaging, and transport to the nearest hospital.

This made for a mess.

It slowed response.

Things got missed.

Today had been a low security day since they were at the club, just Misha's tactical driver. And she didn't see Misha's security coming to protect him.

Misha's driver could be dead for all McKayla knew.

After all, he'd been bringing the car around to pick them up.

McKayla had no Giddy protecting her this time.

This time, she was on her own. *Do or die.*

Patting her skirt, McKayla swelled with relief when she found her phone was still there. The cracked screen worked enough to open with facial recognition.

Still not able to hear anything but a high-pitched note, with shaking hands, McKayla texted Rupert even though he himself was admitted to the hospital after his motorcycle crash: **Blast at Cimberlsd Freens. Misha down. Dob't want to fight rush to hospural. Get medical evac hwlicipter en route. Send to closest best trayma hospital. We r 3 vicitms unscanciius. I cn sit in seet. Msybe.**

She tried to read it over, but the small letters were too blurry. She hoped it was coherent enough that Rupert could make it out. He'd reach out to her team. The team had a plan for most contingencies. They planned and prepared for them. Practiced for them.

Hopefully, it played out in real life like it did on paper.

Her next text was to White: **Exploson go hospural**

Before she could press send, her hand shuddered, and she dropped the phone. Suddenly, her body was shaking uncontrollably. She laid on the ground with an arm under her head to protect herself should she have a seizure.

A man's hand touched her shoulder. *Thank god, Giddy's here.*

She blinked her eyes open to heart-wrenching disappointment.

12

ASHER GIDEON

American National Botanical Gardens, Washington, D.C.

AS SOON AS Mr. Napoli walked away, Mrs. Napoli was a changed woman.

It was a crazy, almost mind-boggling transformation.

The angry, drunken wife—with her scowling face and combative "try me!" posture—dragged a breath in so deep that it raised her shoulders to her ears. Crows' feet radiated out from the corners of her eyes as Mrs. Napoli squeezed her lids together while a soundless whistle slid from between pursed red lips.

And there she was, transfigured into a woman with soft concerned eyes and a shy smile.

Hoover hadn't budged from his place just forward of her toes. He merely tipped his head back until his nose was straight up in the air, watching her.

Mrs. Napoli blinked as she looked down at Hoover. "We can't be friends. You terrify me," she said softly. "I'm so sorry. But I understand that dogs are good judges of character. And you," her voice hitched, "are one of the few people. People—" She laughed. "Beings, I guess, who was on my side." She held up a finger, but it was more to show that she had something going on in her head rather than the stabbing nail-weapon she'd wielded against her husband. "And I won't soon forget that. Thank you."

When he signaled, Hoover rounded to flank Ash.

Mrs. Napoli's sudden shift reminded Ash of a dog he'd seen when he was a kid traveling out with his dad in the interior of Alaska. His dad was a vet that specialized in sled dog care. Ash remembered this one dog that was cornered by a polar bear, it stood there, hackles raised, growling his warning. His dad shot his rifle into the air to scare the bear off. The dog had been ferocious and brave in the face of the enemy, but nearly collapsed with relief when Ash and his dad approached.

The two had been cautious, but in the end, that was one of the sweetest dogs Ash had ever come across.

Hoover looked up to catch Ash's attention.

"Except for you," Ash said, giving Hoover a scritch behind the ears.

With another sigh, Mrs. Napoli shielded her eyes as she looked around. "If you don't mind," she said, turning her focus to Ash. "I'm not up to being social." She pointed at an oak tree with wide-stretching limbs and a thick canopy of leaves. "Come on, Joey, I bet we'll be a lot cooler in the shade."

The child's tumble of thick black curls lay damp on his head from the humidity.

As they set off in that direction, Ash said, "You'll have to excuse me about Joey's water." Thinking that he didn't have all of the pieces to this puzzle.

"He's been anxious with all of the new uhm circumstances," Mrs. Napoli said. "He's had a few accidents that have been poorly tolerated."

And here was a lesson in making judgements.

Ash put a different lens on what happened in the car.

As Mrs. Napoli stooped to drop Joey's green frog backpack with its googly eyes and happy smile, Ash scanned Mrs. Napoli. She wore heavy makeup. Her sleeveless dress had a turtleneck. Thick bangles clanked around her wrists. When she reached up to smooth a piece of hair that the wind trailed across her face, the bracelets slipped down her arm a bit.

She was hiding bruises.

"Bear." Bear announced into his comms to indicate who was sending the radio message. "Heads up. I have a black sedan that's passed me four times. It might be looking for a parking spot, or he's lost. Or it might be *something*. Two men. Big. They extra focused on me and our vehicles. Tinted glass, so hard to tell but one of them might have been videoing on this last pass. New York plates. I texted the plate number to Ortega, and he's looking up the owner's name."

Iniquus operators wore magnetic comms units that they dropped into their ear canals, so they weren't visible, and no one could rip them out of their ears to prevent the team from hearing each other. This was also why they used a button taped to their sternums under their clothes. It was hard to detect, harder for the bad guy to get to.

"Ares. Copy. Heading toward the men's room at the main entrance. Zero view of the road."

Ash pressed his button. "Ash. Copy. Within sight of the road. Moving."

"What's that?" Mrs. Napoli asked.

"I'm being advised that it would be better to find a tree further away from the street," Ash said, keeping his voice gentle and tension free.

Mrs. Napoli's hand came down on her son's shoulder, her breathing became short and shallow as she twisted this way and that, looking for threats.

"I see a similar tree down the hill, ma'am. If you'd like."

She slung Joey's backpack over her shoulder then bent and pulled off her high-heeled sandals. Taking Joey's hand, Mrs. Napoli started off in the direction that Ash had indicated.

"Ares to Bear. We're abandoning our ground game. Assessing our current threat level, I need you to come get Judge and do a perimeter patrol while I stay with the principal. As planned, Judge will have the first forty minutes in the car. We're heading to the bar on the north side of the entry next. Meet us there."

"Bear. Copy. Moving."

Once they were settled in a bowl of land, Mrs. Napoli sat, leaning back against the trunk of the ancient oak, while Joey watched the ants marching in a line up the tree.

She unzipped the frog pack and pulled out her sippy cup, jostled it, then upended it into her mouth, looking disappointed to find it was empty. She turned to Ash. "Do you happen to have a first aid kit with some pain relievers?"

Ash dropped his backpack to unzip it. "Headache?"

"My back and hips." She held out her palm waiting for the medication. "I've had to make do." She indicated the cup with a tip of her head.

"There weren't any meds in the hotel gift shop?"

"I don't know." She turned to a burst of laughter that skated over to them from the party area. "I was told 'no' to any kind of meds," she muttered under her breath as if to herself, but Ash heard.

The sippy cup with booze sounded like self-medication.

"Ma'am, while your husband is enjoying himself at the party, I can take you to the doctor's." Ash held his breath, hoping she would be brave enough to take him up on his offer.

She spun her head and looked at him with a strange intensity. She was thinking hard. Processing hard.

Say yes, Ash sent out the thought hoping it would take root.

Mrs. Napoli rolled her lips in, inhaled, then turned her attention to Joey.

Ash realized that since he hadn't mentioned his observations—and honestly, he was speculating based on what he'd seen in his career—Mrs. Napoli probably thought Ash was concerned she had an illness.

He wasn't clear about the best way to offer help and needed to confer with his team. Ash had found domestic abuse to be a minefield. Easy to set off the perpetrator.

Easy to set off the victim. But Ash would venture this far: "Ma'am, just so you're aware. Iniquus has connections to provide safe housing to women and children who find themselves in dangerous situations."

That could be a reference to issues either domestic or external.

Mrs. Napoli spun her attention back to Ash, blushing. Her gaze dropped to Hoover who lay panting in the heat, his attention pointing away from their group as he scanned.

"He's very protective, isn't he?" Mrs. Napoli asked.

"Yes, ma'am."

Joey pulled a coloring book and crayons from his backpack and scooted over to lean against his mom.

She combed her fingers through her son's curls as he opened a coloring page to a dog with a ball and chose a purple crayon. "I understand that some dogs have a keen understanding of things because their senses are sharper," she said softly without looking at Ash. "And they can communicate things to their humans, somehow." She paused as her gaze scanned over the open field. "I had a friend who was asleep one night, she woke up suddenly from a dream where her dog had said, 'Mom, I have a tumor. I need to go to the vet.' So, the next morning, she took her dog to the vet and told that story. Sure enough, Pansy Face—her dog—had stage one cancer. Catching it so early, they were able to treat her just fine."

"Interesting." Ash tapped out two pain relievers onto her palm, then twisted the cap off of a fresh water bottle and held it out.

After slinging the pills into her mouth, Mrs. Napoli

accepted the bottle. "Hoover, does he speak to you?" She tipped back and gulped half the water down.

Hoover turned toward Mrs. Napoli when she said his name, and her shoulders came up protectively. Hoover turned his attention to Ash to see if there was a command.

Ash held up fingers in the shape of a V and moved his hand left then right, the hand signal that accompanied the command, "Hoover, sentinel," to remind Hoover of his task, guarding his flock of sheep. To Mrs. Napoli, Ash said, "We communicate, yes."

"Our flight leaves at five." She looked over to the party area where applause swelled from behind the boxwood.

"Yes, ma'am."

She turned back to look at Ash. "And you've been hired to see that we get on that flight. That *we,*" she gestured between Joey and her, "get on that flight."

"Ma'am, this is the United States of America. You are an individual who is over the age of eighteen. You decide where you go and what you do. Iniquus was hired to *protect* you from threats."

Their eyes caught. Held. She nodded. But didn't make clear what that signal meant. Yes, she understood? Yes, she was considering going to the doctor?

There was a rumble overhead. The spotty, black-bottomed clouds that had been competing with the sun's rays all day were visibly expanding, winning the fight.

"The weather said only forty percent chance of rain today." Mrs. Napoli shifted around, pressing her hands into the ground, lifting one thigh then the other to adjust her legs, then leaned back against the tree. "Rain would bring relief from the humidity."

"It would," Ash said. "Here in Virginia, we sometimes get heat lightning and your random rumble of thunder." Standing just under the edge of the tree's shadow, scanning three-sixty, Ash pressed his communicator. "Ash to Bear. Can you check the radar?"

"Bear. Wilco."

When Bear got back to the car with Judge, Ash would walk out of Mrs. Napoli's hearing range and discuss the situation with the team. The least they could do was put Mr. Napoli, under some pretext, into the follow car, so Mrs. Napoli had every second available to her to say, "Yes, I'd like to be safe."

The thunder was a cannon blast. The air quivered in its wake.

Joey crawled into his mother's lap, shoving his head under her chin.

"The only public building here is for information and bathrooms," Mrs. Napoli said as she cuddled her son into her chest. "I looked on the website to see if we could be inside away from the heat. There's not enough room for the partygoers. If it rains, will we all just sit in the limo until it's time for the plane?" The way she said it was calm enough. But the look in her eyes said the thought came with a hefty helping of anxiety.

"We're developing a contingency plan. As soon as I have the information, I'll share it with you."

This kind of issue was what happened when a security team was put on last minute, sometimes the normal choices were unavailable for whatever reason, and the operators had to figure things out on the fly.

First steps first. Next steps next.

Ash considered their present situation.

It was true they weren't that far from the cars, which had both benefits and dangers. If the rain started up, the team could get everyone protected quickly. But Bear had been watching that car circle with two large men. Because Mr. Napoli had wanted to get away from his family before Bravo was able to get their tactical set up in place, Bear had never drawn a conclusion about that car's objective.

"Bear. A cell sprang out of nowhere. The map was clear when I left the car. Now, looks like we have a major storm brewing."

Ash's phone blared and extreme weather warning.

"Bear. You got that on your phones, too. Radar is showing burgundy and red levels of precipitation just about on top of us. Take cover now."

A finger of lightning cracked nearby. A roll of thunder pulled their eyes upward. And then, *woosh*, suddenly the sky opened up.

Under the tree, the full force of the rain hadn't reached them yet, but Ash could see the velocity in the way the drops shot the ground, and mud jumped up.

Ash pulled an umbrella from the side pocket of his bag. It was wide enough to accommodate three adults, so would easily cover his protectees and him.

As Ash held the umbrella over his head and reached a hand to help Mrs. Napoli, Hoover circled under to flank him, then stared intently up the hill.

Mrs. Napoli grabbed the items that had been pulled from Joey's bag. She shoved everything in, including her heels, zipped it closed, and slung it over her shoulders.

Wincing as she sprang to her feet, she grabbed Joey's hand and pulled him up into her arms.

The crack of lightning was much closer this time.

Ash could feel the thunder in his chest.

Joey began to cry.

"Ma'am, let's get out from under the tree. We need to get to the car."

Mrs. Napoli was reaching for Ash's hand when her gaze fixed unblinkingly on Hoover.

Ash could send Hoover out into the rain if it would make Mrs. Napoli feel safer. Bravo trained in all weather conditions, it was just another day on the job to be out and wet.

"Ares. We're on the north side of the botanical garden at the bar. It's under a small, enclosed tent. Bear, where are you? Can you bring a car around?"

"Bear. Judge and I are almost to the road. Can you see this? I'm not sure I can navigate the car in this mess."

"Ares for Bear. More information."

"Bear. From the ground up to six feet, there is an opaque blanket of vapor. I can see over it. I can't see anything under it. I can't see Judge or any cars, just rain and treetops."

"Ares. What?"

The temperature was dropping fast. Mrs. Napoli's arms were covered in goose bumps, and she hugged Joey tighter, inching closer, still watching Hoover's posture.

Hoover was a statue of concentration as the mist began to curl down the hillside.

Here was a dilemma, should he move toward the safety of the cars when the cars couldn't be seen, or hide under the tree in a lightning storm? Just last year, four people had been struck in the D.C. area, standing under a tree. Only two survived.

Luckily, the Iniquus-issued umbrellas were made of non-conductive materials. The clients could stay dry without the added danger of holding a lightning rod.

"Ash. I've seen this before when I was driving through Nashville. The asphalt heated up under the intensity of today's sun. When the cold rain hits that heated surface, all that stored energy converts the rain to steam on the road. The heat of the day, the size of these water droplets, that's where all the vapor is coming from. With the temperatures dropping, it'll condense back into water pretty quick."

"Ares to Ash. Any guesses on how quick?"

Yeah, that was the question, wasn't it? If only Ash had a crystal ball. "Ash. Minutes to an hour? My guess here is minutes." He paused to let the sound of thunder recede. The lightning this time left a metallic taste in Ash's mouth. "Ash. Lightning protocol," he called into his comms.

He didn't wait for Mrs. Napoli to inch her way toward him. As much as he hated grabbing at her, that's what he did.

They ran forward.

When they were well away from any trees, Ash had the clients crouch in a ball position, heads tucked, hands over their ears so they were down low with minimal contact with the ground. He stuck the handle for the umbrella into the loops of his pack. If the wind gusts stayed calm, the clients could keep the waterproof shelter over them.

Too many people huddled together created a hazard.

Ash stepped several paces away from his clients and

squatted. He called Hoover to him, but Hoover was hard focused on that vapor wave pouring down the hill and now lapping around Ash's ankles.

Ash paid attention to his K9's body language.

"Bear. Judge tracked us back to the car. We're in. This is crazy!" he called breathlessly into his comms. "I can't see to drive. I can't see anything even with my fog lights on. Sitrep?" Bear was asking for a situation report from his teammates.

Hoover let his chest rumble.

"Ash. The client is in lightning protocol. We're down in a slight bowl. Hoover's fixed on something that's got his hackles up."

Hoover barked a warning.

"We're under the vapor now." Ash fumbled for his amber glasses that allowed him to differentiate shapes better in the fog. "If I stretch out my arm, I can't see my hand." The rain stung with every drop. It pounded on his head and distorted his senses.

Ash cupped his hands around his mouth. "Mrs. Napoli call out." Ash needed to make sure he was heading directly toward her. Lightning or not. With this sudden drop in visibility, he needed to have his hand on Joey.

Kids could panic and do crazy things.

Mrs. Napoli whistled a high-pitched tune that cut through the brutal downpour, and Ash was immediately beside her.

There was a whip of lightning that made everyone jump.

The crackle of embers.

As Mrs. Napoli screamed, Ash turned to see that the

strike had cleaved the oak they had been under, and it was on fire.

"Bear. That was over by you, Ash?"

With his hand gripping Mrs. Napoli, Ash stood. At his height, he could see over the vapor, just like Bear had said. Six feet, then it dissipated enough to see. "Ash. We're ten yards east of the fire. I'm heading your way with the clients. I'll get Hoover to lead. I'd appreciate an intermittent horn honk to give me more information. The mist is crazy thick down here."

"Bear. Wilco." There was the first honk to Ash's ten o'clock.

Ash, once again, cupped a hand over his mouth so he could be heard over the brutal hammering of the torrent. "I need you to carry Joey and hold the umbrella over your heads," he called. "I'm going to help you. We need to get to the car." Ash let go of Mrs. Napoli just long enough to shove his arms through his backpack straps.

"Hoover, flank."

Immediately, he felt Hoover press against his thigh. Ash let his fingers rest on Hoover's fur.

With Mrs. Napoli's hands full, Ash wrapped a hand around her waist, then thumbed his comms. "Ash. Moving."

"Bear. Copy."

"Ares. We're getting into Mr. Napoli's cousin's car."

"Bear. Copy."

The rain made the grass slick, and Ash was glad that Mrs. Napoli was barefoot.

"Find the car, Hoover."

Glued to Ash's side, Hoover was stiff with concentration and hadn't stopped growling since the first strike of lightning. This was his behavior on patrol when the enemy was in the bushes.

If anything out there was under six feet, it would effectively be invisible to Ash.

Gripping Mrs. Napoli tighter, Ash dragged her as fast as he could up the slope. At just over five feet tall without her heels, she was blinded by the vapor.

The Virginia clay soil became slick underfoot, and they were sliding down more than they were crawling up.

Abruptly, Hoover raced around Ash to put himself in front of Mrs. Napoli.

Through the amber glasses, Ash could see Hoover's lips pulled back, menacing the threat with his sharp teeth and vicious warning barks.

Mrs. Napoli was shrieking and wrenching herself out of Ash's grip, trying to get away from Hoover.

Thrashing and hollering, Joey scrambled to get free of the too tight vice of his mother's arms.

It was a clusterfuck, and Ash had zero idea what was going on.

13

ASHER GIDEON

American National Botanical Gardens, Washington, D.C.

SUDDENLY, out of the mist Ash was able to make out two disembodied heads on fat necked men. Linebackers.

They looked every bit as large and dangerous as Ash.

Through the amber glasses, Ash saw the silhouette of guns in the men's hands.

Ash stabbed at his comms with his left hand. "Ash. Contact. Contact. Contact. Two Tangos. Send Judge." With his right hand, he grabbed at Mrs. Napoli's arm and dragged her to the ground, ducking below the mist with her.

Feeling for her legs, he forced them out in front of her. Then, dragging his backpack from his shoulders he laid it on her lap below Joey. As Ash pressed the strap into Mrs. Napoli's hand, he whispered in her ear, "Stay low, move to your right at the bottom of the hill." He tapped her right arm as he gave the direction and felt her nod.

Ash turned his head and through his dim visual field, he watched as Hoover launched forward, locking his powerful jaws around the closest man's forearm, shaking his head viciously until his gun flew free. Hoover fought the assailant on the clay-slick hillside.

With the sound of the tango's agony in Ash's ear, he shoved Mrs. Napoli.

Gasping at her sudden momentum, she fell to her back and skated away from the scene. That clay served as her escape route.

From his place under the mist, Ash watched the second tango wrap his arm across his chest and over his shoulder, winding up his strike to pistol whip Hoover.

On all fours, Ash pawed his way up the hill.

Standing and pressing into his heels, Ash tried to power jump under the gun and block the strike, but his feet had nothing solid beneath them.

Physics had the upper hand.

Scrabbling his feet beneath him in order to stay in place, Ash grabbed the man's wrist in a tight fist.

Downhill were Ash's protectees. He needed to keep as much distance between the Napolis and the attackers as he could.

Dropping his weight and thrusting his shoulder into the man's midriff, Ash yanked the man's arm as he forced him to the ground. In the moment when the tango flinched to regain his footing before he fell, Ash violently shook the man's hand.

The gun flew from the man's fingers then they both hit the ground.

With his free hand, Ash reached for the tango's ear and used it as a handle to drag a leg over the man's chest.

Rising up and torquing his body to get the most velocity behind his punch, Ash aimed his fist toward the tango's nose.

The assailant turned his head to avoid the impact.

Ash felt the bones around the man's eye socket give way as Ash's strike hit with his adrenaline spiked strength. The punch skidded from the tangoes face, and Ash hit the ground.

Lightning flashed across the sky, giving Ash a moment of clear vision.

The tango beneath Ash was swinging a knife blade overhead.

As Ash reached out to gain control of that arm, the tango used Ash's sudden momentum to flip them.

Now, the tango sat on Ash's chest. Three hundred pounds of pissed-off goon.

With Ash's elbow locked and a tightened grip around the tango's wrist to keep the blade from stabbing into Ash's body, their arms quivered as they pitted strength against strength, fighting for control of the weapon.

Ash sensed movement.

Then heard the ferocious growl.

Out of the mist, Judge sprang, jaws stretched wide.

As Judge latched onto the tango's weapon arm, the K9's momentum dragged the tango off Ash.

The air lit with the screams from the two assailants.

Bear reached for Ash's hand and dragged him to his feet. "Go! Go!" Bear yelled.

Sucking in great gulps of rain sodden air, Ash headed into the mist to find Mrs. Napoli and Joey, leaving Bear, Judge and Hoover in the fight.

"Ash to Ares. Dogs and Bear engaged. I'm in search of two protectees."

"Ares. Good copy. PD and EMS en route. Principal secured." Ares indicated that Mr. Napoli was in a safe place.

When Ash called out, Mrs. Napoli whistled her high-pitched tune.

Good thing they had that worked out from earlier, otherwise, Ash might not have found them.

Just as Ash had predicted when Bear had described the weather phenomenon, as the air cooled, the moisture condensed, and the mist was giving way. Ash could see about twenty feet now. The rain had let up for the moment.

Ash jogged their way. Mrs. Napoli had made it a surprising distance.

She stood flat on one foot; the other foot was raised onto her toes. Ash saw blood. She'd cut herself in her escape.

Covered in clay like she'd run a warrior's race in the mud, her arms shielded her son.

Normally, Ash would leave the mother to carry the child, so his hands were free and ready. But Mrs. Napoli was hobbling. She set Joey down and handed Ash back his tactical backpack.

"Are you okay?" he asked as he pulled the straps onto his shoulders.

Joey had wrapped Ash's leg like a monkey on a trunk.

"I cut my foot, and it's badly bruised. It'll be all right. I just can't put much weigh on it."

Ash pulled the child up onto his shoulders. Joey's little hands wrapped under Ash's chin and squeezed so tightly that Ash coughed to clear a way for air to get down his windpipe.

"Hey there, little man, how about you wrap your hands around my forehead, huh?" Ash repositioned the child's hands. Joey was whole-body shivering, part fear, part wet and cold, Ash assumed. Just like his mom.

Ash pressed his comms unit. "Ash to Ares. I have two protectees. Moving to Plan E. Plan E."

"Ares. Copy. Plan E."

Bear was busy with the tangos and the dogs. The team didn't expect his response.

As they made their way to the vehicles, the shrieks of the attackers echoed through the mist. It was eerie as hell, the sounds of a horror film. Ash was sure that Joey would be scarred for life. That or he'd remember it as the greatest adventure with hero dogs. Ash truly hoped it was the latter.

They arrived just as the rain started up again.

Ash opened the door and tugged Joey off his shoulders, gently setting the child inside. "Hey, little dude, how about you go sit in your seat for me. I need to talk to your mom for a second. Okay?" Ash pulled a blanket from his pack and handed it to Joey to wrap up in.

As Joey scrambled to the car seat, Ash shut the door.

"Ma'am those men were intent on targeting you and Joey and not your husband."

"Yes." Up here next to the road the air was thin enough that Ash could see Mrs. Napoli plainly.

"And you know why."

"Yes." She was hugging herself as the rain washed the clay from her hair. She was a stream of red silt.

Ash wanted her to feel the full danger and discomfiture of the moment. He wasn't going to soothe or coddle her.

She needed to make a decision, here and now.

"I can get you cleaned up and on that plane to Italy. But as long as you're in your husband's sphere, you—and more importantly, your son—will be in grave danger. Those men had guns pointed at you. In the mist, no one would have seen anything. They would get away like ghosts in the night had they wanted to shoot you. If they wanted to take you, they just needed to shoot me."

"I'm sorry." Her teeth rattled.

"I'm going to suggest to you that you and your son are better off at a distance from the source of this problem."

"My husband, you mean? Yes. I know. But there's no safe distance. They'd follow us wherever we went."

Ash's gaze took in the sodden dress, clinging to her skin, destroyed by the red clay. He opened the back door, and she crawled in. "I'll get you a blanket."

Ash stepped to the car trunk and pulled out a fleece blanket, using the time to choose his words carefully.

When he handed the blanket to Mrs. Napoli, Ash crouched at the door. "You had quite the fall down the hill. I think you've injured yourself badly during your escape. I think going to the hospital for a thorough examination and documentation of *all* your injuries is warranted. If you want to take a different plane to Italy, we can help you arrange that. If you felt it best to stay here and recuperate, we can contact the right authorities to allow you the space and time to heal. You and your son."

She looked at him wide eyed, she wasn't breathing.

"The easiest time to make that happen is before your husband rejoins us," Ash said quietly so only Mrs. Napoli would hear.

Her body jolted with the sound of sirens whirring closer.

Mrs. Napoli focused on Ash. "I was hurt in the fall. I need to go to the hospital before the police get here, and I'm held up. My husband wouldn't want me to take Joey with me as I get help."

As the police raced up the road, sirens screaming, Ash rounded the front of the limo, got in the driver's side, and inched away from the curb.

14

The Royal London Hospital, London, England

McKayla perched on the edge of her hospital bed, her bare feet dangling over the side. Hugging a pillow to her stomach, this was the posture that best helped her cope with her ringing ears.

She sucked in a shaky breath, then exhaled heavily as John, her security team's number two, came through her hospital room door.

"Sorry to pull you away from your evening," she said with no idea how to modulate her voice.

McKayla had to read his lips when he said, "Seriously, ma'am?"

"Not seriously. I'm grateful to see you."

"Just so you know, you're yelling." He added jazz hands radiating out from his mouth to give her more clues as to what he was saying.

McKayla nodded.

"We couldn't get in touch with you." He walked over, posting her leather tote on the foot of her bed. "Do you understand me?"

"It's better when I see your lips." McKayla spoke so softly she wasn't sure anything but air was coming out of her mouth. "Is this the right level to talk?"

When he gave her a thumbs up, McKayla lifted the phone sitting next to her. "My battery went dead. I was left with the landline by my bed. I had to try to remember your number. Or anyone's number for that matter. Not that I could hear anything. Luckily, you got through to the nurses' station. Hey, how did you figure out I was here?"

John pulled out his phone and tapped voice to text. McKayla held it and read as John spoke. "The pilot called in with the hospital he was routed to with your party."

Her gaze flashed up to his face. "Did they find Ivan? We flew off with four."

"Not that I'm aware of, no, ma'am." As she read, his focus went to the bag. "I packed a change of clothes for you. I wasn't allowed onto this floor until just now. The hospitals have been overwhelmed with casualties."

"The others?"

"I don't have anything for you on anyone's medical status. I'm sorry, ma'am. The roads are swarmed with press. I had to jog a good ways in. We'll need to figure out an exit strategy. I needed to see how you were doing before I considered how to move you."

"I'm off kilter to be honest. You may have to put me in a wheelchair. I'm not up to any kind of exertion right now." She skated a hand out. "Do or die, I'd rally if lives

were on the line, but barring that, I'd rather be coddled."
McKayla pulled her brows together, her lips dropped into a
deep frown. "Did they say when I could sign out of here?
They won't let me leave my room to go see Misha." She
stretched out her feet and exhaled as pain radiated up her
sciatica. "Have you heard from Misha's team? How is his
driver? I didn't see him anywhere at the club after the
explosion."

"No word on his driver. When I spoke to his team
earlier, they said they'd keep me abreast. He was on
comms bringing the car around at the time of the blast.
That's all his teammates know. They were talking to him
then radio silence."

"Bloody hell." She plopped a hand on top of her head
and closed her eyes.

"How's that, ma'am?"

"I texted Misha's driver to pull the car around. I was
impatient to get home. That no one's heard from him…"
She shook her head. McKayla had held this last question
off. "And Misha?"

John shifted his weight from side to side. "They aren't
allowed to tell me anything. I'm not on his security team.
And his security team is trying to get on site. The nurses
are being run ragged and no one's around to answer questions by phone."

McKayla flicked a finger at the tote that he'd brought
in. "Did you happen to think of a phone charger? There's
not even a clock in the room. I have no idea what time it is.
They brought me a tray of dinner, but that feels like hours
ago."

John reached his hand out for her phone then drew a

charged battery from his pocket. "Not quite ten," he said, switching the battery out and testing that the phone came on. "Fully charged." He stretched it out to her. "What's your medical status, ma'am?" he asked as McKayla accepted her phone.

"Sore." She dug through the bag pulling out her clothes. "Covered in glass cuts that weren't a lot of fun to have cleaned out. I have road rash on my arse." She looked up at John, making a face so he'd chuckle. "I won't explain how or why." She reached back into the bag to get the brush and hair tie.

Once McKayla had emptied the tote onto the bed, she set the bag aside. Then looked back to John. "And everything sounds like I'm underwater. So, all told, I'm probably in better shape than I should be."

"Jeremy sent me a news link." He referred to another of her London close protection team. "The club's security cameras recorded good-quality footage of the incident. You're famous now." He paused and grinned. "Well extra famous."

"Wonderful," McKayla deadpanned.

"I understand where the road rash came from. That was a valiant effort, ma'am. Your military training shined."

"Well, thank you. I tried." She winced. "So did it show my rear across all of England?"

"The world, yes, ma'am. Though, surely, people will be focused on other aspects of the incident."

"Have they found the reason for the explosion?" She pointed at the television. "My TV's not working. I haven't any information."

He shook his head. "The authorities are speculating on a gas pipeline rupture."

"Listening to the responder chatter, do you believe that?"

"It makes London feel safer. So…I can't be sure. Rupert has good contacts in MI6. He'll try to drill down on the cause."

"Though I hate to bug him while he's recovering himself from his motorcycle accident and his own road rash, I would really like to have those answers." McKayla reached around to untie the second set of hospital gown ties, trying to hide her wincing. She wanted to be dressed and ready to head out and check on Misha as soon as the nurse brought her release papers to sign.

That, and she needed to get in touch with White.

"Ma'am, I think Rupert would be indignant if he wasn't looped in and doing his job."

"Gas pipeline not car bomb?" she asked again, her brain was still disorganized and anxious, and could be for days to come. That was her experience in Afghanistan, anyway.

"That's what the early reports are indicating, ma'am."

"We were all outside when it happened. When I saw fire, I dove into the club and missed a lot of the concussion. The flash that I saw happened just as Ivan extended his fob to unlock his car. That's not what happens with a car bomb."

"No, ma'am."

"I was thinking about it, as I lay here, I speculated it might be one of those electrical vehicles caught on fire. And just the sheer heat and licking flames that those lithium-ion batteries can put out might have caught the other cars on fire, too. But of course, cars don't explode as a general rule." She started shrugging out of her hospital gown.

John didn't turn to the door while she changed. England had a different level of modesty than she was used to in Pennsylvania.

"You know," McKayla said as she dragged on a fresh pair of underwear. The silk dampened and clung where it came into contact with her antibiotic cream. "I read an article the other day that an E.V. on fire takes ten times the amount of water that it takes to put out a regular car." She slung her bra over her arms, then decided to hell with it and tossed it back into the bag. Too many cuts to make that comfortable.

"Oh?"

"Yeah. And on a regular car you just hose it down, all's well." McKayla wrestled her arms into the sleeveless floral blouse. "On an E.V., they have to get the car up at an angle so they can get the water directly on the battery to cool it." Her fingers were still stiff and shaky. "I'm not sure I can do up these tiny buttons." She shook her hands to give it another go. "And then, if it wasn't cooled sufficiently, the battery can burst into flames again days, even weeks later."

"Seriously? Weeks? Are you okay with the buttons?"

"I've almost got them, thanks. Weeks is what the article said. What do you do in the case of your E.V. catching fire? Take it to a parking lot where no one ever goes and park it there for a couple of months and then tow it to a scrap yard? I can't imagine that it would be a good idea to drive that car ever again. Kind of a lost cause, don't you think?" McKayla opened the elastic waistband on her black yoga pants and kicked her feet into the legs. "The point was, perhaps one of the E.V. cars in the parking lot had been on fire recently and just kind of went poof."

McKayla leaned back on the bed, planted her feet, and lifted her hips to drag the pants the rest of the way on. She needed a physical therapist to rub the soreness out of her muscles.

"Yes, ma'am, I suppose that could have been what it looked like from your vantage point. From the security footage, I'd take that off your list of possibilities."

She lifted a tennis shoe, but her abraded skin screamed when she leaned over to slide it on. McKayla said, "If you wouldn't mind, I can't quite reach my feet. Could you help with my sneakers?"

"Sneakers, ma'am?"

"Running shoes?" She swung her feet onto the bed.

"Oh, yes, ma'am." He grabbed up her shoe, loosened the laces, and wriggled it onto her foot.

McKayla pulled her hair around under her nose and inhaled. "If I can't wash this stench out, I may have to get a crew cut like yours."

"I think it's like skunk, ma'am." He pulled the laces tight and made an efficient bow.

"The oiliness of the scent? Hmmm, you might be right. Maybe I need to make a hair mask of tomato sauce."

"Dish soap and hydrogen peroxide, ma'am." John's phone buzzed. He looked down at the text. "It's Rupert. He's asked me to go to his room."

"If he wants to see you in person," McKayla said, "he might have sensitive information to pass."

"Might well be, ma'am." John quickly got McKayla's other shoe on and tied it. "I'll be back straightaway with a wheelchair. I'll tell you what I learn."

As soon as John walked out the door, McKayla, grabbed for her phone.

15

JOHNNA WHITE

Strike Force War Room, Washington, D.C.

THE TEAM WAS PROCESSING through the data for the mission to the Seychelles. They were watching footage of McKayla to see how she liked to interact with her security team in public.

Luckily for them, it looked like McKayla typically moved through the world on cat feet. Not hiding, just quietly and gracefully present.

She didn't engage with strangers, no posing for fan selfies or signing autographs.

Those made things, from a security point of view, that much easier.

She often used a tactical driver who stayed with the car, car running, ready for quick exits. And one close protection professional at her seven o'clock.

At public gatherings, such as the theater, McKayla

would show up with her four close protection officers creating four corners of a security box as she—or she and Misha—walked in the center. Dressed in the same level of formality as McKayla wore, the team blended in almost seamlessly.

"Tactical tuxes," Lynx said with a smile. "Don't forget your cummerbunds and bow ties. And if she has you all in your monkey suits, I want pictures."

"Lynx, aren't you going to London?" White asked.

"Deep and I will be providing support from here. I'm not field qualified."

White's brows drew together. "The hell you aren't. I've seen you in action."

"I'm trained. I'm not Iniquus qualified. Iniquus only puts ex-special forces operators in the field. Sometimes I land there by accident. But we try to avoid that."

White unfocused from the room as she thought. "Okay. So, four in and two out. When you get to the Seychelles, you'll have to feel the situation out. We need to talk about what systems you'll be taking with you. It's imperative that they're discreet."

"We've been training with new AI language technology," Striker said.

"Oh?" White focused on him.

"We wear our team comms in one ear, in the other we wear a piece that looks very much like assistive technology for someone with a hearing deficit. It picks up ambient languages and translates them in real time. This might be helpful in London if Misha and his friends are speaking in Russian amongst themselves. The AI will allow English and then one other language that's being translated to be heard at the same time. Two languages—English plus another—are the technological capacity as of now. In rooms with a variety of languages, we get a lot of goop by way of translation. So, it's not effective. Under those circumstances, we shut it down."

"Interesting."

"In the Seychelles there will be a variety of languages being spoken at the events," Striker continued. "It's possible that we will have familiarity with some of them. Blaze has Russian. We have some languages from the Middle East and East Africa under our belts. What words or phrases would make us want to home-in?"

White pulled her laser pointer from her pocket and used the red dot to make a circle on the map. "You're familiar with this area here, the Bosphorus Strait in Turkey. It is both the narrowest international shipping channel in the world, and the only outlet from the Black Sea to the Mediterranean Sea and then down to Africa or out to the ocean." She clicked off the laser and stuck the device back in her pocket as she faced the team. "As such it is both incredibly important and dangerously vulnerable."

Everyone was focused on her words.

White had debated whether or not to give them this information. It could create a focus on an individual tree when White wasn't sure that the focus shouldn't be on the wider forest.

Well, here she was going with her gut.

"The CIA was monitoring rockets that were launched into the Black Sea. At first, whoever was launching the weapons seemed to be testing."

"Damned expensive testing," Jack said.

"A great deal of money. They apparently found that those systems wouldn't do what they wanted. Soon after, we tracked drone strikes. The bombs they dropped took out boats with fair precision."

"Who made the drones? Where did they get them?" Lynx asked.

"Good questions." White circled to the other side of the table and pressed her hips back, resting them against the edge. "They looked like they might be Iranian. But some of our analysts are now speculating that they're Saudi."

"Iranian? And they're targeting who? Russia?" Gator asked. "That don't make no sense."

"No, it does not," White said. "To preempt your questions, the answer is I don't know. What I have is speculation. I have to say because the attack is focused on shipping, and because of this specific group of men who are gathering, it smells like the same meal is being served again. One thing we do know is that the bad guy," White said, "if not caught and punished, refines their criminal abilities. They grow stronger and better at perpetrating crimes. More emboldened."

"You said food and starvation earlier," Gator said. "Now, Karl Davidson et al were successful in creating the geopolitical mess that caused Qatar's neighbors to blockade their docks. Qatar didn't make its own food. A good ninety percent got imported. They might've starved if other countries hadn't helped supply 'em—their neighbors and Iran sent planes full of food."

"Yeah, well Qatar learned its lesson after that, didn't

it? They've made huge strides in food security since then," Lynx said. "Africa, as you said, White, has been dependent on grain out of the breadbasket region. Seeing the Russian aggression ahead of planting season, they were able to step things up."

"It'll take some of the danger out of the equation for them," White acknowledged, "but they're still susceptible."

"You think the drones are about stopping grain shipments to other countries?" Blaze asked. "I've been following this, and they're not targeting grain. So far, they've gotten a few military vessels and a couple of fishing boats."

"It would be showing their hand if they did," White countered. "They just need to sink Russian ships. Russia publicly gets mad, and the result is a blockade of the Bosphorus Strait, right? Then the grain can't leave the Black Sea. It's either used by one of the six countries that line the Black Sea or the grain rots. I'd guess that the Kremlin would like the grain to be shipped to the motherland."

"We can't be sure that Russia isn't sending out its oldest most decrepit ships and bombing themselves to have an excuse to shut down the strait, right?" Blaze asked.

"Never say never." White's voice was a clear shade of disdain.

Jack leaned forward. "So, India and African nations suffer to what end?"

"I don't know." White grimaced. "That's why it's imperative that we're gathering everything we can from the meeting in the Seychelles. It's all fun and games until we're watching babies starve."

White held her finger in the air and pulled out her phone, jangling with McKayla's ringtone. She swiped to read the message.

McKayla: **Exploson go hospural**.

White swung her attention to Deep. "McKayla was involved in an explosion in the London, England area. Give me everything you've got."

She tapped her phone to call McKayla. "The text simply reads, 'Explosion go hospital'," White said distractedly. "Her hands were shaking, or she couldn't see because it's all misspelled."

After two rings, McKayla's phone went right to voice mail.

"I have it," Deep said. "At sixteen hundred hours, Greenwich Mean Time, so eleven o'clock in D.C." He glanced at the clock on the wall over White's head. Then said, "Four hours ago, there was an explosion at the Cumberland Greens, which is a social club. Initial investigation indicates that it was a gas pipeline under the west-facing guest parking lot." He read from the screen. "Thirty cars were involved in the fire. One man is confirmed dead, two females and another male were unconscious as they were evacuated from the scene. Many others are hospitalized with varying degrees of injury. Hospitals in the London area are overwhelmed."

"You just received that text?" Lynx asked.

"Just now," White said.

"'Go hospital' not 'at hospital'?" Lynx's brow drew together. "This is from her cell phone number?"

"Yes," White affirmed.

In White's experience, Lynx always was detail oriented and quick to spot discrepancies.

"If McKayla was lucid and ambulatory, she would have found a way to get help hours ago. If she were conscious and able to text, she would have done it hours ago. If she were unconscious and just now able to text, she would have been triaged and put on a helicopter immediately. Perhaps she typed it out and she didn't press send until just now or there was a delay because so many people, trying to use their cell phones, overwhelmed the tower." Lynx pulled the elastic from her wrist and gathered her hair into a ponytail.

White had noticed she did this when she was handed a puzzle to solve, like she was clearing away distractions.

"With her resources and security, surely she wouldn't have queued up for an ambulance ride to just any hospital." Lynx turned to Deep. "Any footage of helicopter extractions?"

As Deep took a moment to search, White tried McKayla's line again.

"Here we go," Deep said. "There's a video on social media that shows three medical helicopters arriving in the clearing to the north side of the clubhouse. The time stamp says within a half hour of the explosion. I'm looking up the company in our database and…" His eyes scanned the screen. "That's a private company. I'm making note of the tail numbers."

"I didn't know that existed in the UK," White said. "They have national health care."

"I can't speak to that, ma'am." He read from the

screen, paraphrasing. "The article says that they triaged and distributed the victims to various hospitals throughout the area based on their injuries." He lifted his chin to see White past his monitor. "We can't just call a single hospital to see if she was brought in." His fingers moved over his keys. "I'm going to see if I can't get hold of tower information to see which hospital they flew to."

There was a ping, and Deep paused for a moment leaning in. "This article just popped up saying a second man died in the explosion. No further information listed."

"Okay, we need to find out where McKayla is and what injuries she's sustained. We need to know if Misha was with her and if he's still alive. No names, Deep? If Misha's dead, this mission is D.O.A."

"Pending the notification of the family, the names will be withheld from the public," Deep read. "I'm looking at a news feed. One second."

"I doubt either guy is Misha," Lynx said. "Misha might have died in the hospital, but I doubt it was the guy who was already found. As a former soldier and a CIA officer, McKayla would put mission first. She would report if she knew Misha was dead, then her own status. Though, sure, it might be that she doesn't know where Misha is."

"Look at this." Deep tapped a key then pointed to the wall screen where a news report was showing high-def CCTV footage. "That's McKayla there crawling out of the door, correct?"

They watched all the way through the image of a man (not Misha) disappearing behind the explosion, two women and a man face down on the sidewalk, McKayla crawled out of the body, checked for viability, then dragged Misha back into the building.

"Ooo-whee," Gator said. "That there is superhuman."

"She's covered in blood," Jack said. "And he wasn't, isn't that interesting?"

"He took the blast." Striker folded his arms over his chest and pressed back in his seat. "She took the glass windows. Which would you rather?"

"Glass," the men said together.

"Deep, can you go back to the—" White's phone rang. She quickly swiped it. "White."

"Hey, so bit of a kerfuffle," McKayla yelled.

"We're aware. We saw you on the news." White peered at McKayla in the video chat. She was pale and had visible gashes on her hands when she scratched her fingers through her hair. "I'm at Iniquus with your new security team, Strike Force. Contracts are signed, and they'll be wheels up at midnight. Which hospital are you in?"

McKayla scowled and White couldn't interpret the expression.

"I'm putting you on speakerphone with a room of people," White said.

McKayla shook her head and pointed at her ear.

"Hearing damage," White told the room.

Deep caught White's eye. "I can give you a secure video conference site that can put up subtitles in real time if that would help McKayla communicate."

White texted: **Sending link with real-time subtitles. 2 secs.**

McKayla read then offered a thumbs up and disconnected.

White's messages pinged.

Deep could work a computer like a wizard worked his wand.

The text was forwarded and a few seconds later, McKayla was up on the war room screen for all to see.

Deep adjusted the monitor's camera to take in the room.

"Can you hear me?" White asked.

"Okay. Fair warning. My eardrums are for shite right now. Sorry if I'm yelling." She squinted and her face came in tight to her phone screen.

They could all see the cuts and scratches over her face and neck.

"Well, hey, I know you." McKayla lifted her hand to her cheek for a finger wave. "Hi there, Striker." She extended her arm again so they could see her whole torso. "Wow, Jack and Blaze. Old home week. Interesting to see you on the screen on the day that I got bombed. Well, according to the news, not bombed just exploded."

"I'm at Iniquus with your new security team." Almost instantly her words showed up on the bottom of the inserted image—the image that McKayla would see on her phone. "Iniquus's Strike Force. Contracts are signed, and they'll be wheels up at midnight. So, we—"

McKayla cut White off, yelling. "I want to go first, please."

And Deep adjusted the volume down.

"That's fine," White said, "but you're screaming so the whole hospital can hear you. We can see the words typed out if you whisper. And please don't say anything that shouldn't be said in public. Which hospital?"

The room could see McKayla's gaze tracking along the bottom of her screen as she read.

Did the explosion completely destroy her hearing? That would be career ending.

McKayla dragged a finger across her lips. "Okay. It's the Royal Something Or Other Hospital. I'm leaving so no worries. My security guy, John, just needs to figure out how to get me to my car. It's parked far away, and he can't pull up for me to jump in. Second, and much more important, I wanted you to understand that going forward, I insist on a tactical K9 as part of my team. One that can alert to explosives." This time, they couldn't hear her at all, but the words trailed across the screen.

White shook her head. "I'm not going to be able to get Langley to pay for you to have a security team on top of a security team. It was hard enough to get this contract to go through. It's not going to happen."

"I'll pay for it. I'm not worried about that. I'm worried about my life. The whack jobs are always trying to get to me, and now it could be that someone is targeting Misha."

"Who?" White asked. "They said it was a gas pipe explosion. Rare, sure. But it happens. Wrong place. Wrong time."

McKayla looked down in heavy concentration, then raised her hand to wave near her head.

Lynx leaned forward. "Okay, so something you saw isn't jiving for you right now, and you can't recall what. I can help you with that later with hypnosis if you'd like. But let's give it a couple of days of not trying to remember so your brain can rest. I'm Lynx by the way. I'll be supporting you from D.C. while you're traveling."

McKayla nodded. "Yes, thank you. I'll probably want to take you up on that if it doesn't come to me on its own." She laid a palm on her forehead. "Look, White, have Iniquus send me the electronic contract for the K9. I'll sign it and have the money deposited. If Iniquus can't get something together for me, I'll hire elsewhere. But it seems that it would be best if we all played on the same team." Her camera turned with her as she twisted to look over to the left, the phone tracking with her turn. "Team 'keep McKayla alive'. Right?" She focused back on White then let her eyes slide over to Striker. "Will you do this for me, Striker?"

"Let me talk this through with Command and the Cerberus Tactical team leaders and see who we have available, okay? I'll do my best to accommodate you. I agree it's optimal if we're all used to working together. And as I understand it, having a cohesive security force is the reason why you're bringing on Iniquus instead of using your regular team."

"Wait," Lynx said. "McKayla, that's not the real reason for the new security team, is it?"

White listened carefully to Lynx. With her ability to read body language, she was picking up on something that White had missed.

McKayla licked her lips.

"Are you willing to share?" Lynx asked. Her voice was warmly encouraging. White would have to practice that tone for when there was a need to 'good-friend' some information out of someone.

"I put together a security team when I became wealthy, and the threats started coming in. I ended my contract with them when I started this mission at Misha's request. The security I'm using were suggested by Misha's team."

"Your present team is beholden to and aligned with your asset?" Striker clarified.

"That's correct. Misha was skittery and nervous about our relationship. As long as there was a security team that was protecting me from whack-jobs, I was fine with them reporting on me to Misha. White and I agreed that since there was nothing for them to see or hear that would upset Misha, that allowing my security to spy on me and report back would soothe Misha's brow, so to speak. But now... Yes, I'm beginning to feel vulnerable. Russia's aggression is having an icy effect on everything and everyone. To the point that I was about to talk to White about moving on. Misha's become a recluse of late. Then, Misha got summoned to the Seychelles."

"And you're taking advantage of the fact that your head of security was in a motorcycle accident?" Lynx asked. "It's the cover you needed to get someone you trusted at your back?"

"Right. I need a team that isn't double dipping," McKayla said. "I need them to be loyal to me alone. And here," she stopped to laugh, "you aren't loyal to me alone. You're loyal to the CIA. Your number one is CIA." Her words were almost silent in the room, but the technology was able to pick up the subtleties and display them on the feed.

"Let me be clear," Striker said. "We have a security and support contract. Our number one priority is your safety and well-being."

McKayla read that twice then looked straight at Striker. "Thank you."

"After the Seychelles, we could see if Misha goes back into his hermitage," McKayla said. "If that's the case, I'm just spinning wheels here."

"You had your outing today with Ivan. That's not seclusion," White pointed out.

"I was surprised that we had a tea today, *especially* with Ivan and Rachel. I was sure there would be something important passed between the two men. But it turned out to be a nothing burger." She paused and looked past her phone again. "Until the explosion that is. Hey, I see my doctor coming down the hall. Let me find out what he has to say about getting me signed out. Then, I'll go see if I can find out anything about Misha."

"You don't know his status?" White asked.

"So far, I've almost zero information about him. I know he was alive on the helicopter. That's it. If I don't call back, then I'll see the team here tomorrow." She thrust her chin forward. "With a bomb sniffing dog. Agreed?"

16

ASHER GIDEON

Cerberus Headquarters, Iniquus

"CATCH ME UP," Ash said as he sauntered into the shower room. It was made for K9 and human alike. "Hey, buddy." Ash said when Hoover locked him in his focus. "Did you have a good day? Huh? Get to bite the bad man?" he asked in a high-pitched reward voice.

Ash would swear that Hoover sent him a grin as his K9 moseyed alongside Bear to go hangout in the doggy dryer.

Judge was standing in the dog tub, where Ares was massaging shampoo into his fur. "Clay is the worst. Every time I think I've scrubbed him clean, I find another patch that makes the water run orange."

Ash toed his shoes off. "How'd it go with the police, Bear?" He wasn't sure if the suit was recoverable. He tugged his clothes off and chucked everything into the washing machine. After he knew if the clay could come out, he'd send it on to the dry cleaners. It was probably toast, though.

Making his way into the shower, Ash turned the faucet and ducked his head under the heavy spray as Bear explained, "By the time the PD got there, I was just letting Judge and Hoover hold their prisoners. The men were too afraid to move, just laid there like statues. Rolled over to get cuffed and patted down. They're being booked at the station as we speak."

"And Napoli?" Ash held his hand under the shampoo dispenser and pressed the button.

"Mr. Napoli refused to give a statement. Out you go, Judge. All fresh and clean. Let's get you under the dryer with your buddy Hoover. There you go."

Ash heard Judges nails clacking across the tile floor.

"Refused to open his mouth," Ares continued. "He wanted to get on the first flight out. Didn't care where the plane was headed, just out. So, I accommodated him."

"What did you tell him about his family?" Bear asked.

"He never asked about his wife or son's wellbeing. Or you, Ash, and the dogs for that matter. He just said that we should continue to cover Mrs. Napoli and Joey until we could get her on the flight to Italy."

"What happened at the hospital?" Bear asked.

"The FBI had a private talk with Mrs. Napoli." Ash did a final rinse and reached for a towel. "From what words slipped out from under the door, it looks like Mr. Napoli and friends are facing some major RICO charges." He used the acronym for Racketeer Influenced and Corrupt Organizations charges.

"Yeah, I got a call from a detective asking what flight I

put him on," Ares said from his own shower stall. "I'm assuming there's a welcoming party waiting for his arrival. So how did you leave it with his family?"

"I waited around until the U.S. Marshal Service showed up." Ash wrapped the towel around his waist and walked down to the dryer to give a quick rub and kiss to Hoover. "Hey buddy, Mrs. Napoli says to tell you guys that you still terrify her, but she loves you for what you did for them."

Ash lifted his voice as he headed into the locker room for a change of clothes. "The Marshals showed up pretty quick and relieved me of my duties." At his locker, he stepped into a pair of boxer briefs.

"And to think Napoli brought us on to torment his wife," Bear said.

"Just deserts," Ares answered as he walked into the locker room unbuttoning his shirt.

Ash caught Ares' gaze. "It's a good thing, though, that she had that ticket out of her hell ride. Not everyone has a viable exit—the financial wherewithal to run. A way to stay safe once they leave. Yeah, it was a rough day for the two of them. But things should brighten up."

"Here's hoping," Ares said.

17

ASHER GIDEON

Cerberus Headquarters, Iniquus

ORTEGA SAUNTERED into the locker room. "Huddle up, gentlemen."

Bear rounded in from the wet room with Hoover and Judge trotting at his heels.

Ortega gave him a nod. "An interesting turn on that assignment. Well done, gentlemen. A quick update on today's mission. Police have custody of the two assailants. Mrs. Napoli, Ares, and Bear have given their accounts to the detectives. Ash, they need a statement from you."

"Yes, sir."

"Mrs. Napoli and Joey have left the hospital," Ortega continued, "and are under the protection of the U.S. Marshal Services as Mrs. Napoli starts her work with the FBI."

Hoover came over to lay at Ash's feet, and Ash

wiggled his fingers behind his dog's ears. "Good news," Ash said to Ortega, then bent to rub Hoover under the chin and accept his dog's kisses. "You did great, Hoove."

"Mongoose is on his way in to give Hoover and Judge a veterinary check." Ortega rested his hands on the back of one of the black captain's chairs. "I relayed your initial assessments that both dogs came out of that takedown unscathed. Hopefully, Mongoose will give them a thumbs up that they're both good to go. With the mission complete, the hotwash is going to have to wait."

A hotwash was the team's opportunity to process everything that had happened while they were working. The good. The bad. And the ugly. They tried to refine what worked and make it muscle memory. They tried to pick apart the weaknesses and correct them.

Ash was definitely going to talk about the suits at an outdoor event. Urban, sure. But that meant shopping, theater, office buildings. Even with the specialized construction of his suit, fighting in that suit jacket in the rain and slick clay today was no bueno.

"There's a mission that Strike Force is developing," Ortega said. "It's taken a turn, and Command is requesting a tactical force multiplier. Ares, Ash—" he nodded his chin at one then the other. "I want you to head over there with me now. Mace is on his way and will meet us in their war room."

Of Bravo's six operator/dog teams, three were designated search and rescue (SAR) and three were scent trained tactical dogs. The SAR dogs were ready to jump at a moment's notice to any mass disaster in the world. The three tactical dogs and their handlers—Ares, Ash, and

Mace—could be lent out to military and civilian operations where their talents could ease the mission.

"I'll stay here with the dogs and wait for Goose," Bear said.

The others headed out the door and piled into Ortega's SUV.

"Do we have a contractor's name?" Ares asked as he shut the front passenger door and reached for his seatbelt.

"Bit of an odd assignment." Ortega leaned forward and pressed the engine on. "The contracting alphabet is the CIA. But they only contracted with Strike Force. The K9 component is a separate contract that the officer is paying for personally." After Ash shut his door, Ortega put the SUV in gear and headed toward the main headquarters building.

"The CIA officer is paying out of their own pocket?" Ash asked from the back seat. "Has that ever been done before?"

"Bob and I started Cerberus, so I know the entirety of its history. I can assure you that this has never been something we've done before. To be clear, whichever operator is assigned—and I'll review this separately with Mace if it's he and Diesel that get the mission—they will be under the Strike Force command structure. You will be using their communications and logistical help. You will answer to Commander Rheas. I will say this here while I can say it privately. You will consider the best interest of *your* client over that of the CIA. And, if you feel that the CIA is endangering the client, your objective is solely to keep that individual safe. The client is the priority. Command will back that up should things go sideways. Your allegiance is to the contractor. Understood?"

"Sir," Ares and Ash said together.

"What operation is Strike Force undertaking?" Ares asked.

"Close protection and support." Ortega turned right down the main campus road that would take the team to Iniquus Headquarters.

"Close protection to the CIA?" Ash asked.

"Their field officer is a celebrity and always has security with her. Strike Force was going in to give her normal team some down time."

"Where and when is this?" Ares asked.

"London. Wheels up at midnight. The client has reserved a private jet for ease of bringing in what equipment we need. That will help with the bulky items like crates and food."

"Late in the game to be pulling one of us in," Ares said.

"Something changed and the officer is insisting on a K9 with a nose for explosives."

"Any ideas?" Ash asked.

"Once the call came in," Ortega said, "I did a quick internet search for London and explosives. Earlier today, there was an explosion at a private social club. Two dead. Lots of injuries. Could be that. Authorities are saying it was a gas pipeline, though. That system's been in the ground and not updated for about a hundred years." Ortega pulled into a parking spot. "I guess we're about to find out."

. . .

AS THE BRAVO men took seats at one of the long conference tables in Strike Force War Room, White introduced herself. "We were about to review this tape again, and it's just as good an introduction to the case as any other." She turned and looked directly at Ash. "Then we can go from there."

The room lights dimmed, and a London news clip came up on the screen. There was a bright flash of fire followed by a concussion that shook the camera. The cars in the parking lot lifted into the air, many were engulfed in flames. Others flashed their lights as their alarms sounded.

Three people—two women and a man—were sprawled on the ground, unmoving.

A woman crawled out of the building.

Hair in her face, clothes ripped, skin soot-covered. Blood.

"Oh, sweetheart, no," Ash whispered from behind his hand.

Ash would recognize her anywhere. That was Dealer. Captain McKayla Pickard. Bajillionaire would-be crypto disruptor. What in the hell was she doing playing there?

Flashes of the roadside bombing in Khandud, Afghanistan over a decade ago, when he'd pulled Dealer from under the rubble and got her onto a pararescue helicopter extraction strobed through his mind.

Ash blinked himself back to present day.

White paused on the face of a man that Dealer was dragging back into the building.

"I'm really hoping he's not dead or gravely injured. We hired Iniquus to accompany these two to the Seychelles end of week." White scanned across the line of Bravo men. "If you don't happen to recognize her, that's McKayla Pickard with her dress up around her waist. And the guy she's dragging is Misha Popyrin, our unwitting Russian asset and key to the Kremlin old boys' club."

She turned to look at the screen. "She says he was alive at that point. She lost track after their helicopter ride to the hospital. If he dies, or can't go to that event in the Seychelles, getting the information out of that gathering is going to be damned near impossible. I don't care how cold I sound. He needs to get himself straightened out. There are too many lives at risk."

White pressed play and they ignored the rest of the scene, focusing only on McKayla with the skirt of her dress tied around her waist, when she powered herself backward with Misha's torso in her lap. Her panties slipped down. It looked like she was scraping the shit out of her backside. When her adrenaline ebbed, that was going to hurt like hell.

"FYI, I know her," Ash said quietly as the video ended, and White pressed the fob to still the frame.

Dealer is a CIA officer? Consider my mind blown.

And to think she'd been playing in his dreams this morning when Hoover woke him up. Premonition?

Looking over her shoulder at the screen, White tapped her fob and brought up a headshot of Dealer.

In this photo, Dealer looked older than when they had

known each other. But then, she'd been twenty-four, and that was a decade-plus ago. Ash looked older, too.

Ash had seen Dealer's pic—*her being Dealer was a lifetime ago, man, that's not who she is now. She's McKayla*. She was back to being a brunette after years of being a blonde on magazine covers.

While Ash recognized the image; he didn't recognize the person. Going after wealth was antithetical to the Dealer he had known.

Dealer was down to earth. She wanted a cabin on the top of a mountain. She wanted boots, and jeans, and flannel shirts. She wanted to be surrounded by peace and the smell of pine trees, to read books and play her guitar for the forest critters. As for money? She had said she wanted to find financial ways to help the women of the world survive without men.

Ash had seen too much in the Middle East and what happened to women and their children when they were wholly dependent on men with no legal way to provide for themselves. He had completely understood why Dealer felt passionate about helping them.

In Afghanistan, a woman, once widowed, was a tragedy. The women weren't allowed to work. They'd gather, hidden under their burkas, lining the streets, like a flock of birds sitting on a phone wire, begging for a bit of bread or a coin to feed themselves and their children.

Some men had soft hearts and would help. Most, though, were abusive, yelling at the women, calling them names, punching at them and spitting.

The American soldiers wanted to help, but if they paid any attention at all to the women, the women could be beaten in the streets. A little creativity sometimes got the job done safely. It was good to think when a family might go to bed without tears from hunger pain.

Many of the women allowed their very young daughters to be married off to much older men. It was a terrible thing to happen to the girls. But with a husband, at least, they'd have food in their bellies.

It was that kind of tortured decision-making that Dealer had wanted to remove by giving the mothers opportunities.

Microloans were what she'd been talking about back in Afghanistan on those long boring days when they lazed about sharing any thought that wafted into their minds.

It had made sense to Ash; Dealer had a finance degree, after all.

Ash guessed something in her changed or De—McKayla wouldn't be a billionaire now.

Billionaire, with a B.

That was just a mind-boggling crazy amount of wealth.

So, when Ash said he "knew her" it was definitely past tense. This was someone who had the same body but was obviously not the same personality as she had been when she dreamed of saving the world.

Dude, did you NOT just learn this lesson with Mrs. Napoli? You don't know what you don't know. Stop with the assumptions. Wait for the facts.

Facts like how do you square it that once De—McKayla had become one of the wealthiest women on planet Earth, she joined the CIA?

"How well do you know her?" White asked.

Now? Not at all.

Ash was doing a balancing act. He owed his team the truth as it could make the difference on a mission. He wasn't about to tell someone that De—*McKayla* and he had been lovers.

Ash's mom had taught him you don't kiss and tell. Like it or not, a woman's reputation was a fragile thing. That rule was just too deeply ingrained for him to not feel it as a duty to protect a woman's privacy.

And just as importantly—more importantly—if McKayla was going into a dangerous situation, Ash wanted to be the one who had her back.

He could feel her vibrating in his bones, again.

"Her call sign was Dealer," Ash responded to White's question. "She spent a couple months as cultural support for our team. She's the one who did all the interface with the local women we encountered. The last time I saw her, she was recovering from being in the vicinity of a car bomb. SEAL Team Three rotated home. I joined up with Striker's team with Jack and Blaze." He tipped his ear toward his old teammates. "I heard through the pipeline that McKayla attached to a Ranger unit and had headed out to the mountains where they were radio silent." He thought he'd sounded matter of fact about all that.

"So, you knew her professionally," Striker clarified.

"Yes, sir."

"And…you had also had a private relationship?" That was Lynx. It was pointless to obfuscate around Lynx, and Ash knew that. It didn't feel like she was doing a gotchya thing, there. Her team was going out in the field, and they needed to know everyone was squared away.

White was looking at him extra hard.

Yeah, there was also the CIA. Ash knew that the people who worked for the CIA had to disclose every damned detail of their entire lives. It made sense, the CIA didn't want their officers vulnerable to extortion.

Surely, Ash's name was in McKayla's file.

So, this was how Ash decided to handle it, "It's hard to categorize our relationship. If we were in the States, you might call it dating. Over there, we were coming and going. When we saw each other, we had some kind of relationship, I simply can't define it for you. After I transferred to Striker's team in Virginia Beach, our paths didn't cross again. It's been…more than a decade since I've had any kind of contact with her."

"All right," White moved on. "We need a K9 to insert as part of McKayla's security. She wants an explosive sniffer." She turned to Ortega. "What have you got?"

"All three of the tactical teams under my command are trained to alert to explosives and boobytraps."

"Okay." White drummed her fingers. "Let's figure out the best choice."

Ash leaned forward with his heart pounding in his chest. "Is McKayla okay?"

White smiled. "She's getting discharged from the hospital. She's scraped up pretty well. She has ringing in her ears. Time will tell if that goes away. But for the most part, she's fine. Thank you for asking."

"How long is this job?" Ortega held his pen over a legal pad.

"Strike Force is contracted for two months, or the mission otherwise ends. Like," she jerked her thumb over her shoulder at the screen, "if our buddy Misha there kicked the bucket."

"A tactical K9 can pose some issues in polite society versus on the battlefield," Ares said.

"Give me some examples." White moved to a chair.

"My K9, Judge," Ares explained, "is a Malinois and ill-suited to sitting at attention for hours on end in a close protection scenario. Unless it was, for example, a parade route or a marathon and we were pacing the client. He's too high energy to be a good fit for urban work, going into polite society. That leaves one of the German shepherds, either Hoover or Diesel."

Mace leaned forward. "Hoover is the most patient of the three."

"Another issue with the dogs is that we don't have the authority to bring the dogs into any private space. We could only be there by invitation," Ortega explained. "Same with many public spaces that don't normally accommodate dogs."

"So, what do you do?" White asked.

"We speak with the management and see what they're willing to put up with and conform to their requirements. For example, they might allow us an appointment before a space opens to the public to go in and sniff it for explosives. But that's really not helpful if the rest of security is lax."

"Do you have a solution?"

Mace looked over at Ortega. "Hairyman Plan?"

All four Bravo men went still, thinking.

"That looks like a good one." White leaned forward, expectantly. "Tell me about the Hairy Man Plan."

"Where all will this mission be taking place?" Ortega asked. "London, right?"

"And the Seychelles," Striker added.

Ares caught Striker's gaze. "Just never in the United States, right?"

"That's right." White's voice was painted with curiosity. "Why does that matter?"

"We've debated this plan from an ethical point of view," Ortega explained. "Our Iniquus ethicist said no to America. But that in certain other countries this is fine."

White held out her hands, asking for context.

"On Cerberus Tactical K9 Team Alpha, one of the team members, Noah, has vertigo from ear damage during his last tour of duty with the military. He uses a stability dog named Hairyman, a Newfie. When Hairyman had a foot injury last year, we trained Hoover to take his place to give Hairyman time to recover."

"Hoover, a tactical K9 acted as a stability dog?" Lynx asked. "Well, Hoover would make sense. He's big for a shepherd and he has the countenance of a service dog."

"Until he's asked for a bite," Ash added. Hoover was no sissy. Today, he was on point every step of the way.

"I...okay," White said. "And since McKayla, too, has damaged ears, you're suggesting that we use Hoover to act as McKayla's stability dog. That way she can take him everywhere with her?" White frowned deeply as she looked at the floor. "Why is that an ethical issue in America and not England?"

"In London, people take their dogs everywhere," Ortega explained. "Dogs, for example, can ride public transportation for free. Service dogs aren't required to be in vest or have credentials—so we wouldn't be lying about his service. He would simply wear a vest with a stability handle that McKayla could hold and people could come to their own conclusions."

"If anyone were to question or make an issue of the dog going in, we cannot use the service dog angle. We'd just have to leave. We cannot lean on disability laws with the ruse."

"And this won't work in the United States?" White asked. "If they were to fly to New York, for example?"

"No ma'am, we won't use that tactic in the U.S." Ortega used his "line in the sand" voice, the one he used when he was telling clients what would be allowed and what absolutely would not. No one challenged Ortega when he used that particular tone. "In America, venues are not as welcoming to dogs. Many who depend on service dogs for medical or emotional support have a rough time of it. Many people who don't understand the laws give them a hard time when they're just trying to move through their day. We've seen it time and again with Noah and Hairyman."

"And it gets worse when poorly trained dogs are foisted onto the public with just a vest bought off the internet, declaring that they have legal rights," Mace added. "We don't want to do anything that would hurt the disabled community that depends on their dogs, like our teammate does."

"So just not in America," White checked.

"Yes, ma'am," Ortega said. "With the caveat that if asked, that the handler not lie. They can say something like, 'This is my dog, when I hold on to his handle, I feel more stable'. It's a true statement and doesn't interfere with the laws."

"McKayla has some ear damage from the explosion. It throws off her balance. She's using a K9 to keep her from falling, holding on to a stability handle. Would that impact Hoover's ability to do scent work? Would Hoover lose some of his dexterity leaping into a fight or have increased risk because of the stability harness?"

"The apparatus has a quick release," Ash said.

"Can someone else handle Hoover, then?" White asked. "Can McKayla? I mean, there's no time to train her on a K9. Once the team is in London, it's two days then you're off to the islands."

"Seeing that very issue if we were ever to try the Hairyman Plan," Ortega said. "Hoover can walk beside someone while Ash maintains command. Ash would walk in close protection formation. McKayla would have her hand on the stability handle. If there was something Hoover needed to communicate, be it scenting explosives, for example, he would signal as usual. If Hoover needed to fight, McKayla would press the quick release, and Hoover would be left with the tactical vest he normally wears in a hot situation."

"Ash and no one else," White clarified.

"It would take a while to train someone to effectively handle Hoover especially at this task," Ash said feeling that the Fates were on his side with this assignment. "So, me and me alone."

White looked over at Lynx to get her read on all this. "Thoughts?"

"I can't think of anything better than to keep a dog by

McKayla's side. And I have to say, I appreciate that Iniquus thought this through and gave parameters. I have a friend who uses a medical alert dog, and it's not easy for her family to be out in public. But McKayla is a celebrity so that should ease things for her in terms of questions especially if there's an article in the papers about her issues. Iniquus can send out a press release to cover the situation. It could include pictures of McKayla and her new pal, without identifying Hoover as a working dog."

White turned her focus on Ash. "I think that hits all of the angles that I had questions about. It's not my call here since it's not my contract." She turned to Striker. "But I suggest we use Ash and Hoover."

Striker looked at Lynx, and she gave him the nod, saying, "I think that Ash is the right man for McKayla." Then Striker slapped his hands on his thighs, sealing it. Done deal. "Looks like the Hairyman Plan is a go."

Ortega stood. "After a violent takedown today, Hoover is getting a well check from his vet. As long as Goose says Hoover's mission ready, Ash, looks like you're heading out. Go home, get packed for the long haul, grab Hoover's paperwork, and your passport. You can write your after-action report for the D.C. P.D. on the plane and email it to me. You're wheels up at midnight."

18

ASHER GIDEON

Heathrow, Private Hangar, London

THE INIQUUS TEAM pulled out their phones and turned off airplane mode.

Immediately, they all dinged and pinged as the messages from the last seven and a half hours dropped into the message folders.

Striker pressed number two on his quick dial to bring up the war room.

"Deep."

"Striker here. We've landed. I have you on speaker phone with the team. The pilot left the plane. We're clear to speak. What have you got for me?"

"I talked with McKayla. First, we were able to have a normal toned conversation. She said she still has some tinnitus, but she can hear okay and thinks she can modulate her voice. I agree. She did fine. I didn't need to repeat myself to her. That's good news. Second, she said she contacted Misha. He's alive and was lucid enough to have a conversation with her on the phone. She hasn't seen him in person to know what his medical status is. She made plans with him to go for a visit this evening. He said he had lots of tests scheduled for the day."

"Copy that."

"Next, McKayla sounded a little skittish when we were talking about her security team. I'm sure she can give you more information about that when you get there. She's told them that she's going to go lie down on a friend's bed and be spoon fed soup."

"And in reality?" Striker asked.

"McKayla has a cottage in the country that is her secret retreat when she's had enough of being under a microscope. I have that address. She asks that the dog person go to her address without her London security team knowing that the dog exists. She thinks it'll be a better cover if the dog doesn't look like it's attached to Strike Force."

"She's correct," Ash said. This was better than he could have hoped for. Ash wasn't sure how he was going to react seeing McKayla again. He'd prefer that it was a natural reaction rather than him trying to stand there, coldly professional in front of his team, when all his thoughts since he'd boarded the plane were heated.

I remember you, Dealer. I remember us.

"McKayla has requested that Strike Force," Deep continued, "go on to her penthouse and meet with her security team. There will be three. The fourth, their lead, as we've been told, is hospitalized with an accident unrelated to the explosion. Once you're comfortable, there will be a changing of the guard and her team will start their R&R."

"And once they're out of the picture," Striker said, "we can all join up and plan next steps. Sounds perfect to me. You'd think she was operationally trained or something."

"Or something." Deep's voice held a grin. "I'm here for the next four hours, then Lynx will take over my post to provide assistance. If you need something that she can't provide, I'll be on campus and available. We'll be switching back and forth. Someone will always be in the war room. Here's to Fair Winds and Following Seas."

"Thank you. Striker out." He swiped to end the call, turning to Ash. "You have that address?"

"I do. The text says there's a rental vehicle waiting for me outside the hangar. And there's a gym that Deep's rented out for training purposes near the secret house."

Striker gave him a nod. "After we get through with the customs agent, how about you and Hoover head on over to re-introduce yourselves to McKayla—it's going to be hard to get used to that name change. For me, she's Dealer."

Blaze and Jack nodded their agreement.

Ash decided to lay low and not respond.

"We'll all do the best we can with that." Striker turned to Ash. "Go reintroduce yourself to McKayla. We'll handle your gear for you."

"Thanks."

"Just let us know if you need us to bring anything to the gym."

"The bite suits," Ash said.

"Fun times," Striker said. "Take McKayla to the gym and teach her how to work Hoover with the stability vest. Make sure she can quick release without thought. Then, the three of us will join you. Those bite suits will let us train McKayla on how we want her to react if there were to be an attack and give Hoover a chance to protect McKayla so he's clear on his duties."

"Exactly." Ash nodded toward the window.

"Then, we'll head on to the hospital and see what's up with Misha." Striker stood and stepped toward the door. "Could be this mission folds before we really get started."

ASH TUCKED his vehicle under a tree in front of the secret country house and sat there for a minute trying to stop his hands from shaking.

Flashes of Dealer had taken up way too much brain space. Ash had needed every bit of his SEAL focus training to get out to her house, making sure he stayed on the left side of the road without zoning into autopilot, and sliding into the habit of the right side—well, the wrong side, in this case—putting the citizens in jeopardy.

What would McKayla think of his showing up in her life again?

Hoover whined beside him, snaking his head under Ash's arm, and resting it on Ash's thigh.

"I'm nervous as shit, Hoove." He opened the door and unloaded Hoover, trying to screw his game face on. He looked at his watch, fifteen minutes early. "Hoover, go potty, have a bit of a run."

Part procrastination, part taking care of his K9.

"She knows it's me who's coming right?" Ash had asked White at least three times.

"I told her your name."

At the time McKayla and he knew each other, she was Captain Dealer.

Ash had been Ensign Gideon as one of the very few SEALs that started out as an officer with a four-year degree. The SEALs had a healthy dose of disdain for the "cake-eaters," the folks that sat around the office making life-or-death decisions about the SEALs with very little understanding of what a body could actually do and not do.

Major hint, they couldn't do what Hollywood said they could. Yet, they were humans that willingly worked through illness and injury. Through physical and mental pain.

Ash got the whole cake-eater issue.

But Ash had never lived that lifestyle, he'd gone from boot to selection.

Going in as an officer meant he wouldn't be punished for failing Hell Week like the others who tried. For an enlisted sailor, it was a huge risk and took considerable bravery just signing up. If a sailor failed, they'd spend the rest of their career scraping paint and doing other crap jobs.

Ash hadn't known what might be heading his way as an officer if he rang the bell and called it quits; he just assumed it would be crap, too.

Though, Ash never really considered the possibility of failing.

It wasn't his mindset.

You go in, you figure it out.

Still, there was an extra big target on his back from selection through SEAL Team Three.

It was a distinction that made things uncomfortable until he made the move to the East Coast and was on Striker Rheas' team.

Yeah, when he knew Dealer, Ash was Ensign Gideon. Call sign Giddyman.

With teammates with names like DeathEater, Comet, and Danger, Giddyman was Team Three's way of punishing him for having the nerve to show up with a university degree and an officer's paycheck.

Ash let it all slick off his back like water off a sea lion hanging out on the rocks of the inland channel back in Juneau. Just shake it off and move on.

When Ash transferred to the East Coast, Striker's team rechristened him as "Ashes" and was later shortened to just "Ash."

Seemed lame since his given name was Asher.

But this one was an honor. Ash had been tasked with a very delicate demolition job. The Goldilocks of all demolition jobs. Too little? People died. Too much? People died. Ash had done it just right and everyone got home whole and healthy.

"Ashes" from the children's rhyme. *"Ashes, Ashes, we all fall down!"*

Relative to McKayla, that was recent history.

Back when they knew each other, she'd called him

"Giddy." Or when she was horny, she'd call him "Giddy-up" with a broad smile and a shake of her booty that gave him a rock-cock.

Ash was glad that Hoover was taking advantage of the command and was doing sprints around the grass.

As new images of Dealer sprang to mind, Ash needed a minute to cool his jets.

19

McKayla Pickard

The "Friend's Place" Cottage, London, England

McKayla was expecting the knock on her door. Her eyes sought out the wall clock as she covered the phone's receiver and called out. "Hello! Come on in." Two on the dot, the guy was prompt, she'd give him that.

She spun toward the far wall so she could end her conversation, without having to make her first contact with her new K9 security guy a finger wave and a mouthed, "just a minute."

"Look, I have someone at my door, Misha. I need to go. But I'll be to the hospital this evening after dinner the way we planned. Is there anything I can bring to make you more comfortable?"

"No, but please make sure you come." Misha's voice sounded weak but urgent. "I have something important we need to talk about."

"Is there news about the explosion?"

"Downing Street is assuring my embassy that it was the gas line and not an assault on Russian citizens."

"Can you imagine if that led to World War III? Some terrorist targeting Russians in London? Good that it's not. Listen, my stability dog and his trainer have just arrived. I'm being rude to them."

"Tonight," Misha insisted. "Promise."

"Of course." McKayla pulled the phone from her ear, looking at the screen as she tapped the red dot to end the conversation. She turned to greet her K9 security team.

The door held wide, the operator stood there frozen, his hand resting on the knob.

Asher Gideon, call sign Giddyman.

Her heart stopped.

White should have warned her.

She had to have made the connection. When McKayla went through the checks to gain employment with the CIA, she'd had to list everyone whom she'd had a sexual roll with and Asher Gideon was one of the few names that graced that list.

White had called this guy "Ash" no last name.

So, McKayla had heard that as a call sign like "Striker" and "Blaze." Even "Jack" wasn't Jack. His name was James and Jack came from "if you give me problems, I'm gonna jack you up." Or some such SEAL shite they used to spew.

McKayla's mind was stuttering around, throwing out thoughts that were padding. Insulation from the crazy that was happening in her body.

She felt her face drain of color, and she damned well thought she was going to faint.

She'd been in an explosion yesterday. She could blame these sensations on that.

Though, she knew it was just the systemic blow of seeing *him* again.

Here.

Giddy.

He looked *nothing* like he did in Afghanistan.

His hair was cut short, his face clean shaven.

His eyes were the same—intelligent and kind—more wrinkles radiated from the corners. Some would call them laugh lines, McKayla knew they were hard earned, squinting into the horizon in the desert sun, looking for insurgents.

She'd never really seen his face before, only imagined what lay beneath the frazzle of hair, always dry and prickly, full of desert sand and wind debris. None of the oiled and tended beard-glam that was popular with some.

He stood in her living room.

Pristine in his Iniquus uniform.

So *very* odd.

"McKayla?"

Her real name on his lips made her body jerk as if she'd sustained a shock.

She had.

"They didn't tell you it would be me showing up?" Smooth as butter on a bun. Just the melt into her bones richness of his voice made her slick with need.

She still wasn't able to get her eyes to blink.

Ash slowly turned toward the door. Silently shut it and

threw the lock. He made a gesture and there was a clunk that pulled McKayla's attention. Her gaze slid down Ash's powerful frame to the enormous German shepherd who followed a silent command and laid down, tongue out, panting.

I feel you there, pooch. Me, too.

Ash turned back, and they just stared across the space, neither one breaking the silence that built between them.

For her, it was a storm of need.

Her heart squeezed down. Her jaw dropped as she tried to find oxygen.

"Dealer?" Ash lifted his arms out to the sides. Could have been a question, a welcoming gesture, the beginnings of a hug…

It looked like surrender.

Her body was moving.

She lunged forward at the same time he did.

Wrapping her cold fingers around his precious face, her mouth banged against his, teeth hitting teeth, tongues whipping wildly.

She gripped at him, sinking her nails into his flesh as their lips bruised each other in desperation.

She kissed him as if this was her one chance to grab all the passion from him that she could before life dragged them apart again.

It was the last gasping breath of a drowning person.

It was the last anguished scream before the fatal shot was fired.

He kissed her with every bit as much intensity.

Pawing at his belt, unbuttoning, unzipping, dragging

away the clothes that kept their skin from touching. They were tossing, kicking, scuffing, and prodding.

She worked a moment on her garments, then reached out to tug at his.

The dance of the frantic.

Naked, his skin was hot against the marble coolness of her shivering desire.

Reaching down, his powerful hands grasped her thighs, lifting her up so her arms and legs could wrap him.

She was the anaconda of lovers. A huntress looking for satiety.

"Bedroom," he demanded.

"Here. Anywhere," her mouth was on him again.

"Bedroom," he demanded.

She could feel his cock tapping on her ass with every step he took, following the direction of her pointed finger.

Kissing along the way, they banged into this wall in the hallway, then that. Like an old-fashioned pinball getting whacked toward the desired position, until he fell toward the bed. Turning gracefully to be on the bottom, as soon as their momentum settled, he rolled McKayla under him.

Her legs fell open to welcome him.

Up on his elbows, staring down at her. "Thank god," was all he said before she made angry love with him.

Furious love.

Years of frustration and recrimination, boiling through her.

Years of pain, turmoil, and self-denial.

They howled and gasped, growled, and mewled.

This wasn't *their* kind of sex.

Their kind of sex was furtive. It was a fox in the hen house.

She was the only woman on the base.

He was the only officer amongst his team of enlisted men.

Giddy and Dealer being a couple was okay by military standards. They were taboo in the eyes of every man inside the razor wire.

If they knew she was having sex, if they heard her moans and orgasms, she would be endangered.

Outside of the mores of polite society, there was military discipline that held the smallest key to the smallest lock imaginable.

McKayla would wake up in a sweat, panting with the images of rabid, hungry men snarling and ripping at each other to get to her. To strip her of her clothes and her dignity. To leap, one after the other onto her bones, taking their pleasure at her expense.

It was terrifying in a way that a man could never fathom.

In a way that she'd never given voice to—not even to Giddy.

Speaking the words of her terror out loud, who knew what goblin or demon might snatch them from the air and form them into the monster of action.

No, Giddy and she had had *furtive* sex.

The only woman in the only woman's tent, Giddy would sneak on his SEAL-trained silent feet, moving shadow to shadow until he slid into her tent.

The rule was no words. No sounds. Not even heavy breathing.

She would be ready for him, masturbating in the darkness, imagining him creeping toward her. Gliding callused hands over her curves, her breasts, imagining how it would feel once he had his hands on her body. The gooseflesh of excitement. The gasp that desperately wanted to escape her lips held back for survival's sake.

In the black of night, she'd been too afraid that it would be some other soldier with similar build, with the same shaggy Special Forces beard and long hair that moved into her space. How horrific that would be to make desperate love to a rapist?

Only Giddy was welcome to lie between her thighs and disappear into her body.

Moving on cat feet to the end of her cot, Giddy would squat and reach out a single index finger.

One tap for "I." Hold.

Four taps for "Love." Hold.

Three taps for "You."

She'd reach down and pull his hand, sliding it up her leg, covered with hair like a man's because there was little water at the base. She was lucky that she had diaper wipes to give herself the most cursory of baths.

He didn't care. Not even a little.

Time was short. They gave themselves fifteen minutes tops.

Giddy and Dealer had barely moved lest the cot joints called to the others, letting them know that while they'd been wrapping a fist around their own hard-ons and rubbing their own dicks raw, Ash was luxuriating in the velvet folds of a lust-slick pussy.

Amidst the clamor of her thoughts, Giddy stilled.

Kayla turned to see him holding up a blood coated hand.

The raw abraded skin on her arse wasn't yet ready to be stretched with her ankles over his shoulders, so he could bury himself so deep inside of her that each stroke had a bite of pain.

"I'm not on my period." Who cared? "I was in an explosion."

"Fuck, Dealer." He had stopped, was holding completely still.

"That's right," she exhaled. "Fuck Dealer. Fuck *me*. Don't you dare stop." She pulled her legs down from his shoulders, wrapping his waist, tightening the muscles of her thighs to hold him where he was. Desperate that he shouldn't try some gallantry shite and pull out before she'd had a chance to scream out this orgasm and every orgasm she'd had to swallow down all those years ago. She softened her voice from the angry desperation that she'd heard in her own tone. "Please, don't stop."

"Never." He bent, his mouth hard on hers.

With that kiss, he seemed to be drinking her in, absorbing her, lost in the tangle of their tongues.

But the frenzied energy dissipated, melted into the ether.

Ash slowed the dance.

As he stroked gently in and out of her, he explored her face and neck with his fingertips and butterfly kisses.

She thirsted for this attention.

Back in the desert, after Giddy and his team had moved on to their next assignment, McKayla was out with a team on a day so brutal that she'd ended up with heat stroke. No hospitals around, a CIA officer took her to a hotel with a bathtub and running water. Parched and blistered by the noon sun, skin bright red from boiling in her own blood, McKayla had soaked in the tub, drinking from her liter bottle, trying to regain the fluids from inside and out, in order to survive.

That's what she was doing here. What she felt Giddy was doing here.

Feelings, desiccated in the desert wind so long ago, McKayla needed this attention like the flower needed rain, to regain its strength and beauty. She was the resurrection plant that had survived, curled into a little ball, until it was time to bloom again.

Now, even those memories drifted away.

Her brain quieted, and McKayla could just listen to her body. Here. Now. In Giddy's arms.

She floated on the sensation.

She focused on the energy that welled in her veins.

Then the cork was pulled from a champagne bottle with such velocity that it pinged around the room, breaking things, then ricocheting on to the next. All the fragile glass tchotchkes sitting on her emotional shelf that represented loss and sorrow, longing and self-imposed deprivation, were smashed to bits, like the raining glass shards from yesterday's explosion.

As she lay there wrapped in the warmth of his arms, McKayla was exhausted from the power of her orgasm.

Why had she denied herself his love?

A mysterious self-punishment.

Some kind of self-flagellation.

She lay there both sated and yet desperate for more.

A starving person who had shrunk her stomach down from lack, looking at the buffet and only being able to hold so much.

Only so much joy.

Only so much love.

Too much, all at once, could make a starving person sick.

It was called "refeeding syndrome" and she'd learned about it in Africa. If nourishment is given too quickly serious complications could happen, further harming the body. Seizures, comas. Heart failure.

McKayla didn't have the emotional strength for another round of heart failure when it came to Asher Gideon.

She needed to pace herself.

20

MᴄKᴀʏʟᴀ Pɪᴄᴋᴀʀᴅ

The "Friend's Place" Cottage, London, England

"Wᴏᴡ, ʏᴏᴜ ʟᴏᴏᴋ…ᴄᴏɴꜰʟɪᴄᴛᴇᴅ." McKayla came out of the bathroom where she'd washed herself up, smeared antibiotic ointment on her cuts and abrasions, and pulled on a pair of white cotton panties.

In the time she was gone, Giddy had changed the blood smeared sheets and climbed back in. The top sheet tented with his dick in the ready position. But he wasn't wiggling a finger trying to entice her to jump on and go for another joy ride. He just looked at her with his beautiful eyes so intense that they hurt. "I knew that seeing you again was going to be a kick in the gut."

"Nice to see you, too." She stalled.

He threw back the corner of the sheet, inviting her back to bed with him. "Oh, sweetheart, no. Seeing you is a miracle. Just—" He pushed himself upright and scooted back against the headboard, scrubbing his hands over his face. "Man, that was a bad idea."

"Thank you." She crossed her arms under her naked breasts. Standing there, suddenly feeling cold.

"No. Not what I meant."

"Better start saying what you mean because you're starting to piss me off. And here I was in a nice little semi-coma from that orgasm."

"Exactly."

"Giddy, I'm not a mind reader." She climbed in next to him and pulled the sheet over her. "Ash, I mean. Sorry. I'll need a little practice."

He closed his eyes and shook his head. "It's complicated." Reaching out a hand to her, McKayla accepted it.

Ash drew her into his arms to cuddle her, dropping a kiss onto her nose as she looked up at him.

"Complicated. Isn't that the defining sentiment of our knowing each other?" McKayla asked.

"It is indeed." He stroked his hand over her hair, rubbing the ends between his fingers before reaching up to cradle her head and kiss her.

"Let's talk through the complications," she whispered.

"I thought I had a handle on my feelings for you. And I do *not*. I was coping up until you turned around and I saw your face."

Her fingers played with his smattering of chest hair. "What was the reason that we didn't get together after we were both out of the military?"

"The habit of secrecy and pretending that our feelings didn't exist. That's my guess. At first anyway."

"Oh, yeah, that. That habit kind of sucks. So that was

at first." She twisted to kiss his shoulder. "What happened at second?"

"I honestly assumed that you were in a relationship with someone and my showing up, hat in hand on your doorstep, was kind of pitiful. Magnify that after your face started splashing on all the magazine covers. Very glam. Very much a world that I couldn't fathom and *nothing* that I wanted to be part of."

"Oh."

McKayla was remembering who she was before she had lost herself in the crazy world of money and power.

She hated it. All of it.

All she'd wanted—all she'd dreamed about when they were in Afghanistan—was a cabin on a snow-covered mountain, a hot cup of sweet cocoa, a good book, and Ash bursting through the door, stomping his boots with an armful of logs he'd cut to keep her warm. Dumping them down, sweeping her up, and love making.

"You looked like you but not," Ash was saying. "I thought you had to have just gotten sick to death of MRE's and sand on your toothbrush and went one-eighty. If I approached you, I might look like I was trying to hitch my horse to your wagon. Which I had no desire to do. Be with you? Yes. Be with a celebrity and prance around at all of those swanky parties? Not a chance. I loved who you were back when I knew you and felt happy that things were going well for you now."

"I see." She rolled off of him, so she was lying flat on her back, looking up at the ceiling painted a cool summer blue. "Well, I haven't changed. The celebrity? That all took me by surprise. I have to say, I hate all of it." She let a smile slide wide. "Except for my on-call massage thera-pist. That's a definite positive in my life." She tipped her head away another few inches, scrutinizing his expression. "What's that look on your face?"

"I had an interesting life lesson handed to me yesterday about reading a situation based on the veneer. I was completely wrong about a client and the circumstances of their behavior. Happenstance helped me to see the problem and allowed me to offer a solution to her situation. It flashed in my mind, when I found out you took a job with the CIA that might be true about you and your wealth. I apologize for that."

"Accepted," she said. "But that's not the complication."

"Series of complications."

She pressed the heels of her hands into her forehead. "Bollocks," she exhaled.

McKayla came upright thrusting her face close to Ash's. "You're married," she accused as horror washed through her system. "You have kids." And out of nowhere, her stupid fragile emotions that had been surfing her nervous system since she dove through the doorway during the explosion, opened the flood gates, and she started to bawl.

It was the ugly, lips peeled away from the teeth in a grimace, nostrils-flared, eyes-squeezed-tight kind of bawling a five-year-old does when a bully breaks her favorite toy, and the world comes to an end.

Ash just shook his head, waiting for a break in sobs so he could say. "I'm not. Never have been. Not even close.

McKayla, listen to me." He reached out and jostled her shoulder. "That's not it."

She rubbed the back of her hand under her nose to catch the snot, so she could reach for a tissue.

"Still rattled by the accident, I see. Adrenaline and shock are hell on the system."

McKayla liked how he labeled this outburst matter-of-factly—just a human system doing what human systems do.

She felt like a jellyfish.

"Let's start with Hoover," Ash said.

"Hoover?"

"Is my dog. He's at your front door wondering what all that noise was about."

"Call him." She blew loud and long into her tissue. Then pulled another from the box to blow again.

"Yeah?" Ash checked.

With her nod and another honking wet blow into her tissue, Ash threw a sheet back over her before he called out, "Hoover! Come!"

There was a thump and a bump then clattering nails, racing over the wooden floors.

"Here, Hoove!"

An enormous German shepherd leaped onto the bed, stopped when he and McKayla were eye to eye. He looked confused. Then turned to Ash as if asking for an explanation.

"Hoover, lay down and meet McKayla." Ash put his hand on his dog's shoulder, showing Hoover that he was to lie down between their knees.

"McKayla, Hoover. He'll be your stability dog as you

deal with disequilibrium from damage to your ears in the blast."

"Yes." She held her hand out for Hoover to sniff. "White had me using a walker so that we could make that scenario work. Hello handsome. Aren't you magnificent?"

Once Hoover seemed satisfied with the intro and dropped his head onto Ash's lap, McKayla rubbed her fingers into his fur. "Mmmm. Dog medicine."

"Hoover is the only K9 we have who has the personality of a service dog, the training to act as a stability dog, the ability to scent explosives, *and* the ability to assist in takedowns should that be required."

"Superhero dog." She leaned down and kissed the top of Hoover's head. Already falling in love with him.

"Without a doubt." Ash bent his knee and shifted around so they were eye to eye. "I'm the only one who is trained to work him through all of those roles."

McKayla shook her head. She didn't see the problem. That was what they'd come here to do. "Okay."

"And then we have us." He gestured between them. "It's crazy how years just fold over. My feelings for you are every bit as intense as they were when I left you at the end of that mission."

She grinned as joy radiated through her body.

"It's crazy, how it's like not a day has gone by without my loving you and having you in my life." He took her face between his hands and looked deeply into her eyes. "I fucking love you, McKayla."

She held her breath. Hearing those words from Ash's mouth needed a minute to process through her system.

For so long she had been so cold. An icicle.

Composed of the same components as always, just frozen solid. She needed Ash's heat to warm her back to her normal state of fluidity. *"Melt me",* her mind called out.

Crazy internal words.

She didn't care. This felt crazy. Transformational.

And yet, there had always been barriers to *them.*

It was like fate was having a good joke.

"Yes. Me, too," she stammered. "I love you, too."

That didn't take the "But…" out of his eyes.

"I'm glad we're on the same page about that," she said, confused.

She was a balloon floating to the Heavens, only to have the air let out and tumble back to earth when he said, "It's such a bad idea for me to be your security point person. As emotionally involved as I am, it might get in the way of my professional performance."

"Okay, let's start there." Pragmatism was McKayla's forte. She could land on a solid fact or plan. Emotions? She wasn't as good at dealing with those. "Why would this be different than when you were with the SEAL team, and we were at the forward operating base?"

"I wasn't contracted to provide for your safety. You worked alongside us. We weren't even in the same branch of the military. Though, I did everything I could to keep you safe back then."

"The explosion in Khandud."

He kissed her hair. "Exactly. But, like there are rules with doctors medically treating family members or friends, it's similar with close protection. I need to be tactical, working with cold precision."

"I don't understand that. I mean you said you loved me. It seems that you'd *extra* protect me."

"I might act on emotion instead of on training."

"You'd do that for a brother. You love your teammates, right? You love Hoover?"

"Not the same. I'm contractually responsible for you."

"Okay, we need to drop that piece because I don't understand. I'm sure there's ethics involved. But frankly it's starting to piss me off. What else is a problem?"

"I love my job at Iniquus. I mean *really* love my job. Hoover is part of me. We're one and the same. But he's not my K9, he's Iniquus's hundred-thousand-dollar investment."

"A hundred-thousand." McKayla shrugged. She'd write a check if there was a problem. But what was the problem?

"More than working with Hoover and my brothers. I get to take all of the skills I built as a SEAL and apply them to relief missions, saving innocent people. We go around the world and pull babies from under the rubble and give them a chance at life. It's the best career in the world to have a hand in helping like that."

"I'm hearing a no 'fraternization clause' in your contract with a strict enforcement that means immediate termination."

"I'm going to have to report this to my superior. I'll deal with whatever outcome they feel is correct. Iniquus hangs its hat on its reputation, and I will do nothing to hurt my company."

"But the CIA didn't hire you. I did."

"Which makes it that much worse, I would suspect."

"No. Sorry. Not my point. I contracted a K9 handler. I signed the contract. And that contract starts tomorrow at noon. When I signed the contract, Command thought tomorrow would be the first chance they could get a plan together, and a team headed to London. Today, we have no contractual relationship. Tomorrow, we do. There's no breech to talk about." She looked up and caught his gaze. "Besides, you'd never kiss and tell. I am a hundred percent sure that's true."

"In this case, I would allude. But if the contract starts tomorrow, then I haven't done anything contractually wrong. Though, it's a shade of gray in my own assessment of these circumstances. Clarifying, the gray refers to the ethics of the circumstances. About making love to you, that was perfection."

McKayla showed her agreement with a long, thorough kiss.

The Hoover whined and tapped his paw on her thigh asking for attention, too, making McKayla laugh.

Shifting his hips closer to the headboard, Ash sat up a little taller. "Just so you know about that kiss and tell piece, I brought it up with the team—that we had dated."

"White knew for sure." Kayla scooped her hands under Hoover's snout and brought their foreheads together. She breathed in the clean doggy smell of him, wondering why she didn't have a dog of her own. When she sat up again, she said, "There were a whole lot of questions about our time together from Langley back when they were considering my application."

"I thought as much."

She turned to catch Ash's gaze. "Iniquus sent you anyway?"

"Lynx—she's not in London, she's back in D.C."

"She was on the video call last night. Really young to be sitting in that room. She had a certain authority about her, too. Even White, I noticed, seemed to be walking on eggshells around her. But she seemed very sweet. Friendly."

"She's kind of a big deal around Iniquus. If Lynx wants something to happen, it usually does. Her yes vote seems like gospel with her team." Ash let a grin spread across his face and his eyes glittered with merriment. "She said I'm the right man for you, and everyone kind of nodded. Done deal."

"You're the right man for me? And everyone agrees?"

The grin fell off. "I haven't asked your opinion yet. After this is all over and that contract isn't tying my hands," he canted his head, "what do you think?"

21

ASHER GIDEON

The "Friend's Place" Cottage, London, England

AS MUCH AS Ash wanted to laze around in bed, making love to McKayla, they had work to do.

Striker expected McKayla to be dexterous with the stability harness by the time he showed up at the gym wearing a bite suit.

During those exercises, Ash would have to make darned sure that anything physical was gentle.

While McKayla said she felt fine, and that their love making hadn't hurt, the scrapes on her booty, though superficial, had to feel raw. Her exposed nerves had to burn.

"We're only slightly behind schedule," McKayla said as she pulled her front door shut then checked that it was properly locked.

Ash laughed.

And McKayla responded with a knotted brow. "What?"

Checking Hoover for any sign that he had something on his radar, his own head on a swivel to clear the area, Ash said, "You have a bit of a British accent now."

She tipped her head. "When in Rome."

When Ash pulled the fob from his pocket, McKayla jerked her body, bringing her arm up to protect her face. She must have realized what she'd done. She dropped her hand back to her side and gave herself a shake.

Must have been some visual trigger from the explosion the other day.

Ash used the key to unlock the door instead of fobbing it open, then pulled it wide for her.

As she got in, Ash opened the back door and turned to Hoover. "Here we go, buddy, load up. You're in the back this time." He shut the doors, rounded the front of the vehicle, and slid under the steering wheel. "When in Rome, you'd have an Italian accent."

"Would it be Italian or Latin do you think?" She tugged her safety belt and clipped it in place.

"Depends on the era the saying came into being. Italian was formalized in what? The fourteenth century? What does that sound like, a Latin accent?"

"No clue." She rocked from one thigh to the other, looking like sitting was uncomfortable for her.

Ash wouldn't bring it up unless he had a solution. McKayla hated to be seen as incapable of taking care of herself. "It's strange hearing you say shed-yool instead of schedule." He pitched his voice up to sound feminine, *"We're only slightly behind schedule,"* he teased.

"It's strange to hear you at all." She knotted her fingers in her lap. "This is quite the déjà vu."

"And that would be in France." He pressed the engine button, put the car in gear, and headed them down the road, following the directions on his phone.

"I thought we'd take a linguistic tour of Europe." She gave a half smile.

"Britain left the EU." He reached over and squeezed her hands. This was how they'd banter back in the day. There was an edge to it right now. Ash decided to keep going and see if they couldn't get on an even keel.

"Touché. Which means we're still in France." She fell silent until they were on the highway. "White said there's a plan afoot."

"Afoot? Now, we're time traveling? Who said that, Sherlock Holmes?"

She leaned her head into the window. "If you're going to keep teasing me, we can't be friends."

"I'm your security for now. Not your friend."

"Today you can be anything you want to be. My contract with you starts tomorrow. Noon, remember?"

"Still. We're not friends. I don't make love with friends." Then it hit him. "Shit, De—McKayla. I'm so sorry. I wasn't wearing a condom." He pulled a hand down his face as his heart thumped hard against his ribs. "I can tell you that I just had my yearly physical with Iniquus, and they are extremely thorough. My STD list is clean. We can go and get you a morning after medication."

"We're all right. My 'very thorough' physical, was last year. And I haven't been with anyone since then. So, check that box. And I take birth control to keep the cramps at bay. We're good to go."

He swung his gaze to catch hers.

"We have until noon tomorrow." She batted her eyelashes.

And damned if she didn't give him rock-cock, again. This assignment was going to be painful. He laced his fingers into hers. "God, I've missed you."

DEEP WAS good at his job, Ash would give him that. Even from across the ocean, with short notice and a five-hour time difference, all of Deep's logistics were golden.

With Hoover guarding McKayla in the vehicle, Ash went in with his equipment to check for video cameras. Surely, Deep didn't identify their client. But curiosity might make someone try to set something up.

And if they saw McKayla's face, the video would be a cash cow to the media.

He went back out to give McKayla the all clear and to get Hoover and his equipment bags.

"This is going to be pretty easy once you get a little practice under your belt," Ash said as he locked the door behind them and dropped the bags. "Hoover will be taking his commands from me. If you want Hoover to sit, say, 'sit.' I'll signal him, and it will look like he's obeying you."

"He won't obey me?"

"Not if I'm around. He's taught that he's to answer to his handler and no one else."

"Oh."

"But I'll be around whenever you're in a public space. Just like with your past security team. Only where they stood at your seven o'clock, I'll be standing at your five o'clock. Hoover will always be on your left side. I'll hold the doors, checking behind them first. When I tell you to move, you move."

"Yes, sir." She gave him a sarcastic salute.

"Not like that. More like, if I say, get down, you don't think, you do."

"Yup. Been there done that. And that's the protocol I've been practicing for the last few years. Well, without the dog."

"Get dressed." Ash gave Hoover's command to stand still so he could strap the tactical vest into place. This version of the tactical vest had the addition of two metal boxes on either side where the stability handle clicked into place. Ash twisted to look over his shoulder. "This is a summer vest. It's not ballistic, though it is stab resistant. Our prep research says that knife attacks are the issue in London." He pressed up to stand. "When Striker gets here in his bite suit, I'll show you what Hoover can do when a knife is presented."

"So, at a restaurant, no steak?" She looked at him innocently.

Ash didn't take the bait. "If a knife is being wielded in an aggressive way, smart aleck."

"But what about that?" She pointed at the grip handle he pulled out of the bag. "Why wouldn't someone just grab that and control Hoover?"

"That's what I need to show you." Ash held the handle

on the free ends out toward her. "Take this in your hand. Wrap your hand comfortably around the grip. That's right." Ash let go to adjust McKayla's hand just because he liked touching her. "Where your thumb naturally rests, do you feel a button?"

"Yes."

"Quick release. If you think Hoover needs to shift from stability work to threat work, press the button and pull up."

"Okay. Press. Pull."

"Right now. Let's say it's a bigger fight than we anticipated. Hoover is attacking Bad Guy A. I'm defending against Bad Guy B. Here comes Bad Guy C."

"Right. Well, I have *some* skills, you know."

"Do you keep up with them?" Ash asked, remembering she certainly seemed to have her soldier's mind set when she was getting two hundred pounds of unconscious Misha back in the building after the blast.

"I do. My security team works with me on all that."

"So, they know your actions and reactions?"

Her brows came up. "Is that bad?"

"Not unless they turn out to be the bad guys or are giving the bad guys information. They double dip with Misha is my understanding."

"And you think Misha's a bad guy?" She gave him a one-sided smile. "I'll sum him up for you. He's got a lot of money and wants to be left alone."

"Back to our scenario. Bad Guy C comes onto the scene. He has a weapon and so do you."

McKayla held up the handle. "Yup. I'll stab him in the face with this. Look how sharp the ends are."

"Exactly." Ash positioned himself behind McKayla.

Reaching around, he moved her fists on either side just near the top handle, ends pointing away from her. "Good?"

"I guess."

He dropped his hand and walked over to the martial arts equipment stacked neatly on the shelves and picked up two short sticks. "Ready?" he asked.

"Okay. Go!" She dove forward.

Ash easily sidestepped the assault. "You jumped the gun. Get ready."

"K." She moved back to her assault position—dominant foot forward, toes and energy pointed toward the threat.

"Now, instead of lunging forward, pull your arms apart."

When she did, the stability bar separated into two short sticks with little tabs down near her hands that would help stop someone from pulling her weapon from her hands.

"Well, would you look at that?" She smiled.

"I know, right? Pretty cool. Our engineers have been working on this for us."

"Are we going to fight?" She put herself in short stick position—left arm over head for a downward strike. Right arm across her body ready for a sweeping rib blow.

Ash shook his head. "Not today, sweetheart. Today is a good day for you to heal. Your body's been through a lot." Ash took the weapons from her hands, clicked them back together. "Magnets." Then attached the support bar into the connections on Hoover's tactical vest. "Right now, we need to practice. We're going to walk around and around and when I say, 'Action' you're going to press and pull."

"Action? Like in a movie? Not release?"

"'Release' is Hoover's command to open his biter after he takes down a bad guy. 'Action' is a verb that means motion. You need to be in motion."

"Got it. Okay, so when I hear 'Action' I push, pull, then make weapons?"

"If you think you need to fight. They work either like short sticks or you can stab someone. Not as sharp as a knife, you'll have to get some momentum. Use your leg strength and body weight."

Her brows went up to her hairline. "Wait. You think I can skewer someone?"

22

MᴄKᴀʏʟᴀ Pɪᴄᴋᴀʀᴅ

The Gym, London, England.

Sᴛʀɪᴋᴇʀ, Jack, and Gator had shown up to help her train at the gym. It was odd to see how Striker and Blaze had aged. Not old. Older.

They were cocooned in the thickness of bite suits that had neck guards and face shields.

McKayla had never seen that before.

The Hoover that she had met at the cottage was hardly the kind of dog that would chomp your face off.

And that was McKayla's life lesson for today.

Hoover was a sweetheart, until Hoover saw a threat.

They were running the scenario again. And again. And again.

McKayla only had this practice session to get this into her muscle memory.

Striker rounded the corner blade in hand.

The rumble in Hoover's chest was a shock wave in McKayla's bones.

She knew—just like she knew there was air in her lungs—that Hoover was deadly serious about protecting her.

It was the most astonishing revelation.

It made her feel…too much to process.

But for sure, the emotions brewing in her system from the explosion, to seeing Ash, to this very moment made her feel like she was struggling to keep her head above water. The sensations from deep in her being were dragged to the surface like the moon shifting the oceans at high tide.

And Hoover's determination to keep her safe, even from Striker and Jack as the make-believe bad guys made her want to bawl, again.

You experienced this the last explosion, too, McKayla reminded herself. Any act of kindness or support felt almost too tender to bear back then.

And now.

But McKayla refused to let those emotions flow freely twice in one day.

She locked them down tight as she faced bad-guy Striker.

"Action," Ash called from her five o'clock.

Without thought, McKayla pressed the button, pulled the handle, then stepped to the side.

As Striker swung a plastic blade through the air toward McKayla, Hoover leaped forward.

Striker's face twisted with pain as Hoover's teeth locked around his wrist. While the bite suit stopped the teeth from digging into Striker's flesh, it didn't stop the pressure of those jaws, clamped down tight. Nor did it protect Striker's tendons when Hoover furiously shook his head, making the weapon fly from Striker's fingertips.

McKayla was mesmerized until she heard Ash call out. "Action," a second time.

Out from the doorway jumped another bad guy in a bite suit.

McKayla stepped back as Ash swept Jack's legs out from under him, and they were rolling each other with Judo moves, trying to lock the adversary's joints into submission.

This wasn't play.

This was like being at The Farm where the CIA taught her all the dirty tricks, all the ways to destroy the enemy so she could live to fight another day.

Ash said action, McKayla reminded herself. She pulled her handle in opposition to make two short sticks and aimed for cover.

A third man ran out from the locker room area.

McKayla jumped back and wound her arms into short stick strike position.

The room swam in McKayla's vision. Up was the same as down. The ceiling, walls, and floor swirled around her like she was on some chaos ride at the fair.

With a high-pitched siren blaring in her ears, lighting her nerves on fire, McKayla stabbed her weapon forward trying to create space between her and the assailant.

And then she was up, floating in the air, unable to breathe.

"Hoover, release." Ash's voice was right near her ear. "I've got you McKayla. Breathe."

Ash dropped to a knee and laid her gently onto the exercise mat.

This was the fourth time that Ash scooped and carried her in this training session. But the first three times were scenarios, so he could practice how to hold her without dumping her over his shoulder in a soldier's carry. The team didn't want McKayla's head upside down after the explosion.

"Get her some water, Jack." She heard.

Air wafted over her face, and she blinked up to see Gator, still in his bite suit, fanning her with a legal pad. "You okay, ma'am?" She heard his rich Cajun accent like the pine-scented smoke from a campfire wafting past the riot of noise in her head.

"Whew," was what she managed.

"Too soon," Jack said, crouching with a water bottle in hand. "Too much. We overloaded your system, I apologize." He reached under her shoulder and lifted her enough to hold the bottle to her lips.

As McKayla sipped, she glanced over at Ash. His face was a storm. But it was coldly distant. She knew that expression. It was the face he'd made when he wanted to protect her in Afghanistan but the best way to protect her was to seem unaffected.

He'd told her how it just about killed him to stand there when his instincts told him to plunge in. But he lived up to the oath she'd made him swear to her back then, that nothing could give away the secrecy of their feelings for each other.

She'd said it endangered her.

McKayla knew that Ash had seen enough shit in enough bases to know what female soldiers had to deal with. He'd simply said that anything she needed him to do to feel safe, he would do it without question.

Then he followed through with not just the letter but the spirit of her law.

Those distant yesterdays in the sandbox, now here today in London, she mused. Nothing much had changed, had it?

All McKayla wanted at that moment was to go back to her secret house. To curl back into bed with Ash and cling to him until tomorrow at noon.

But she was a CIA officer, and she had to go talk to her asset.

This so sucks.

"What do you need, McKayla?" Ash asked.

"Nothing." She took the bottle from Jack and sat all the way up. "The water's helping. My brain misfired. It was a good exercise. I'd like to try it again in a few days. I really needed to see how that works with Hoover and Ash being engaged, how I could defend myself."

"Remember, your job is just to get to safety," Striker said. "Don't stick around and try to save Hoover or Ash. If you're in the mix, they have to focus on you instead of putting the bad guy down."

"Right. And you said they'd be able to find me from my watch?" McKayla asked.

"We'll go over that in just a bit. Rest for now. We're going to get out of these suits and shower up. Then White wants to talk to you." Striker paused. "You good? You need a doctor?"

"No. No. My ears." She flapped her hand near her head. "I really did just have a moment of vertigo. My doctor said that was a possibility."

Hoover came over and sat between her knees, head on a swing, looking for anyone else who needed a bite today.

McKayla leaned forward to wrap her arms around Hoover's broad body. "You really are a magnificent beast." She laid her cheek on his back and closed her eyes.

Striker patted McKayla's shoulder, then stood. The three Strike Force men went off to get cleaned up while Ash stayed with her.

Ash turned and watched the men round the corner, then he slipped behind her and eased her head back onto his shoulder.

Hoover turned and rested his chin on her thigh, McKayla stroked a soothing hand over his head. For his sake and hers. "Good boy. Such a good boy." She peeked up at Ash, who smiled at her.

He combed his fingers through the length of her hair. "Good girl, such a good girl."

She smacked his hand. "Stop."

Ash looked toward the locker room, then, seeing the coast was clear, dropped a kiss onto her lips. It was soft and lingered as if he didn't want the sensations to stop.

She didn't.

"You scared me," he whispered.

"And you scooped me. I mean I was going down, and then I was floating."

"Mmm."

"Yeah, all session. With your lifting and carrying me to safety, you knew what you were doing. How did you learn to lift and move a woman around like that?"

He paused, considering her.

She spun around, resting her head back on Hoover as her pillow.

After another swig of water, she said, "It was surprising how much it made me feel beautiful and graceful—how you moved me. It was very...Well, from that, I can understand the allure of a damsel in distress trope." She breathed out by way of a laugh. Then lifting the bottle toward Ash as an emphasis, she pressed. "That didn't come out of nowhere."

"No, I trained," he said quietly.

She raised her brows. "Sex classes? Dance classes?" She slowly came up to a sitting position, testing the waters and deciding the weirdness had passed. Hoover thunked his wagging tail on the mats as McKayla shifted to sit cross-legged, facing Ash.

"Figure skating," he said.

"In Juneau?" Her brows pulled together. "That's not something I see you doing by choice. In my mind's eye, I always see you tromping about the great white bleakness with your snowshoes strapped on."

He stared into her eyes for a long moment. "I don't want to tell you this. It'll change that dynamic—put a different picture in your head—if I'm lifting you or tossing you around. It's the opposite of sexy."

"Oh, now, I'm really curious." Setting the bottle aside, McKayla put her hands down behind her and leaned her weight into her arms. "Now that you've put it that way,

I'm going to be gnawing on that bone until I get an answer. I'll wonder right when I want to be focused on the sensations of freedom and hahaha exquisite femininity." She trilled the last two words and batted her lashes.

"That's how it feels?"

"It does." She gave him a sad smile. "I'm afraid the damage is already done. You might as well explain."

"My cousin, Ginny, had some medical issues and a good outcome wasn't possible." He reached over to capture a strand of McKayla's hair and slid his fingers slowly to the end. "Partners skating was on her bucket list." He brushed the strand back and tucked it behind her ear. "I couldn't do anything about her health, but I sure as hell could give her something that distracted her from some of the crap she was going through. Before her diagnosis, she loved to skate more than anything."

McKayla felt her heart squeeze. "That takes a lot of energy, skating."

"She was mostly in my arms. It was my job on the ice to protect her and let Ginny know she was safe, at least in that moment. I wanted her to feel beautiful and graceful the way she described what she saw on the television." He pressed his lips together, his mind seemed to drift away, then he focused on McKayla, again. "When you said that's how you felt when I lifted you, that was a gift, thank you." He took a beat. "It tells me that Ginny probably felt that, too." He held the flat of his hand straight overhead. "When I balanced her and spun around really fast, she said she felt free." He swallowed, and his gaze flickered away from her face to the back wall. His voice was gruff when he quietly said, "I'm lucky to be athletic, so I could do that."

"Wow." Tears made Ash's face swim in front of her. With all the evil that McKayla had waded through as an adult, it was soothing to know that there were men like Ash out there in the world. "That's intense. How…uhm…" She swiped her fingers over her eyes.

"Ginny died when I was seventeen."

McKayla's mouth pulled into a deep frown.

"I miss her like crazy. We were close growing up."

"I'm so sorry," McKayla whispered.

"I'm not. Honestly, I'd never want anyone to suffer the way she did. My pain is her gain. Now, I see her in the clouds." He traced a finger in the air. "You know when they have the swirling lines like the trail left by a skate blade?"

McKayla nodded.

"That's her, letting me know she's up there having fun, graceful and free." His gaze came down and there was an intensity in there that was a bit overwhelming to McKayla. "Can you do me a favor and let this conversation go?"

"Yes, I will," McKayla whispered. "Just one more thing. You said if you told me this story that it would change our dynamic."

"I plan on lifting you, twirling you, and tossing you around my bed like a rag doll. And I don't want this to pop into your brain. I mean," he lightened his tone back to teasing, "you learned things along the way that might show up in our future sex life. I never speculate about how you developed your magic way of getting me off. I just appreciate the sensations. But I have a guy brain. And in my experience, women's brains are a lot more complex, I don't want this tangling up your enjoyment."

"Complex." She let that word play across her lips and tongue as if she were trying it on to see how it fit. She dropped her voice to a whisper. "After the hospital tonight, what you're saying is that you *are* taking be back to bed, right?"

"Yes, ma'am."

"Say it again." She smiled. "I kind of like that."

"Yes, ma'am." He reached out as if to brush a hand through her hair and stopped himself. "Man, this mission is going to suck."

"Wait." McKayla drew her brows together. "I thought you said that once the contract started that wasn't allowed."

23

————

WHITE

Strike Force War Room, Washington, D.C.

FROM THE LOOKS OF THINGS, the team was outside in some kind of shelter sitting around picnic tables. The roof cast a nice shade over their faces, but the trees were bright with the setting sunlight.

The five-hour time difference between London and D.C. was always a challenge.

"White here. I'm in Strike Force War Room with Lynx."

"The team and McKayla are present." Striker looked around. "Ash swept the gym for electronics, and it was clean as far as he could tell. I feel safer out at the park. The only chance that anyone could hear us is if they knew we were here and had a parabolic ear on us."

"Thank you." White gave a nod. "So, McKayla. Are you happy with my choice of teammates for you?"

"Fun times." McKayla let her gaze wander from team member to team member, then back to White. "I read in the paper the other day that with social media, the six degrees of Kevin Bacon game isn't correct anymore. It said the average distance between any two people is only about three and a half degrees. And that's of all five billion of us."

"Crazy," White said. "Then what I'm about to tell you will come as no surprise. Strike Force has familiarity with more players than just you on this mission."

"Oh?" McKayla leaned forward. "Who?"

"Karl Davidson, Nadir al Attiya, Rajja al-Saidi."

The muscles in McKayla's face tightened. "Context?"

"That's not a mission you've been read in to," White said matter-of-factly. "Let's just say Gator was there when the bullet flew that got Karl Davidson his amputation and prosthetic leg. Blaze had been on the mission prior to the shot. Striker and Jack were supporting the mission."

McKayla spun to Gator. "Did you do the shooting?"

"No, ma'am," Gator said.

"Does Karl *think* you did the shooting?" McKayla asked.

"No, ma'am, he's aware of who shot him."

When Gator turned his focus to the camera, White figured he wanted permission to give more information.

He did not have that permission. White sat mum.

McKayla would just have to stew. That's the way of things. You got to know what you needed to know. And. That. Was. It.

"White, you seem to have a handle on what happened then and what's happening now." McKayla scratched at the back of her hand and must have snagged one of her scabs because a deep maroon bulb formed then rolled a red smear down to the webbing between her thumb and forefinger. McKayla was either unaware or ignoring it because, unaffected, she continued. "You must think our strategy going forward is going to be effective."

"I do," White said.

McKayla turned briefly to Ash, who was dragging a first aid kit from his pack. "Do you know the men I just mentioned? Davidson, al Attiya, or al-Saidi?"

His saying, "No, ma'am," to McKayla like she was just a client amused White to no end.

McKayla looked like she was trying to be patient as Ash cleaned the cut and dressed it.

"Okay. Bonus that we have a fresh player," White said. "Ash is the one who is going to be public facing because of Hoover. Frame it this way, McKayla, your team has successfully thwarted this crew before. Since they have history, Strike Force is the best equipped to get the job done." White looked down at the list in front of her, then refocused on the computer camera. "McKayla, you and Hoover are still planning to see Misha this evening?"

"I am."

"Good," White said. "I'm very interested to see how that plays out. And to that end, I'm going to introduce you to two pieces of surveillance equipment that are available through Iniquus and one of the reasons Langley signed off on my hiring your new team. Striker?"

Striker reached into his bag and pulled out a smart watch and a clear bag that seemed to hold a contact lens case, mirror, and wipes.

McKayla fingered the bag.

"Those are video camera contact lenses," White explained. "Blaze and Gator have experience with them and saw how effective they can be on our last mission together."

"Yes, ma'am," Blaze said, shooting a glance toward Gator then focusing back on White. "The reason we're doing that? What are you hoping to capture?"

"McKayla and Ash's use will differ from Strike Force. McKayla and Ash, the two of you will need to wear this technology whenever you are with—or think you might stumble upon a player—be it Misha or one of his associates."

"Video contact lenses?" McKayla scowled.

"You've worn contacts before to change the color of your eyes."

"Yes, ma'am."

"These won't feel much different. There is a microscopic video recorder," White explained. "I'll leave it to your team to teach you how to use them. But let's go ahead and get your systems properly synched."

McKayla pulled the bag closer. "Where does the information get stored?"

"That smart watch. The images are encrypted in the contacts and flow to the watch, up to the satellite, and out to our end where it is unencrypted."

"Wow." McKayla mouthed.

"The teams' watches will also pick up the audio component. Once the data is sent, it's no longer stored on the devices. The audio and visual are stitched together. If there's no uptake, for whatever reason, it can store up to twenty-four hours' worth of data then it will dump the oldest information."

McKayla reached for the watch. "So, if anyone were to get hold of this…"

"The information is encrypted and hidden beneath other data. If a bad guy were to get hold of your watches and try to figure out what's on them, all they'll get is your step count for the day and what alarms you have set."

"When you say, 'us' who are you referring to?" Lynx asked White. "Surely, the information comes here. It's one of the ways we track the safety of our people."

"Both here in your war room and we want that feed at Langley," White confirmed. "Like with your computer systems, my office will use AI to separate the various noises and conversations and have them translated for anything of interest." White focused on Striker. "Our interests extend beyond the mission we've hired you to undertake. You will not need the breadth or depth of the data we're collecting. Your focus is much narrower than Langley's."

"Yes, ma'am," Striker said.

"But my understanding is that Iniquus has cutting edge capability that exceeds that of the CIA," White continued. "So, you do you. And we can compare conclusions if you'd like." She turned back to the rest of the team. "McKayla, the visual is important so we can see if a facial expression is indicating that something is of significance. Sometimes a phrase sounds innocuous, such as someone passing information via code. But as Lynx, I'm sure would agree, body language and eye contact changes when someone is trying to create emphasis around a hidden phrase."

"Yes, ma'am," she said.

"Good. Now, for Strike Force, I'm limiting the use of the contacts as it pertains to the CIA. For me, I would like the team to wear both the watches and contacts during the times you're in the Seychelles at group gatherings." She lowered her voice to tell Lynx, "Iniquus, of course, can choose how and when you wear the devices." Then spoke once again to the group. "Let me add here that, when Misha and McKayla are out at the various parties, I'd like her to use a four-man team. The more eyes and ears the better. To answer your question, Blaze, we're looking for who clusters with whom, who avoids whom."

"Yes, ma'am," the men said.

"Whoever is on duty, you have to do a balancing act. Langley wants as much data as possible. Again, we need names, faces, who encircles whom. Facial expressions. Lynx." White turned and sent a smile to Lynx. "Anything you can pick up with body language would be a huge bonus." She focused back on the camera. "McKayla, take a moment and try on the contacts."

This was probably going to test Lynx's ethics. Strike Force shouldn't be in any kind of danger on this mission. Mission success on data gathering external to everyone's safety might be another story.

While White couldn't imagine Lynx doing anything that would put either her team or the world in jeopardy (even if White was unclear of what jeopardy was in the works), she *could* see someone with Lynx's strategic brain capacity—and the means to play a vengeful game against

White and her cohorts in the Color Code—double cross the CIA.

And White would never know.

In White's calculus, this was how it could play out: Lynx picks up some clues that put the puzzle together—that was her job, after all, as the Iniquus Puzzler. She holds onto one of her "rabbit from a black hat" magic tricks where she figured things out from the most random of random observations. Then, Lynx walks that info to Iniquus Command. Iniquus Command would then bypass the CIA to move the information into channels it preferred.

The CIA comes up dry. Someone else "magically" lands on the truth.

Money wasted? No. Not at all.

The bad guy needed to go down; that was *all* that was important.

Babies shouldn't starve; that was *all* that was important.

But funding went to those who pulled successes from their pockets.

White needed a win to keep the purse strings loosened.

She deserved that. After all, White had invested a great deal of political capital in making this mission happen. Iniquus didn't come cheap. McKayla's mission could certainly be handled by security teams without such an elite pedigree.

Of course, McKayla had offered to pay.

But then McKayla would have been in the driver's seat. And that dynamic of leader and follower would have been a mess. In White's mind, anyway.

Yeah, Lynx was making White nervous about picking Strike Force over Tidal Force.

True, though, Tidal Force was doing training exercises out in the direction of the Seychelles off the coast of East Africa. If things got out of hand, the two teams could simply switch roles.

White didn't know the logistics folks in Tidal as well. That might be a good thing.

Yeah, White was second guessing herself.

When Lynx leaned her head back just a bit and raised her eyebrows a little higher, White felt like Lynx was eavesdropping on her inner dialogue.

It was an odd sensation. To White, it was like someone was in her bedroom rifling around in her underwear drawer. It was a little too intimate to be comfortable.

White turned her attention to Striker. He was an interesting man to be engaged to Lynx. He was a philosophic stoic; nothing seemed to rock him.

And, yeah, White could admit to herself that she found Striker attractive in a non-shiny, good-guy kind of way.

Six-foot three, he looked great standing next to Lynx.

Visually, they worked together as a couple, he with rusty brown hair and soft green eyes, she with long blonde hair and blue eyes. Not all couples fit as nicely in the same picture.

Sometimes, there was something incongruous about a couple that made people squish their brows together and try to figure it out. Age difference, style-difference, it could be almost anything.

Sometimes, White wondered if the visual match wasn't an extremely crucial element to a successful coupling. If people liked the fit, and decided the couple belonged together, did it make it easier? If people were always a little uncomfortable, a little judgey because of some vague disquiet about how the two looked standing side by side— a hyper fit woman with a pizza eating, gamer dude—did that subtly drive the couple apart?

Did the energy toward them from others make a couple question themselves?

It was an interesting thought experiment.

White always considered the visual when she put couples together in the field. And so far, she was batting a thousand on couple longevity after a mission. It was a game she liked to play—when it made sense to play it.

If she ever got tired of saving the free world—White thought as McKayla finished wiping her fingers with a disinfecting cloth—maybe she should go into the match-maker game.

White considered Asher and McKayla sitting side by side. They were a good visual fit.

McKayla lifted her wet hands up like a surgeon to let her fingers air dry.

With Ash holding her phone camera up as a mirror, McKayla carefully popped a contact into place and blinked.

Asher Gideon was one of the few men on McKayla's intimacy list. There was still something between them. White could see it in the studied way they didn't look at each other. The careful indifference in their posture.

White and Lynx turned toward each other. There was laughter in Lynx's eyes and improbably, Lynx gave her a wink. She saw it too.

Yeah, both visually and chemistry-wise these two were a good fit.

McKayla was blinking watery eyes and held a tissue under her lashes to catch a tear. "I hate contacts. So, sucky."

"Noted," White said. "Okay, from there you have your watch." White turned back to Lynx. "You have her up and running. All synced?"

"Working on it," Lynx said.

"White." McKayla blew her nose on her tissue. "I know you have your heart set on discovering something of importance in the Seychelles. But Misha is not a brave man. He tries to lay low, tries not to get tangled in anyone's webs. He'll avoid anything and everything he can. My bet is that he uses the explosion to stay in London."

"This is true. And I've thought about what should be done. Right now, he's an unwitting asset. We can always turn him so he knows that we can make it look like he was very disloyal to his father and the Kremlin. I've decided that we will take baby steps in that direction."

McKayla tensed. "I'd like to discuss that with you further. That and my role in this game. I'm comfortable enough in my deep undercover role. Because of my international recognition, telling *anyone* that I have an employer would put a target on my back for the rest of my life. The least of it would be that I would be *persona non grata* around the world. No one wants to invite a Russian assassination team to their party. And no one wants to deal with a dead guest. What leverage I have with my fame and fortune would be squandered. On what? Misha Popyrin?

He has nothing more for us than what I've already gathered—except of course for possibly the Seychelles. He's not going. I promise you that."

"We'll see what he says tonight, but I'd like the pressure from our side to start."

"How?" McKayla asked.

"Get any newspaper from today and flip through. You'll find that, last night, one of the most prominent Russians in the meat industry fell from the third story window of his hotel where he was vacationing."

"Again?" McKayla pinched her nose, covering her mouth. When her hand released, she said, "You know Misha won't even come to my penthouse? He won't go anywhere that is higher than the second floor. Well, except for the hospital. He's on the fourth floor."

"You show him the paper," White said. "Then, you tell him you're done with your agreement."

"Why?" McKayla asked, rubbing the tape on her bandaged hand.

"White," Lynx said. "I have her up. Everything's a go."

"For all of them?" White asked.

"No, ma'am, your directive was for McKayla to wear the lenses when she's interacting with any of the players and for Strike Force operators to only wear their watches, which provides us with audio and geolocation."

"That's correct. Your visual diagnostics are an expensive component."

"Lots of man hours from our AI department," Lynx pointed out.

White tipped her chin down as she leaned back a bit. "Agreed."

"Real time, I can track the vital statistics, safety, and location of all members. At the same time, I can manage a single conversational grouping. For that, I select the conversation with the highest probability for needing immediate intervention. All other data points are gathered and stored for research."

"And that would definitely be McKayla who is our priority. Thank you, Lynx."

"White, I asked *why* you want me to tell Misha our agreement is finished," McKayla said.

"Because you want to go to the Seychelles, and you say Misha won't go. So, if Misha wants to keep you in the role of his significant other, then he has to provide you with the opportunity to see behind the curtain of yachting uber-wealth."

"Okay," McKayla said. "I'll take a run at it."

24

McKAYLA PICKARD

The Royal London Hospital, London, England

McKAYLA DREW in a deep breath and squared her shoulders before she knocked at Misha's hospital room door.

With Misha's feeble, "Come in" Ash twisted the knob and pushed the door wide, holding it for McKayla.

Hoover looked from Ash to McKayla, waiting for a signal telling him what to do next.

Gripping the stability handle, McKayla moved toward the bed, with her internal announcer proclaiming: *And McKayla Pickard, in a run at an Emmy, acts her little heart out as the concerned and caring significant other of Misha Popyrin. Who, in turn, seems to be going for his own award as man with the manliest man-flu that ever-managed many... manipulations. Too much? Probably.*

Definitely. Come on, smile sadly, shake your head with pity. Let's do the damned thing.

McKayla had been studying Misha for almost a solid year. And she could tell he was pressing the pitiful-me pedal down a little too heavily.

"Wow, look at you with tubes and wires everywhere." She stepped forward to stand near his hand. "What are the doctors saying?"

Misha looked over the edge of the bed at Hoover. "What's this?"

Ash brought a chair closer so McKayla could sit. And when she found her place, Ash signaled for Hoover to lay down.

"This? This would be what they call a 'dog' in English."

Misha brought a hand up to rest it over his heart. "Don't be mean to me, McKayla."

"It was teasing, not being mean." With her fingers wrapped around the stability bar, she reached down with her free hand and scratched Hoover's ear. "I told you I was getting a stability dog until the vertigo improved. This is Hoover."

"And him?" Misha didn't look toward the door or otherwise recognize Ash standing there. Men that Misha didn't have on his approved list were all opportunities for McKayla to cuckold him.

And given the opportunity, she had done just that. McKayla's inner announcer continued.

"'Him' would be Ash." She sat back up and looked Misha in the eye. "He's a close protection operator with Iniquus Security."

"Iniquus. I know this name."

"World famous." McKayla held up her hands, razza-matazz. "You look upset. Ash is part of my temporary security team. Do you remember? We talked about this. Rupert and the motorcycle accident?"

"How do you know them? How did you bring them on? My privacy is of utmost importance to me." He stabbed a finger into the air. "You know this. It's why we switched out your security to Rupert's group."

"The new guys are contractually discreet. I have the usual—a four-man team. Three of them are ex-Navy SEALs. Very skilled. I'm pleased. How do I know them? When I was in the military, I worked with the three ex-SEALs, including Ash here." She tipped her ear toward Ash who stood at parade rest beside the door, looking vacantly at the industrial green wall in front of him. "I went out with them on missions to interact with the women."

"Feel them up is the way you described it," Misha grumped.

McKayla ignored it. He obviously wanted to be pet and coddled. She wasn't in the mood. And it would be counter to White's directives. "They have a fourth guy who was a Marine. I never went out on missions with the Marines. His name is Gator." She smiled. "He's from the bayous of Louisiana."

Misha shook his head.

"Gator is short for alligator. The water there is full of them. Very dangerous creatures. I'm sure he earned that call sign for something other than his accent."

Misha frowned at her.

"What's going on?" She lifted her chin toward the machines. They seemed to be within the normal parameters to her, but she only had her own experiences in the hospital to gauge that from. McKayla decided to keep the readings in view of her contacts.

She'd try anyway.

Her team had talked her through how the system worked. That it was the position of her eyeballs and not her focus that mattered. Just like on a smart camera, one could put a focus box anywhere in the picture, but the aperture would include the background information.

"I should feel better, if—" Misha turned his attention to Ash. "Excuse me, but would you stand outside for a moment so I can speak to McKayla privately, please?"

Ash caught McKayla's gaze, and McKayla sent him an affirmative nod.

After the door shut, Misha said, "My family prefers Omega Security when we're in America."

McKayla let her face harden. "Like I said, I've never heard of anyone with a better reputation than Iniquus. I knew some of the Omega goons when I was in the Army. As a woman," she looked down and affected her most vulnerable posture, "I don't feel safe around them."

"I'm sorry if my tone was insensitive. If you feel that these people are best for you—"

"I do."

"He's—how you say—nice on the eyes."

She let the fragile woman energy go. "How *I* say? I've never said anything remotely like that."

"He's handsome. You don't agree?"

McKayla shrugged. "I put paintings on my walls because I like attractive things. I don't screw them."

"Language, McKayla. Why must you always speak like a sailor?"

"Not a sailor. Army."

"Still." Misha frowned. "Here you look like you're an intelligent, cultured woman and then you open your mouth."

"Too salty? If you don't like it or me, I can go." She gripped the safety bar and hoisted herself to her feet.

Hoover watched for his command.

"Stop." Misha put his hand over hers. "I apologize. I'm in pain and in an unbelievably bad mood. My friend died."

McKayla took her seat again. "Who?"

"Ivan died in the blast." The heart monitor showed his heartbeat quickening but only slightly.

Clasping her hands together, McKayla pressed them to her heart, whispering, "Who told you Ivan died?" She shook her head vigorously. "No. No. That can't be right. It's not in the papers. They don't even mention Rachel and her friend. I've heard nothing."

Misha reached out a hand to wrap McKayla's entwined fingers in his, a gesture of comfort. "The authorities are speaking with the Russian Embassy. And the Embassy is speaking to me. I only know of Ivan because he was a citizen and of Rachel because she was married to a Russian and has rights. Visas or something. Of that, I'm not sure. She's in critical condition." His eyes teared up and McKayla wasn't sure why. She'd never seen him emotional that way before.

There was a knock at the door, and John stuck his head in.

Ash sent a glance toward McKayla to make sure the intrusion was okay.

She gave Ash a curt nod, and he shut the door.

"John," she said, "I thought you'd be drinking cocktails on an island or something. You're off the clock."

"Yes, ma'am. I was checking in on Rupert before I left. And I saw Ivan and Rachel's daughter in the hall. I thought I'd quickly update Mr. Popyrin and you. How are you, sir?"

Misha raised the top of his bed then pulled his hospital gown until a bandage peeped over the edge of blue fabric. "I had surgery on my heart."

"What?" McKayla's hands flew to her cheeks. "Is that why they wouldn't let me see you?"

"When I arrived on the helicopter. They were quite concerned with my vital signs. All the stress of the explosion made me go into an SVT—my heart was beating way too fast. They had to rush me into surgery."

McKayla scowled. "And the prognosis?"

"As always. I live with the risk. They were able to fix what they could fix." He turned to John. "You spoke to Ivan's daughter? How is Rachel?"

The hospital room stench—blood, sweat, and stool, which had only been lightly disinfected during a cleaning was overlaid with the scent of adhesive and rubbing alcohol and burned the cilia in her nose. "Misha was just telling me her status is critical?"

"Yes, ma'am. I'm told she's suffering from primary blast lung and blast abdomen."

"That makes sense." McKayla had to shift her grip as Hoover moved to the other side of her chair to look at John.

John focused on Hoover then brought his gaze up to meet McKayla's.

"It's a difficult injury. But she can come back from that."

Misha reached out and caressed her hand.

"Yes, thank you for the information, John." McKayla gave John a smile and a dismissive nod.

"Have a lovely holiday," McKayla added.

As the door shut behind John, McKayla snatched her hand back. She didn't like Misha touching her. And the feeling was so much worse knowing Ash was standing guard outside the door. "That could have been you." McKayla tried to force a warble into her voice.

"Fortunately, it wasn't." Misha's face drained of color.

McKayla shot a glance at the machines. The readout was steady.

"Did you speak to your family about your condition?" McKayla asked. "I know you try to keep your life private from them, but if the embassy is involved, surely someone in Russia reached out to your dad. You don't want him to think you're hiding anything." When Misha didn't answer, McKayla added, "I don't want them to think less of our relationship because I didn't reach out."

"You have suffered the effects of the bombing and rescuing me. You are recovering."

McKayla pushed herself forward. "Bombing? Is there new information?

"No," Misha said quickly. "I misspoke, explosion."

"I've been thinking about that. It doesn't seem like the Kremlin-y thing to do. Those deaths—usually they involve windows and stairs. People beating themselves to death or nerve toxins."

"Hey!"

"I need to know if you think that you've caught the ire of anyone that might want to make an example of you."

"With you in close proximity?" His voice was painted with derision.

"Of course. This isn't a love relationship. It's a mutual aid package."

Misha stared at her darkly. The heart beats were still holding at a rate more rapid than when McKayla had come in. She decided that the threat she'd just made was sufficient. With his medical history she could only push but so far. McKayla would hold off on the newspaper article that White wanted to use as emotional leverage.

"It doesn't look like your trip to the Seychelles is a go for tomorrow," McKayla said. "I have the plane and crew on standby, shall I stand them down?"

Misha grabbed at McKayla's hand, and Hoover sat up straight, eyes intense.

Protecto Pup.

"I cannot go," he whined. "It's impossible. But McKayla, I need you to go in my place."

"What?" She whipped her hand away from his. "No. Why? No. I'm not going without you." If Misha wasn't going, and if Misha wanted her to be in certain places acting as the go-between…

Not ideal. But White would be jumping up and down celebrating.

If McKayla didn't resist, Misha might get suspicious.

"Please. I'm doing this for my father."

"He'd understand. You were bombed…well, exploded."

"My father is extremely stressed right now. We ship. There is *nothing* to ship. Nothing coming in. Nothing going out."

"Okay. We've talked about this before. Why are you bringing it up now?"

"There's more and more pressure on our families. Western governments are freezing oligarch's assets."

"Still, I don't understand. You knew that at any point… accidents happen. You told me you wouldn't go back to Moscow, and you don't want to work in the family business. All of that will fall to your brother's shoulders. I don't have a good understanding of what's happening here. Other than your being Russian, this doesn't affect you. You have money in offshore banks. *Plenty* of money in the banks."

Misha closed his eyes and shook his hand through the air. "It's all very complicated."

"Are you being threatened?"

"It has been requested that I go to this event in the Seychelles. An evening at the botanical gardens. An overnight party on my uncle's yacht. After those events, if you're not having an enjoyable time, come home. But it should be very posh. And the mega yachting culture, I have not yet introduced you to that lifestyle. Very lovely. Uncle Niko, you've met him, you know he'll make sure you're comfortable."

"Requested by whom?"

"Required is a better word."

"Who? To what end?"

"My father and Uncle Niko wish me there. The subject is shipping. It's business. You will do nothing except represent the family name. Showing everyone that we are present and ready."

"Ready?"

"For shipping."

McKayla sat back in her chair and stared at him as long as she could keep herself from blinking. "I'm thinking we might be at the end of our relationship." It was cold. A hammer striking an anvil.

"I've lived up to my end of the bargain." He used his deep growly bear voice—the one that Misha used when he wanted to intimidate McKayla. After all, *he* was the man, and as such, his will would not be denied.

From the heart monitor, McKayla could see that Misha was panicking.

"As have I. Yeah, we've talked about this. This relationship is nice and all. It's served my purpose of exploring the unknown world. However, I'm not dying for the opportunity."

"My family has friends in the right places. They'd warn me if that were the potentiality." He made a fist and shook it with frustration.

In McKayla's imagination, Misha's fist was a man's hand around a chicken's throat, and he shook the bird to break that neck. Seemed like an apt metaphor.

"Really, Misha? I was blown up in an explosion, and you want me to go to a party? I have to use a stability dog to keep myself upright. I'm just now beginning to be able to hear."

"It's *extremely* important."

"Give me one good reason I should go. Why is it so important? Tell me like I'm a five-year-old, so I can understand."

"My father needs a representative from my family on his yacht or my family will be out of the global shipping picture. We will be bypassed should opportunities arise. And we cannot afford to miss any openings. Now, you have already received the itinerary with dress codes as well as the security information. You have your jet lined up. The reservations are in place. You will simply be going unescorted. But you have Iniquus, so you won't be going alone."

"Uncle Niko isn't family enough?" McKayla pointed to her chest. "I'm less family than he is."

"I told my father that you are pregnant with my baby and that the baby is safe following the blast."

Okay. That was a stunner. McKayla went with those emotions and let her jaw drop as she blinked vacantly at Misha. "What in the *actual* hell?"

"My brother just fled to Finland afraid of conscription. He's been disowned. My father was in such a state. He was threatening. Everything is very tender in Russia right now. And my father is afraid of pulling any more attention to the family given the economic circumstances."

"What has this got to do with me being fake pregnant?"

"Your pregnancy would prove that I am having sex with you."

"No, it doesn't. I could be fu—sorry, *copulating* with anyone. A turkey baster."

"Would you consider that?" He thrust forward looking excited.

"What? No!" McKayla thrust back in her seat getting distance from Misha. "You're not even up to the act of filling a turkey baster. Are you out of your mind saying something like that to me?"

Misha fell back in his bed. "I'll come up with some story. It will work out. You will have to have a miscarriage where there are no medical records."

"If they could look up medical records, they could look up your heart stuff." She waggled her hand toward his monitors.

"They wouldn't think to. Listen, as pregnant with my heir, you are, therefore, pregnant with a future oligarch."

"I...what?" McKayla felt cold wash over her body. He'd put a target on her back.

"Yes, and as such this makes you—"

"An incubator for your imaginary family DNA. And as long as I have this fake baby in me, they think I have your family blood in me, too?"

"Correct."

"Who thinks that way?" McKayla shook a confused head at him. "That is so messed up."

"My father and Uncle Niko. They need a family representative to go and make assurances to my friends. You know many of them already. Our friends will be there— Karl, Nadir, and Rajja. We just had a nice evening together with Nadir and Rajja. Others that you already know will be there, too."

"If they are the people who need the message, they should come and speak to you in London."

"This is not as complicated as you make it out to be," Misha yelled, red faced. "It's simply week-long party where my family needs to be represented."

Hoover jumped to his feet and put himself between Misha and McKayla.

Mckayla stroked Hoover's head, then planted a kiss. "Excuse me, morning sickness. I'm having trouble focusing on you past the nausea."

His voice was icy when he said quietly, "Don't play cute with me McKayla. I have lived up to my end of the bargain—you have seen behind secret curtains. This is your *duty* to our agreement."

McKayla stood up and stalked out the door, pleased with her success.

25

McKAYLA PICKARD
   McKayla's Penthouse, London, England.

THE WOOD PANELED dining room felt warm and richly cozy for a space that could comfortably seat twenty. The walls, brightened with art that evoked the peace of nature, gave this space a relaxing, familial ambiance.

But McKayla didn't feel calm.

Her whole body buzzed with an internal alarm— danger on the horizon.

Nothing to be done about that. Hers was a dangerous business.

The team fixed plates of snacks that McKayla's cook had set out before he was dismissed for a week of paid leave.

Tapping her phone to end her conversation with her stylist, McKayla let a smile tickle her lips as she listened to her cook sing made up words to a pop tune about his surprise and delight at a week of "Free-dom! Freeeee-dom! FreeDOM!" The words drifted off as he moved through the kitchen and left out of the servant's exit.

"Who was that you were on the phone with?" Striker asked. "You gave them all of your

Seychelles plans?"

McKayla slipped her phone into her back pocket. "That was my stylist. If I didn't tell her my plans for this trip, it would have been grossly out of character, right? I just told her the events, the dress codes and weather. She doesn't know the dates or location."

Striker set his plate down and bladed his hands onto his hips. Not aggressively, not punitively, more of a "help me understand" kind of stance.

"Look, my stylist was recommended to me by my very English," McKayla swirled and elegant hand in the air, "very fa-fa etiquette teacher, Mrs. Peabody-Strumpkins." McKayla lifted her chin to look down her nose at Striker— hard to do when he towered almost a foot taller than she. "Mrs. Peabody-Strumpkins is about a hundred years old. But she is *fabulous*!" McKayla let the last word stretch long and sing-songy.

"You're making that up." Gator, sitting at the table, lifted a sandwich with fixings piled taller than McKayla thought his mouth could stretch. Gator was an interesting combination of gladiator body and boyishness with his smattering of freckles across his nose. Both fierce and endearing. The kind of man that a mom would look at with pride and think, "I put some good into the world."

"What am I making up?" McKayla asked.

"Mrs. Peabody-Strumpkins?" He shook his head. "That's gotta be a joke."

McKayla hugged herself. "Isn't it the most scrumptious name? It sounds like something warm and gooey you'd put in a bowl and top with ice cream when you needed comfort carbs."

"This stylist person, what does she do?" Gator asked, then surprisingly was able to take a bite of his monster sandwich.

"In this case, she'll come over and pack my suitcases. She picks out everything I need for a look." McKayla made air quotes around look. "She takes a photo of the outfit and often draws me a little picture so I can see how she wants me to wear the thing. She has alternatives for each event and casual wear for in betweens." McKayla looked at her watch. "She'll be here in an hour. When I get back to the Penthouse tomorrow morning, the suitcases will be impeccably packed and placed beside the door for my driver. Which will be one of you."

"Penthouse in the morning?" Striker asked, pulling out a chair and setting down his plate.

"You all will stay here tonight in the security wing. For me, I'm heading back to my cottage. I'll take Hoover with me and then," she glanced over at Ash, "I guess Ash to handle Hoover. And anyone else who wants to sleep on the fold-out couch. I only have my room and a guest room. It's just a cozy little cottage retreat."

"Ash, do you need support?" Striker asked.

Ash paused as if thinking it through. "It's a safe location. With Hoover there, no one's gonna sneak up on us. She's right, though, not a lot of room."

"In that case, I'd like you to sit down with us first, McKayla. I need to know what the schedule looks like. We need to make decisions about security attire. How many will go to which events? All of that. Blaze and I have a plane heading out to the Seychelles at twenty hundred hours this evening to take care of our advance work."

"Okay. Uhm, I'll call the hotel and make sure you have rooms. My reservations for you all are for tomorrow. I'm going to my office to make copies of my itinerary for each of you and take care of that for you. Give me two seconds."

WHEN MCKAYLA CAME BACK IN, she rounded the table, handing her stack out.

Striker thumbed through his copy. "They indicate what security is allowed where."

"You'll be on Niko's yacht for twenty-four hours exploring the Seychelles," Jack read. "Dress code island chic. Tropical-formal attire for dinner. Security will be provided."

Striker put the pages down. "I don't like that."

"How do you think I feel?" McKayla asked. "However, both White and Misha say that the yacht party is imperative. Misha says that Nadir, Rajja, and Karl will be there. White believes that's my best opportunity to figure out what's going on. Do you think my watch will work? Can it be interrupted with scramblers?"

"They won't do that," Jack said.

McKayla turned his way. "Why not?"

"Yeah, I've been out on a boat with some men who

would have liked to evade any signal getting out," Gator said. "I was wearing the contacts and watch, and I never had an issue. See, the captain is running GPS to know where they are. Jammers run on low power microwave signals. They work by creating noise to overwhelm satellite signals. Where they'd stop the watch from contacting the satellite, they'd also stop the satellite from sending the right GPS location. Running into another vessel, or heck, into land, it's too dangerous, they ain't gonna do it."

"You'll have us at your back even if we aren't on the yacht. Tonight, while you're at the cottage, my team and I will put this together. We'll bring Ash up to speed on the plane ride."

"Ten-and-a-half-hour flight. Seychelles is GMT plus four hours." Blaze calculated on his itinerary. "If we leave out here at ten in the morning that puts us on the island at twenty thirty hours London time, but midnight plus in that time zone."

"Good," McKayla said. "I don't want to get there any earlier. I don't want to worry about running into anyone, straight off. I like to have time to get my legs under me in a new place."

"We need to leave from the Penthouse to the airport around nine, then." Blaze circled the number on his paper.

"I don't like her not having anyone on the yacht, though," Gator said. "We need to think that through."

"She can at least have Hoover with her." Ash rubbed under Hoover's neck, eliciting a moan of satisfaction from his pup.

"How would that be?" McKayla asked. "A dog on the boat?"

Ash tipped his head down to receive his Hoover kisses. "You have stability issues. Are they going to tell you no?"

"Maybe?" She shrugged. "I would. Food and water lead to bathrooming needs. You said you run him ten miles a day. High energy dogs and all that."

"Food and water are simple. Exercise—I run him before he gets on and when he gets off. Or you run him on the treadmill. Hoover's comfortable on open water. We take all the Bravo K9s out on boats regularly."

McKayla shook her head. "He can't go twenty-four hours without a potty break, Ash."

Ash smiled. "He's potty trained."

"I get that," McKayla said. "But I've also seen the volume he voids out even if there was some kind of post, he could wiz on. Surely that won't be allowed. Not on a mega yacht."

"No. I'm not saying he's house broken. I'm saying he knows how to use the toilet."

"No, he doesn't. Does he?" She looked down. "Do you?"

"Bravo trained all of our big dogs because we're often on boats, and it was the simplest solution. While Hoover knows how to use the toilet, the only issue he might have is if it's not a lever flushing apparatus on the toilet. But otherwise, that's what he does on a boat."

"You're kidding me," Jack said.

"Not at all. He's very proud of himself. Gives him a bit of independence around the house, he doesn't have to wait for me to walk him."

"Doggy door?" Gator asked.

"Would be dangerous since my condo is the top floor on a ten-story building."

"Ah. Okay. What made you think to train him to do that?" McKayla asked. "I've seen people post videos on social media, but I thought those were actor dogs, learning tricks for films. Come to think of it, I've never seen a dog using the bathroom in a movie. That's not a thing."

"I was doing an ultra-marathon," Ash started.

McKayla pointed at Hoover splayed out at her feet. "With him?"

"No, we were staying with a…friend of mine."

McKayla didn't really want to hear about the ex. While McKayla wasn't generally the jealous type, she'd just rather not let her imagination fill in the picture right then. "Can I see? Do you think Hoover needs to go now?"

"If he doesn't have to pee," Ash said, "he can at least go through the motions for you."

"And number two?" She wrinkled her nose. "I mean… it's easier to dispose of I guess."

"Not a problem," Ash assured her.

"The story about the ultra-marathon and Hoover's skills?" Blaze asked.

"I twisted both my ankles," Ash said. "The hill dropped right where a runner lost his balance. He went down. I tried a little trick we learned in the SEALs on how to run down a steep slope. By the time I got to the guy to grab him off the tree he was hanging from, my ankles were pretty much toast."

"He was okay in the end?" Jack asked.

"Eventually."

"Well, I'm glad of that, but are you trying to convince

us that because you couldn't walk to take Hoover out, you trained him to use a toilet? You are so bluffing." McKayla was grinning as Ash took off Hoover's harness. "You're going to tell me he's pee shy or something. Should I turn on the water and give him privacy in the loo?"

"You joke. But you'll see. And it's good." Ash folded the vest and put it on one of the dining room chairs. "Hoover can go to the bathroom in his vest if needs be. But not with the handle sticking out. And he has a little more trouble with getting bound up when he's getting into position. I make it a policy to take off the vest."

"Wilco," McKayla said.

"If you're going to be alone with him, you need a couple of hand gestures."

"I've seen sit. And load. And lay down."

"Then you're almost golden. The hand signal to use the potty is the American Sign Language sign for toilet. Okay, first come stand in front of Hoover, I'll be doing the signals with you because while I'm here, he won't follow other commands.

"K."

"McKayla, fist up for sit."

When McKayla made the move, Hoover looked at Ash. Ash held up a fist and Hoover sat.

"Okay, pay attention, you hold your fingers out in a peace sign or V shape that points at Hoover then swing them around to point at your eyes. Yes, that's right. It means move your focus up here to me. I'm communicating with you. Good?"

"Yes."

Hoover was looking at Ash.

"Next sign is toilet." Ash reached out to demonstrate the signal. "You make a fist. Your thumb pushes through your pointer and middle fingers." Ash waited for McKayla to get her hand in position. "Good. Now, twist it back and forth like this. Like you're jiggling the water toggle to flush."

Hoover stood up and went into the bathroom.

Everyone trotted along behind him.

"Wait, how'd he know that was my bathroom?" McKayla was aghast.

"He can smell a drop of gasoline in a pool of water," Ash explained. "He knows where the bathroom is."

"That's—" McKayla made a face. "Yeah, it makes me feel like my latrine isn't clean."

"You're fine. Just assume he smells the soap and towels."

Hoover was over to the toilet where he worked his snoot between the lid and the rim. Bouncing his nose farther and farther under he got the lid on his head, then pushed it up.

McKayla sat on the floor in the doorway, so Strike Force could lean their heads in and watch, too.

Hoover stood in front of the toilet facing the tank and placed his front paws on the seat. With a push of his back legs, he jumped his rear legs up to sit. Balancing there, wiggling his hips a bit, soon there was a plop.

"No way!" McKayla whispered.

"Did you hear that?" Gator's voice was pure glee.

A stream of urine followed.

Hoover gave another little bouncing shake then jumped down. Using his nose, he let the lid fall back into place with a clatter. Then, he pawed at the lever until the toilet flushed.

Everyone broke out in cheers, clapping their hands.

Hoover came to sit in front of Ash. Ash handed McKayla his pull toy. "Now he gets a high-pitched reward. Tell him what a good boy he is and let him fight you for his toy."

That was the fun part. Hoover radiated pride with a happy tail thumping the ground as he crouched belly down and tugged at McKayla.

When Ash took over with the rubbing and more praise, McKayla gestured for the group to follow, and they all made their way back to her den.

"Okay, you never finished the story," McKayla said, curling up at the end of the couch and hugging a pillow to her. "Why can Hoover do that? The girlfriend wasn't able to exercise Hoover."

"She tried. She rode her bike alongside him as far as she could. She wasn't an athlete. She could do about three miles. I needed to figure out something to exhaust Hoover. There's nothing like teaching a dog a new trick to use up their energy. An engaged thinking mind is a tired mind."

"Isn't that the truth?" McKayla asked. "Foreign languages, new situations, when my brain is engaged, it's exhausting." She held up a finger. "No smart cracks."

Ash said with a grin, "None from me."

And with that grin, McKayla was ready to have Ash all to herself. "Speaking of being exhausted, gentlemen, I'm heading to my cottage. I look forward to hearing your plans tomorrow." She stood up. "We're going to the

Seychelles, gather the information we need, and we're all going to get home safe and sound."

But as she tried to pronounce that last sentence, fear grabbed hold of her imagination, making the words thick and sticky in her throat.

26

ASHER GIDEON

The "Friend's Place" Cottage, London, England

MCKAYLA HAD LOCKED the door to her cottage, and with her hand on the stability bar, she and Hoover set off over the short distance to the vehicle. It was zero eight hundred hours and with traffic, they needed to get on the road to meet the team in an hour.

Ash's brow furrowed as he watched her move. "Are you okay, McKayla?"

She swung her head to look over her shoulder at her five o'clock, Ash's close protection position. "I'm fine. Why do you ask?"

"You're not walking like you normally do."

"I'm a little—" She cleared her throat. "A little tender."

"From the explosion?" He reached for her elbow.

She sent him a mischievous grin. "No, it's from all the mad romping through the night. Getting tossed around my bed like I was a rag doll." She came to a stop by the car and turned to Ash. "It's been a while for me—read that as over a year—since I've had sex. And any woman will tell you, with that much sex in such a limited amount of time, it's expected that I'd be… uhm…sore."

His eyes scanned the environs then came to rest on McKayla's warm brown eyes, full of laughter. "Sweetheart." His voice was hushed. "I'm sorry I hurt you."

The smile fell off, and she rolled her eyes at him. "I'm a big girl. I know my body. I made my choices. Stop making that worried face at me. I'm not made of glass. I'll be fine. I plan to go to my bedroom at the back of the plane. Take my book. Take a nap. I'll be right as rain by the time we land in the islands."

He placed his hands on her shoulders so she would look up at him. "Do you need a doctor?"

McKayla laughed. "That would be a no. Stop already. I can take care of myself."

"Obviously." Ash opened her door. "But I'd like an opportunity to take care of you a little bit, too." He took her elbow as she lowered herself onto the seat. "Especially if I had a hand in making you uncomfortable."

"No, Ash, it wasn't your hand that did it." McKayla gave him a wink that had him grinning ear to ear.

Last night had been a hell of a good time. Finding McKayla in his arms again, miraculous. The best part was being able to make love to her the way he'd always wanted to. When they were deployed, her rule was not a sound, not even heavy breathing. He got the why of that—and it terrified him. He always wanted her in arm's reach. Keep an eye on her. Keep her safe.

He did what he could.

Sex between them had always been good in her little one-woman tent.

But listening to her mewling and begging for more last night? Shit. That was gold.

He wasn't sure how they could make a relationship work, but Ash was determined not to let life pull them apart again.

He had hit the jackpot with McKayla. She was *everything*. Just an amazing, surprising, wonderful woman.

And in a few weeks, he could tell the world how he felt.

He was walking on air.

After loading Hoover into the rear seat, and taking another sweep of the area, Ash climbed behind the wheel.

The silent drive was interrupted when McKayla said, "So we were pretty busy last night, and I didn't ask you what you think of Misha?"

He turned onto the main road and joined the traffic. "I don't have enough to go on. I was only in the hospital room for a few minutes."

"Gut?"

"Yeah, my recent batting average with gut impressions isn't what it normally is." He watched a car come up in the rearview going way too fast. Teenager in the driver's seat. He changed lanes and disappeared down the street. "There was a mission I ran the other day. It kind of threw me."

McKayla swiveled in her seat to better face him. "Tell me about that."

He looked her way, wondering what he should say. McKayla had always been a good sounding board. She always had some reasonable input. "There was a woman, I smelled alcohol around her, and she seemed be swaying under its influence. I thought she was drunk. Tipsy, at least. But really her instability came from a significant injury she was hiding."

"And the smell of alcohol?"

"She'd poured a scotch from the hotel mini bar into her son's sippy cup, trying to find relief."

"Hard to get drunk on minibar bottles."

"Every turn, I misread. Really nice woman. Really terrible situation. It's doing a number on my head."

"In the field you work with what your senses give you."

"Right."

"Ash, it's not safe to second guess yourself. In SEAL training, you were put in a shoot house where you had a split second to decide if a guy had a weapon or had weapons-free hands. You trained your brain for years to see and perceive."

"Same mission," he said, "that piece came in handy. In a low-vis situation, I was able to pick out the weapons."

"Don't start doubting yourself, hesitate and die."

She reached out and put her hand on his thigh. And his cock danced to attention. He would think he'd had enough exercise and would take a damned break. Their brief window was closed for now. He moved his thoughts away from her hand and back to the mission fail. "This is more of a judging people call. It keeps playing through my mind, I've had this sentence circulating through my head since I took this assignment: 'Don't trust what you're seeing'."

"As it applies to me?"

"You're not a seeing, sweetheart. You're a feeling."

"What feeling is that?" She painted her fingers down her bodice as she stuck out her boobs provocatively.

Ash pulled her hand from his thigh, lifting it to his lips and said, "I want to lick your smile, so I can taste happiness." He kissed her hand. "That's what I'm feeling right now."

She laughed and joy spread through him.

Mission. He reminded himself.

"You asked me my gut on Misha. This is one of the issues we talked about me having feelings for you and knowing this guy gets to play the boyfriend. How does that affect me? Am I prejudiced from the get-go?"

"*Prejudged.* Prejudging isn't being prejudice. Prejudice is when you lean into stereotypes, and you aren't open to changing your mind when the facts present themselves. Did you change your mind about the woman?"

"One-eighty."

"So not prejudiced. Prejudging is a brain survival instinct. We prejudge everything until we test it."

"Toe in the water."

"We blow on food before it goes into our mouths if we think it might be hot," she said. "We pick up books and judge whether we're going to enjoy it or not by the cover."

"I still feel bad." Yeah, it was going to take him a while to get over his insensitivity to Mrs. Napoli's situation.

"Did you make it right?" McKayla said softly.

Make it right? Ash pressed his lips together. Close. Damned. Call. "I took the steps to make it safer. Right? That wasn't in my capacity. And I'll never know—client privacy." He turned to catch her gaze—warm, concerned, supportive. "I hope so anyway."

"Problem is—" McKayla shifted around to look forward again, adjusting her seat belt. "And I'm just reminding you of this since you've studied this *ad nauseum* in your training—our brains take in so much information. Millions of pieces of information. Some people are more aware than others. If you're an artist, you might pay more attention to shade and hue. If you're a musician, you might hear beats in the soundscape that might get lost on other ears—either pleasant or cacophonous. Heck, if you experience OCD, you might be fine-tuned to find that *one* thing that's out of place. That can be overwhelming in some situations, but surely there's a job where it's a highly prized skill set. You, my friend, were trained to find threat. To assess who, in any given situation, might cause problems. You go on what's available to you. It's an imperfect system at best. Maybe give yourself a break?"

He didn't answer. What did he say to that? Sure, he was trained to find the threat. But real people with real lives depended on him not making any mistakes.

She must have seen him debating that in his own mind because McKayla added much more harshly, "Okay, let me put it another way. You need to give yourself a break because if you're second guessing the situation, it can get people killed. Like *me*."

Ash gripped the steering wheel and sent a ferocious scowl her way. "God, McKayla, don't say shit like that to me."

27

McKayla Pickard

The Penthouse, London, England.

McKayla had texted Jack when she and Ash were ten minutes out.

Jack and Gator were waiting on the sidewalk near a black SUV. Not hers. They must have rented it.

Just like her normal security team, Ash had parked so she was on the sidewalk side of the car.

After Ash put their vehicle in park, McKayla popped her door to move to the back seat since she was the shortest of the team. She had been told that Jack would be driving her vehicle. Ash would be shotgun.

It was kind of funny, kind of cute how when she exited the car, the men were in go mode. Heads on a swivel. Their stances formidable.

"You have my bags?" McKayla checked in as Jack

held the door for her, using his body to block her from public view.

"Yes, ma'am. In the lead car." Jack, like the other members of her security team, was dressed in the Iniquus close protection uniform of charcoal gray tactical pants and a black short-sleeved polo that made his biceps look like he could punch through a brick wall.

Black hair. Intensely blue eyes. Even taller than Ash's six-foot-three height, Jack was the prototype for some action figure doll.

People on the sidewalk were turning around to stare. Yeah, the men and their doings did spark curiosity.

Just from the visual of these two, McKayla couldn't imagine anyone approaching, let alone attacking her.

McKayla smiled to herself, thinking what Misha would say if he saw her Iniquus security team all together. Poor ego-hurt guy.

"Did Striker and Blaze get to the Seychelles okay?" McKayla stepped back, allowing Jack to open the passenger door for her.

"Yes, ma'am," Jack said. "They landed on Mahé just fine. They've settled at the hotel and have started their processes."

"Good to know." McKayla pushed in next to Hoover. "Hey buddy, I get to ride next to you." She reached for her belt, checking the time readout on her super-secret spy watch. "Okay, let's get going." She'd told her stylist that she wanted to wear thick bangles all week. That should hide the comms unit well enough. McKayla wondered if the designer had considered women's fashions when planning this device. Sure, the men could hide them under their tux cuffs. But it was much too utilitarian for her gowns.

Gator, in the car directly ahead of them, tapped his break lights, signaling that he was ready as Jack adjusted the mirrors in her car.

Ash stood at his open door. One last scan. He popped in, and before he settled, the cars took off.

McKayla swiped her hand across her stomach.

She had a churning-pit-of-the-belly kind of thing going on.

The men swerved evenly and comfortably through traffic. She thought about an old car commercial where the guy was in the back seat cutting a diamond. The idea was that the ride was so smooth that one didn't feel that the diamond was at risk.

It wasn't the ride that was making her feel queasy.

Maybe it's fake morning sickness? McKayla tried on a little gallows humor. Didn't work. She wondered how far along she was supposed to be. She'd been so surprised by what Misha had done that she hadn't put it through her CIA processor to imagine the ramifications of not knowing the details of this stupid story.

McKayla had no idea how to act like a pregnant person.

The further they drove, the more dread formed in the pit of her stomach. She didn't want to feed the sensation by paying too much attention. Whatever was causing this, there was nothing to be done about it at this moment. Right now, it was a car ride to the plane. A very long southeasterly flight. Then, she could better assess.

Her instincts told her this was going to be a shitshow.

As McKayla focused on Ash sitting in front of her—the breadth of his shoulder and the softness of his dark hair, she wondered what—if anything—was in store for them as a couple. Ash had been very clear that he wanted nothing to do with her wealth and fame.

Ditto, she thought, neither do I.

Was this a fun tumble for him? Didn't seem so. Ash asked for a relationship after this mission was complete.

He said he loved her as much as ever.

Ash also said he loved his job and had his little freak out after their passionate reunion, thinking he might get fired. Most men McKayla knew would just brush the act under the carpet—no harm, no foul, no reason to mention their wild sexcapades to the boss.

But honesty and responsibility were cornerstones for Ash.

And that integrity seemed like the kind of solid foundation McKayla would like to build a future on.

How could they possibly resist all the things that would tug them apart?

McKayla didn't love her job with the CIA, she'd freely admit. Even for what good she'd been able to do, it still felt like spinning wheels in a mud bog.

She thought this work would help soothe her soul, but in the end, yeah, McKayla didn't like having to prance around in high heels and makeup and *that* was the best part of it.

In other words, living in this world of the entitled *sucked*.

She longed for a mountain top. A fire. A good book.

And with that, McKayla remembered that one of the

ways that she used to like to calm her nerves back in the day, as they bumped over the dirt roads on their next foray outside of the wire, was to listen to Ash talk about his home state of Alaska. There was something about his tone that changed when he spoke of home. She could picture the vast seclusion. The cold on her face. What wouldn't she give to be there today?

"Did you know that Ash considers us all to be outsiders?" she asked Jack.

"Not in the way that that sounds. I'm from Juneau. Everywhere that's not Alaska is considered 'outside'," he said.

"Oh?" Jack glanced into his rearview then over to Ash. "Huh. Learn something new every day. What was the hardest thing for you to adapt to when you left the frigid north?"

"The noise. Now let me be clear, Alaska has its own noises. But city noise is a lot to deal with. Crowds. I hate crowds."

"When we were in Afghanistan you talked a lot about the dust," McKayla said. "And filth."

"Oh, Alaska can be dirty. Lots of mud. But yeah. The cold keeps most of that down. Juneau," Ash looked over at Jack, "where I was born and raised, is the deep south of Alaska. "

"They drink sweet tea and say y'all." McKayla laughed.

Ash swung his head around, pulling his brow together. "Nah. Life wasn't that exotic." His tone was light, an exchange of teasing banter. But he must have heard something in her voice to make him look worried like that.

Ash was doing his due diligence, head on a swivel, checking mirrors, scanning the roadside.

McKayla, too, had never given up the habit of searching the roads for the thing that was out of place. Any sign that a roadside bomb was waiting on them. She wondered if that kind of awareness, that hyper vigilance would ever leave her system.

"You have to imagine that it's basically one road called The Road."

"Clever nickname." McKayla reached out to rub Hoover's head.

"Isn't it?" Again with Ash's worried face searching hers. "Starts at Auke Bay and runs about forty-five miles to Echo Cove."

"Echo Cove is a romantic name." McKayla dug her fingers into Hoover's fur for a little dog magic. "In a kind of 'Oh my darlin' Clementine' kind of way. Wistful."

"The road doesn't connect to anything?" Jack asked.

"The only way out of Juneau is to fly, boat, or hike. Once you're there, you're there."

"What kind of work is in that area?" Jack put on his signal and followed the lead car into the turn off. "Fishing, of course."

McKayla realized that Jack had to know all this. Ash had been on Striker's SEAL team along with Jack at one point. Those men had to know everything about each other. Nice that Jack was playing along.

"So 'the bush' is the name for interior Alaska. That's where my dad worked. He'd go into the remote wilderness, cabin to cabin, checking on the dogs, giving them their vet care. Almost all of the dogs that dad worked with were on competitive sled teams. Athletes. Mom worked in tourism during the cruise ship season. From September on, she made crafts to sell in the tourist stores the next year."

"Get this, Jack. Ash's mom owned a sightseeing boat and captained it to take folks to see the whales. I want to see whales. Why haven't I gone to see the whales, Ash?"

"Couldn't tell you. They're amazing creatures."

"Not only did Ash's mom captain her boat but the bus driver that picked up the tourists from their cruise ships was a female." McKayla pulled at her safety belt, starting to feel trapped in the backseat. "The naturalist who helped everyone understand what they were seeing was a woman. It was a woman powered business from start to finish. Cool, huh?"

"I thought there weren't that many women in Alaska," Jack said.

"More in the cities than out in the bush. But, yeah, the male to female ratio is a heck of a lot better down in the lower forty-eight."

"That's how you got going with the dogs?"

"Yeah." Ash had angled his head and was watching the side mirror. "Jack, heads up. There's a black SUV powering up on my side. Six cars back."

McKayla twisted around to see, then watched it veer off at a petrol station. "We're good."

"When I got older, whenever school was out," Ash picked up where he'd left off. "Dad would take me with him to help with the dogs' care."

"And that's when you fell in love with dogs?" McKayla asked.

"Not all dogs, to be honest. I like the athletics of it."

McKayla recognized the approaching turnoff for the back of the airport. "Like Hoover."

"Hoover is the Zen doggo of all dogs," Ash boasted. "He's an alpha."

"This sweet guy?" McKayla bent to kiss Hoover, and Hoover thumped his tail. "I'm not sure I agree with you."

"When a man says, I'm an alpha male, one hundred percent of the time he is not." Jack flipped on his turn signal and now they were driving along the fence line to her hangar.

"Agreed," Ash said. "The best special operators know what they are. They don't need to swagger around getting people to agree. The best, you'd never guess their skill sets."

"The least aggressive?" McKayla asked. "Well, no. The most aggressive when aggression is required and when…ah, I get it. No need for Hoover to posture. He's the real deal."

"Exactly."

"What's it like to have a plane ready for you at any time?" Jack pointed ahead of them as the lead car came to a stop by the blue building. Her jet sat ready on the runway. "The freedom of knowing you can be almost anywhere on the planet by the next day."

"For me?" McKayla released her belt as Jack maneuvered their vehicle over to where the rest of the team was getting out. "I don't use it all that often. I have it to lend out."

"Rent it?" Ash asked.

"No, you know, to *do* things. Someone needs a supply of something to get someplace to help someone. I have a logistics person who fills the plane, and my crew gets the things or the people where they need to go."

Jack put the gear in park. "Like a charitable thing?"

"I just think about it as an opportunity thing."

Gator was reaching for her door handle.

Jack popped the locks. "That's never in the papers."

"No." The door opened to the smell of jet fuel. "And I hope it never is," McKayla said as she got out, holding onto Gator's extended arm for support in case anyone had binoculars on her. After all, her flight plan had been filed. Anyone could find out when she'd be at the airport today. "It would turn into somebody saying that I'm trying to rehabilitate my reputation," she continued as Jack got out and could hear her. "I don't really care about what other people think about me. I care what *I* think of me."

Ash was getting Hoover from the car and strapping on his stability vest.

With everyone out, they stood together to discuss next moves.

McKayla shielded her eyes with the blade of her hand, watching her flight crew approaching to welcome her. "You know, Jack, to answer your question. I really don't like knowing I can take a plane anywhere at any time. I don't enjoy being wealthy. It takes away so much. Too much. There's no reason to dream, I can do anything I want whenever I want it." She took hold of the stability bar on Hoover and released Gator. "Thank you."

"My wife's from a very wealthy family," he said. "D-Day hated all that. She's in the Army now. Similar to you, in some ways, she wants to serve, and she likes a challenge. She said it takes the fun right out of everything when things come too easy."

"Exactly. I enjoy the feeling I get after I've had a good strenuous workout. That sense of accomplishment and fatigue from a job well done. I really liked that in life. I miss it. I'm still trying to figure out what to do about it. One thing I know is I can't put the genie back in the bottle."

28

ASHER GIDEON

Grand Paradise Hotel, Mahé, Seychelles

AND HERE WE GO. Ash left his room, twisting the knob to check that the lock had engaged.

He had been to a lot of high-end places in his work providing close protection, but nothing like this. Nothing even close.

The Grand Paradise Hotel was insane.

It turned out McKayla had rented the entire top floor of this wing. Ten rooms instead of the five that would more than suffice, saying it would make security easier.

Each room had an astonishing vista, white sand beaches on the west and granite cliffs to the north. The décor was a marriage of opulence and tiki shack. Some-how, it worked.

At a thousand dollars a night per room, McKayla would be out fifty grand during their five-day stay.

Fifty grand.

And that only paid for their rooms.

Mind boggling.

Obscene.

Ash adjusted the sleeves on his tux. Like the Iniquus suits, the close protection tuxes were built for free movement. And like the suit Ash wore to the last botanical garden party he'd attended; his reinforced waistband didn't support a holster and gun. The laws against firearms, or even having ammunition, in the Seychelles were extremely strict. And the punishment for breaking those laws, fifteen years in the poky.

White had wanted four men with McKayla at each event.

The invitation indicated that security would be provided.

Reticent to follow the team's suggestion that Ash use Misha's invitation, lest word get back to Misha and he feel cuckolded, McKayla called the host. After explaining the recent events in London, and the use of a stability K9, she asked that she be allowed one of her close protection team to manage her dog and assist her should she have a medical incident.

Who could turn that down?

Ash's name had been added to the guest list. The host instructed McKayla to identify Ash as her "medical aid," not her security or she might cause unrest amongst those who had left their close protection with their cars in the outer ring lot.

Blaze would be guarding the floor here at the hotel, making sure no one got into the team's gear to sabotage it. He was the only one dressed in tactical pants.

Striker would drive tonight with Gator riding shotgun. They were already in the vehicle in the front entrance, waiting for McKayla.

With Ash as her "aid," Hoover was the weapon.

Ash reached past Blaze to knock.

Stepping back as the door opened. Ash's breath caught. His systems froze.

Who was this?

Ash remembered digital-camo-McKayla with her dirt smeared face. Hygiene in their forward operating base had been hard to come by. Her hair had been dusty, scraped back into those tight military buns.

Here? It was hard to recognize her.

The one shouldered dress shaped along the curves of her body. It was the color of the ocean that he could see from his hotel window. The silver stitches were like the foam roiled by the waves crashing against the shore.

Her makeup was flawless. Her hair, held back from her face on one side with pins made of precious gems, flowed in a cascade of rich satin over her shoulders and down her back, the ends were soft curls that he wanted to play with.

She was royalty.

Ash's brain was misfiring.

Blaze leaned in. "Contacts?"

She batted long mascaraed eyelashes.

Ash wasn't used to her in makeup. Wasn't used to the seductiveness of her eyes like that. Yeah, she looked amazing. Yeah, his body was responding. But Ash's brain wasn't on the same page.

"Audio?" Blaze asked.

McKayla moved her jangling collection of bangles out of the way to show the watch underneath. And Ash remembered Mrs. Napoli. She, too, had used bracelets to hide her secrets.

Ash looked down, checking on Hoover with his wagging tail, then bladed his hand toward the elevator.

He trailed McKayla at her five o'clock.

They were silent until the doors shut. "Is everything okay?" McKayla asked.

"I'm just…who are you?"

"An actress, playing a role."

This was, in the flesh, the woman Ash had seen on the magazine covers.

When they left the "Friend's Cottage", Ash had been so sure that everything was going to be fine between them. Even in her penthouse, everything was fine.

But here? McKayla like this? Not his comfort zone.

While his contract with Iniquus had made Ash a comfortably wealthy man, this?

This was antithetical to his nature.

Ash didn't know how to navigate such conflicting emotions—loving McKayla and hating her lifestyle.

"Wow," McKayla said under her breath as the doors open. "You keep thinking that hard, and you're going to wear the tread off your brain wheels. It smells like burned rubber in here."

She stepped out of the elevator with Hoover prancing contentedly alongside her.

Ash at her five o'clock.

This was the problem of Ash being McKayla's close protection.

It was a mindfuck.

29

McKAYLA PICKARD
Eden Botanical Garden, Mahé, Seychelles

STRIKER PULLED the black SUV forward, stopping when the passenger door was in front of McKayla.

He and Gator looked appropriate for evening in their dark suits and crisp white shirts.

Ash opened the door and assisted McKayla in.

She *wasn't* happy.

That elevator ride was like getting steeped in Ash's judgement and censure. It felt selfish on his part. And he should cut it the hell out.

After loading Hoover into the cargo area where a blanket was laid out for him, Ash rounded the vehicle and jumped in next to her.

They were off.

"Ash checked on your communications?" Striker asked as he rolled them forward.

"He did." McKayla was watching the sunset out of her side window, trying to draw in the beauty and peace.

"What's the plan tonight?" Gator asked.

"See who shows up. It's tricky with the instability issue. I'll be conspicuous wherever I walk. And if I walk too much, that will seem odd, too."

"Ash is wearing video contacts as well," Striker offered. "He can't leave your side but panning the room will look normal for him."

"I'm trying to work out a reason why I would leave my dear Misha's hospital bedside to be partying in the islands. Seems gross. I'm hoping Uncle Niko will come and treat me like a fragile flower. This dress makes me look plenty delicate, I think. And Hoover helps that image. I'll play that angle." She brushed her skirt. "There's dinner and then a breakaway. Men in one direction, women in the other. The men will discuss business. They've organized a flower arranging class for the women. I'll go with the men." McKayla took in an unsure breath. "I'm going to try, anyway. I'm here representing the Popyrin family, after all. The men who are here are very old school in their thoughts about women. I figure if word of my pregnancy and," she stopped to point at Hoover, "instability get around. They will see me as innocuous."

"I grew up with a mother who was out there breaking down stereotypical molds for whale loving tourists. With the military, it was eye opening to move into diverse cultures where women weren't even seen as fully formed human beings. They were treated like children," Ash said quietly. "I have to say that from your work, and that of other cultural support team members, I learned how men negating women's intellect and capabilities was a fool's game."

"I saw the same thing when my wife was trying to dig up intel at a shindig like this for uber-wealthy folks," Gator said. "D-Day was playing a role, same as you're doin' now, McKayla. She had the same issues with the cultural view of women. It made it hard for her to get her ear in the right conversations. Oooowhee, did she hate every minute of those designer clothes," Gator said. "Have to say, D-Day threw me for a loop when I saw her there. Not at all who she normally was. And there she was looking like she was a movie star."

Gator seemed to be adding little bits of "wife parallels" into the conversations. McKayla wondered if—having lived through a similar situation as McKayla was with Ash —he wasn't trying to add context and normalcy to the thoughts Ash might be having.

"They suck. I want elastane in my pants, I want big old flannel shirt comfort." McKayla's hand skated down her bare leg to her feet. "These shoes," she said pitifully, "are Medieval torture devices. Ah well, when in Rome, I guess."

Striker chuckled. "Hopefully, you won't have suffered in vain." He nodded toward the line of cars. "We're here."

McKayla closed her eyes, took a breath, fixed her Mrs. Peabody-Strumpkins-approved smile on her face, and waited for Ash to open her door.

After moving through the reception line where the hostess verified her invitation, McKayla, with her hand on Hoover's handle, wended her way amongst the islands of orchids and tropical fronds in the arboretum. A group gathered to her left to go into another building that was filled with butterflies.

There was a long line at the bar, and the men walked away balancing three and four drinks in their hands.

No drinking for her tonight. She passed a server and requested some water.

His hand went into the air, and quickly after, a woman arrived with a goblet balanced on her tray.

A skewer with an orange rind and small purple orchid made the drink fancy.

Mckayla was on the search for Uncle Niko.

As she rounded the column, McKayla spotted Rajja. Turning the corner to join him, she found the trio of friends were there.

"You brought your dog," Karl Davidson said from where he lounged on an eggplant-colored couch.

McKayla smiled and looked toward the empty seat, she'd wait for an invitation and if it didn't materialize, she'd sit down anyway.

"Come, join us," said a man with a heavy Russian accent.

"Good evening." McKayla took her seat.

Hoover laid down in front of her rather than at her side.

Ash didn't correct Hoover, but followed his dog's gaze to Karl, before he moved to stand like a piece of statuary by the wall.

McKayla curled her hand to her chest. "I'm—"

"A disruptor who started new ways of dealing moving monies." The corpulent man rocked from hip to hip to inch himself to the edge of his seat. "You will enjoy this conversation." He obviously knew who she was but had brushed by the introduction.

McKayla hoped someone at Iniquus could identify this guy or that she'd find a way to ask politely a little later. "I wasn't moving money so much as showing how wealth was an illusion. You tell someone 'this has value,' if they buy in, it has value. This is true in the art market, in fashion, even in intellectual property. My business simply gave people another thing to call valuable."

"Until it was not," Russian guy said. "You were smart to sell when you did."

"I try to be smart in everything I do." She smiled and lifted her glass of water to show she was teasing.

"Here is an example of smart." The man stabbed a finger in the air. "This brings me so much, mmmm, I will use the German word schadenfreude."

"Oh?" McKayla raised her brows.

"You know this word?"

"Yes, we use it in English, too. Like we use the foreign phrase *joie de vivre*. Though vastly different meanings."

"For me," he said, "much of my *joie de vivre* comes from my schadenfreude." He chuckled.

"Okay." McKayla lifted her hand graciously. "Tell me about money and schadenfreude, why are you gleeful with the pain of others?"

"Oh, you have come in during a discussion of the child's play of manipulation. No one can stand up to the propaganda machines of Russia and her friends from the

Soviet Era. We are much too good for the average person to resist. We lead them by the nose, and we get from it what we want. The difference in America and Russia is that democracy is impatient. Our government plays the long game. And we have known since Aesop that the turtle beats the hare."

"Oh. Well. Is this a general observation or were you thinking of something specific?" McKayla asked.

"I read just today, some guy working on the U.S. presidential campaign was convicted on six counts of laundering Russian money to pay for the expenses, and the candidate didn't even win. This kind of thing is so easy to hide. How was it that he allowed himself to be caught? I tell you. Greedy in the front. Impatience in the middle. Leads to jail in the end." He threw both hands into the air. "They should have worked through my communications business. With me, it would have been whisper quiet. Successful."

"So, you're happy that this man was caught and convicted because it makes you look good to others. Or because you offered your services, they turned you down, and they were caught."

"Yes, this." He stabbed a finger into the air again. His hand landed on McKayla's knee, and Hoover lifted himself to sit at attention.

"Misha's father, Victor, is a great friend of mine," the man said. "He told me you would be here, and I should look for you, Miss McKayla Pickard. You are every bit as beautiful as the pictures he sent to me."

"I'm sorry, I missed your name." She held out her

hand, but the guy turned to Karl as Karl groaned beside him.

Leaning his weight into an arm, Karl used his other fist to pound at the muscles in his hip.

"If you were a Russian, young man, you would be happy that you have an amputation. Though, the way things are going right now, I cannot promise that they would not make you go to war as you are."

Karl blinked at the man as if completely dumbstruck by his saying such a thing.

McKayla had never seen Karl taken aback before. That was kind of fun. McKayla experienced a bit of that schadenfreude the guy had mentioned earlier.

"I heard that they're just rounding up men in the streets," Nadir said. "We have a sudden influx of young Russian tourists in Qatar, those who plan to stay for as long as their tourist visa will allow. Money of course, can extend these fairly easily."

"The troops. Psh," the Russian said. "They were culled from the back woods of Mother Russia. Places with no education and not even toilets. The poor sad peoples. No one cares if they are buried in the ground. It only gets worrisome for the Russian people when they try to harvest our young men from the cities. From Moscow. The educated, the ones that make things tick."

"I heard on a news report, that a copilot was sent to the front without anyone telling his airline. Not to fly mind you. To walk through the mud with a rifle," Rajja said. "When he didn't show up to work, there was no one to replace him next to the pilot. A pilot cannot fly alone.

Everyone needed to get off the plane. No flying when you send your pilots off to war to fight the ground game."

McKayla wanted the conversation back on propaganda, and better yet, if she could get them talking about shipping. "Misha's father, Victor, have you seen him recently? How is he doing?"

"He's, how shall we say, doing a fine job of both keeping his head above water and staying under the radar. This is a finely tuned skill. Not many have it." He lifted his head as he caught someone's eye. "You will excuse me?" He struggled to his feet and walked away.

McKayla tried to keep her contacts trained in the direction he took, so Iniquus could figure out whom he was talking to.

"You need wine." Nadir pulled her attention back.

"No, thanks. Doctor's orders." She put her hands on her stomach. "No wine for a few more months."

Nadir shot a startled look toward Karl. "Ah so?"

Karl let the look glide over to Nadir. McKayla wasn't sure what to make of that other than perhaps they had speculated amongst themselves about her real relationship with Misha. Perhaps they, too, had listened to the speculation put out by the Simonas of Misha's past model-dating life.

McKayla somewhat understood why Misha had said she was pregnant. Her carrying a fake oligarch grandbaby did tie her to the family in a way that she could not be tied even with a marriage license. A marriage could end in divorce. But a baby—yeah well, one would hope that an innocent baby would be safe. The ties that bind.

Nadir told Karl, "We were just visiting with Misha and Ivan in London."

"Did you know that Ivan died?" McKayla asked.

"Wait, who?" Nadir asked.

"Ivan Krokov," McKayla said, adding. "Shipping."

Rajja leaned forward. "Ivan Krokov. Dead, you say?"

"How?" Nadir was equally agitated.

Interesting. She thought she'd hit two nerves with that information. One, they were surprised by a friend's sudden death, and the second thing, McKayla didn't understand. Something there was upsetting them. Business deal?

"There was an explosion at Misha's club. That's why Misha's not here." She gestured toward the room.

"Did he mention an explosion to you?" Karl asked Nadir.

"He said he was in the hospital after an accident." Nadir looked at her. "This is why you're covered in scabs?"

"Scabs? Yes. I was cut by the glass. It was in all of the papers. I guess he assumed you knew." McKayla pulled out her phone and queued up the video with her pulling Misha inside. "Yes, well the accident was a gas line that blew up. Here." She tapped the video on. "See for yourself."

The men huddled in. Their faces grim. Questioning looks passed from one to the other.

"That's you?" Nadir asked. "In your condition?"

McKayla put a hand to her chest and went for an "offended" expression. "Misha and I are a couple. Do you think I'd leave him outside with the red-hot metal debris raining down on him like that?" When they handed the phone back, she added, "It doesn't show the frames that happened before the explosion. Ivan, sadly, was standing very close to where it happened. And he didn't survive it." McKayla looked down and took a moment. When she lifted her gaze again, the men were hyper-focused on her. "Ivan's death isn't in the papers, yet. I was told it's because they need to contact his family. I assume his Russian family because his wife, Rachel, knows. She was in the explosion as well."

"Not killed?" Rajja asked insistently.

"No, I only know she survived and is in critical condition but nothing more, I'm sorry." She took a sip of water. "Misha said that the Russian Embassy believes that Ivan didn't suffer. He was there one moment and gone the next. But I'm sorry for my shocking news." She touched her heart. "And I'm sorry for your loss."

Something was definitely up about this piece of information.

For three men who sneered at the world, this level of disquiet was remarkable. She hoped White picked up on this when she saw the videos come through.

Since Misha had made the slip and said bomb and not explosion, McKayla had wondered if it wasn't, in fact, a bomb.

And if it was, did the CIA know?

And if they did, why hadn't they shared that with her?

Beyond their response to this news, there was something about these three. More than met the eye. McKayla just didn't understand the dynamic.

And, of course, White wouldn't explain.

Whenever they were around, McKayla simply performed White's directives: watch, listen, report.

Strike Force knew. Well, knew something.

But McKayla had served with those men. She knew their integrity wasn't a badge pinned to their uniforms, something for show. Integrity was the marrow in their bones.

But man, was she curious about who shot Karl.

Karl was the kind of person that many would like to shoot, she thought as the three men's heads came together and they started a private discussion in Arabic. Not one of McKayla's languages, but Lynx or Deep were back at Iniquus Headquarters recording all of this.

She'd let them think their conversation was private.

Who shot you, Karl?

McKayla only had two clues. One, Gator was there when it happened. Two, Karl knew who shot him. Nope, one more: Three, the circumstances were classified. The sum of all of that was that it wasn't the story that Misha had told her. Misha had said that Karl and some friends had gone hunting at his father's Tanzanian lodge and a rifle misfired. An exotic way to lose a leg.

Yeah, something had always seemed just a little off about that story.

And off about Karl, too.

McKayla never enjoyed the company of the ultra-bored, which was her way of describing the uber-rich. But something about Karl's face just kind of turned her stomach.

The other thing that McKayla had caught was some

weirdness about Gator when he heard that Karl was going to be on the yacht.

"Do you enjoy yachting?" McKayla asked when the three broke huddle. "I understand that we'll be enjoying each other's company again tomorrow on Uncle Niko's craft."

"We're very much looking forward to a leisurely ride past some of the beautiful tiny islands and atolls," Nadir said, his eyes slid to Rajja,

Rajja's gaze slid to Karl.

Karl stared at Hoover who was staring very hard back at him. Swirling his drink, Karl licked his lips and asked, "How are you going? You are dependent on a stability dog."

"Yes, he's quite amazing. Not only is he comfortable on boats, but," she dropped her voice conspiratorially, "he's been trained to use the head. And the why of that?" McKayla was making this up on the fly. "Because if he is partnered with someone with stability issues, they wouldn't be able to let him go out and go potty, right?" She caught Karl's eyes then gestured toward the corner of her lips, the universal cue for wipe your face, buddy.

"And exercise? Are you going to tell me he gets on a stationary bike?" Karl asked, rubbing the white linen napkin over his mouth.

"Treadmill. I put Hoover on the treadmill then I sit and listen to a book on tape." She smiled sadly. "I'm having trouble reading since the explosion."

"With as damaged as you are, I'm surprised your doctor allowed you to come."

"I was relieved my OB decided it was the best plan for

me. Honestly, I needed a change of atmosphere, someplace warm, kind, and beautiful with family and friends." She generously moved her hand in front of the three to indicate she was speaking to them. "London can be too cold and gray. Besides, my Russian family requested I come. And to them, I never like to say no."

30

McKayla Pickard

Eden Botanical Garden, Mahé, Seychelles

The bridge to the island housing the mega yacht marina was in sight.

Ash reached over and squeezed McKayla's hand.

"What were you thinking just now?"

"I was remembering visiting a friend in Florida. The temperatures dropped to freezing. We bundled up and went out looking for frozen iguanas."

"What?"

"We had a wagon, and we lined it with a battery-operated electric blanket set on low with a towel over it, and we laid them in there until they defrosted."

"Iguana popsicles?"

"They were still alive. Just frozen stiff until we warmed them gently and took them back to her garage."

"And why were you thinking about that?"

"Don't know, just some random memory that popped up. I guess it's because I'm here with the beaches and warm temperatures. It's cold and rainy in London year-round. Misha likes it there, he's not big into traveling. He's a bit of a homebody. But last year I went to visit my friend, and I was excited for sunshine and warmth even though it was winter. And I didn't get what I expected. I got falling iguanas. Why, what were you thinking?"

"Not about frozen iguanas, that's for sure." He squeezed her hand twice to let her know he was going to release his grip, then tapped the turn signal. "You won't be alone. The team is already on our own rental yacht. While we'll try to stay off Uncle Niko's radar, we'll have water scooters that can get over to you quickly if need be."

"No weapons."

"No *guns*. Anything can be a weapon."

She held up her watch. "You'll be able to hear me even on the ocean?"

"Remember, those units send signals to satellites. We should be able to hear you just fine—us, Langley, and the war room back at Iniquus."

"Too bad I won't be able to hear you, though."

Ash pulled into a parking spot. "Reviewing: Striker and Blaze brought your luggage and Hoover's equipment, and the boat staff has you unpacked in your room."

She nodded.

"Hoover's food is packaged up. Just empty the bag into the bowl. He has four bags, one for tonight, one for the morning, two more because—"

"Two is one and one is none." McKayla slid her sunglasses from off her head to her nose to get some relief from the sparkle of sun on the water. "You are still *such* a SEAL."

"If the seas aren't rough, and you feel like it won't interfere with your surveillance, Hoover would love a run on the treadmill. Best practice is to put Hoover on the treadmill for his run first. Food second. He tends to puke on his run if we do the food first. And McKayla, once you put the food down, pull your hand back immediately. Hoover has his name for a reason."

"Got it. Potty. Run. Food. Relax." She climbed out of the car and stood holding on to the open door while Ash got Hoover's vest on and walked him over.

Hoover crouched down as they moved toward a cluster of seagulls.

"Hoover," Ash said, reminding him he was on the job and wouldn't be chasing birds that morning.

Ash rounded the vehicle and McKayla took the support bar.

"After being on the Russian yacht," Ash said, "our combat rafts might not have the same charm for him. Good thing you're not going to be on it for long. He might think that luxury is the life he prefers."

"Meh," McKayla said. "There's only so much that's luxurious then it becomes overkill. It's not the thrill one would think."

"Says the b-b-b-billionaire."

"Shut up." She stood there looking at the enormity of the yacht. Two hundred feet of sleek design. It was beautiful.

"We're tracking your GPS, and we'll be watching and listening. It would be nice if you could take a tour and slowly look around each space, sort of talk us through what you're seeing conversationally if you're with the staff."

"I can do that. How does that help?"

"Deep will stitch the videos into a cohesive 3D computer view. He can identify where you are on the yacht, and who is in what vicinity."

"See who's clustering."

"Exactly."

She was just standing there shaking her head back and forth, unable to get her feet to walk forward.

"What's going on?"

"Just an off feeling about this trip," she whispered.

"About them telling you that you couldn't have security?"

"Not really. About that, I've been trying to sort this out in my own head. It may be as simple as me not wanting to be away from you." She blinked her eyes wide. "Wow, did that sound clingy. It's not the right take. I had a place for you in the back of my mind. And now that I have you here, knowing it will only be for a short time, couple of months at most, I selfishly want to absorb as much of you as I can into my system." She exhaled. "That probably sounded worse." She brushed her hand through her hair as the tiny flyaways tickled at her skin. "Let's set that aside. Whatever those Ash emotions are…because I've concluded it's not the basis for my, mmm, unrest. Disquiet."

"You learn to trust your instincts when you're out on the battlefield."

"Exactly. I'm bringing it up. Here are some truths. If you were on board, you wouldn't be allowed a weapon. If you were on board, people within Misha's close orbit would be scrutinizing me and by extension you. I love how you look at me when we're in private. Surely, I slip, from time to time, and I look at you in a way that shows the intimacy of my emotions."

"Go on."

"The owner of the yacht is Misha's uncle. Misha's uncle insisted Misha be here. To do him in? No. It would be easy enough, while Misha is in the hospital to go and threaten him or extort him. If he were to die, it would look like the natural course of things. Or someone could just let him go home and then they put a pillow over his head. With his heart condition, the Russian Embassy could ask that a doctor sign off on the death certificate and fly his body home. They didn't invite Misha to do him harm. Since I am here representing Misha, bringing news about him, and acting as intermediary, I am not a target. We will be on the water. We're not straying outside of the area of the Seychelles. Uncle Niko has security. No one else will. Businessmen won't attack me. There's no reason to."

"And yet?"

"I have that low level hum. I'm fairly convinced that what I'm going to find out is going to be horrible. Like soul-burning awful."

"Do you have any idea what White thinks is going on? Why she's so jazzed about you being here?"

"Zero. And I'm sure that's where the anxiety is coming from. What if I miss it and there's a global implication? Or someone dies. Or… I don't know, my imagination can go nuts, so I try not to think about it." She turned her face into the wind to breathe in the salty fish scent. "I don't think she trusts me very much. I honestly just go look, listen, and report. Never any context."

Ash knew. Even if he didn't know everything, he knew *something*. McKayla could tell from the shadow that crossed his face. How his body was just a little more rigid.

"I hummed the day of the explosion in Afghanistan. I hummed just before the cyber-business I developed tanked, even though I wasn't involved." She stopped to frown at him. "I hummed the day you arrived."

"All day when I arrived?"

"Mostly."

"So maybe it wasn't the day I arrived as much as I arrived on the day you were humming?"

"Is there a difference?"

"I think so. I mean you said you hummed the day of the car bomb in Afghanistan, right? I saw the explosion, and I ran in. I knew you were there, and I found you. Maybe your humming is like a beacon for me to locate you." He grinned.

"And ride to my rescue?"

"I think I'm more in a supportive posture right now." He lifted his mirrored sunglasses to look her in the eye. "No explosions, do you hear me?"

"Is that special ops speak for 'break a leg'? You aren't soothing my nerves here."

"We won't be further out than you can swim. If you don't like the guests, jump overboard. Long swim, though, so grab Hoover, grab something that floats, get in the water. We can follow your GPS signal. We have one in your suitcase, too, so if you do jump in, we'll know you've separated from the vessel."

"Encouraging."

Ash tapped his sternal button on his comms. "McKayla is a go. Bring up audio visual."

When he nodded at her, McKayla said, "Check. Check."

Ash paused. "They have you loud and clear." He looked like he was reaching for her then shifted the motion down to Hoover. "Be a good boy for me. Do your job. Be smart. Okay?"

Hoover pawed at Ash's leg, and Ash crouched to receive his doggy kisses.

Wiping the slobber off with the back of his hand, Ash stood. "McKayla, the team table topped a scenario where you jumped ship, I wasn't teasing about it. We'll be to the seven o'clock of the bow. Should you need us at any point, we have a plan. And a contingency plan. And a contingency of the contingency plan."

"Got it."

"You have to map the yacht for us. And trust that we've got your back."

31

ASHER GIDEON

Fair Winds Yacht, The Indian Ocean

WITHOUT ANY KIND OF SALUTATION, Lynx started, "I think we have a problem."

Blaze and Gator dragged their chairs closer, so they could see the computer monitor. They were sitting in the dining area of their yacht. Nothing even close to the size and splendor of the Russian yacht, but it was manageable for their team without any added staff, and it was their best choice for blending in and looking innocuous.

"I was dreaming about Antisthenes," Lynx said.

"As one does." Striker turned to her on the screen with a "this is gonna be good" grin.

She lifted her chin looking at someone coming into the room. "I have the team together."

"Good." That was Deep's voice.

Lynx pulled the ponytail elastic from her hair, shook her

head, then gathered her hair into a handful. "The dream was about a Spyder lesson," she said with the elastic between her teeth. She wrapped her hair into a messy bun on the top of her head, wrapped it in the elastic, then looked straight into the camera. "The quote is 'Pay attention to your enemies, for they are the first to discover your mistakes.'"

"Oh, shit," all three of the Strike Force members said in unison.

The energy in the room shifted dramatically.

Ash had never worked with this woman, Lynx. She had a reputation though. She pulled magical rabbits out of hats. She made connections that were invisible to mortal eyes, and once they were pointed out, they were obvious as the nose on a face.

Her title was bizarrely "Iniquus Puzzler", and with the tickle of danger at the base of his skull, Ash thought he was about to see first-hand why this woman was held in such high esteem from Command all the way down the Iniquus ranks.

"Okay, let me walk you through what I saw. What Deep and I did. And some speculation that I don't know what to do with from a tactical perspective. But I think you all need to put your oars in the water, so to speak."

Striker pulled a pad and paper closer. "Ready."

"I dreamed that I was a doctor in the hospital. It was imperative that I diagnose the patient. I couldn't see the patient, but I knew he was a man. I thought that he was probably Misha. So, as I lay trying to remember any details—" Lynx focused on Ash. "My mentor Spyder McGraw trained me to ask a question before I go to sleep.

This allows the subconscious mind to sift through all of the data that we took in but maybe didn't know to pay attention to. My team is used to this tool that I use. I want you to know, so you have context."

"Thank you," Ash said. He'd admit that when she led with she'd had a dream, he had taken this conversation lightly until the team's dynamic shifted so abruptly. And now that she said that she used her dream time to access information—like many of the Inuit peoples that he knew growing up—yeah, that tickle at the back of his neck radiated shivers down his spine.

Did this have to do with McKayla? Did it put her in any kind of danger?

"Since my dream took place in a hospital, I asked Dr. Jeffers to come down and take a look at the file information we have on Misha's health. Data that McKayla had been gathering over her year under cover. Also, we had the audio and video from her visit with Misha for Dr. Jeffers to assess."

"He did that already?" Striker asked.

"He did." She turned to accept a mug of coffee, then Deep sat down beside her, and they were both on the screen. "Deep, can you run just the first little bit of the hospital? The part where Misha is telling McKayla what's wrong with him?"

Deep slid to the side, and they could hear his fingers on a keyboard. Then a split screen of Misha saying, "All the stress of the explosion made me go into an SVT—my heart was beating way too fast. They had to rush me into surgery."

"Stop please," Lynx said. "Ash, what was that? What are you seeing?"

"I'm watching Hoover's posture."

"Good." Lynx smiled. "I always trust my dogs. Explain what Hoover's telling you."

"Yes, ma'am. Hoover was trained to be able to go with me into a setting where I needed to conduct business amongst people that were…to use a condensed way of putting it, evil. Let's say that I had to go to a tribal council with war lords, and we all had to be chill and hospitable to get through negotiations. Neither Hoover nor I could be reactive. Hoover's personality and training are such that— when we're lent out as a force multiplier, either for an Iniquus operations team or a contracted entity—his behavior conforms to my command. Hoover's command at the time this video was captured was to act as a stability assistance K9. Now, the thing you should know is that Hoover gets that he's playing a role and his outward behavior is for show."

"Undercover doggo." Lynx smiled.

"Exactly, he always knows that his real job is to protect and defend. Hoover and I communicate with each other. I signal him with voice and hand commands. He signals me with his posture and focus. I always know who the bad guy is. Or, in a room of bad guys, I know the one who has the power to make things go kinetic. That's not always the highest rank. With that explanation out of the way. What I see Hoover signaling is that there are two bad guys in this room. Misha and the security guy who just entered, John." Ash pointed at the guy in the corner of the frame.

Striker said, "He's second in command of McKayla's security team."

"Hoover says he's not just bad but dangerous. Hoover's watching for a weapon."

"Would Hoover jump at a weapon?" Deep asked.

"It depends on his command," Ash explained. "The day I got assigned to this mission, I was out with a family. The command was for him to guard his sheep. Two assailants showed up, and Hoover grabbed the gun arm and crushed the man's bones. He didn't need a special signal. The command was to guard his sheep and that meant he should follow his instincts. Bad guy plus weapon equals takedown."

"And if he's playing the role of stability dog?" Jack asked.

"He'll do his best to stay in character. He might pop a lip up to expose his teeth. He might rumble a bit in his chest. He would protect under three trained sets of circumstances. One, he responds to a command. Two, his person is down and unconscious. He will stand over the person and protect them."

"Seems like a problem," Deep said.

Ash canted his head. "How so?"

"What if they needed help? Mouth to mouth, an ambulance ride?"

"Hoover knows who the bad guy is. He'd let a good Samaritan in."

"You've tested that theory?"

"I know my dog, and I trust him. Period."

"Okay, another question." Jack set his mug down as he leaned forward. "He's trained to protect. Let's say he was in that same role where he pulverized the gunman's arm. What if it was a good guy who held the gun? For example, a police officer thought your client was a criminal and pulled their gun on them. Would Hoover attack?"

"Let me give you a similar scenario," Lynx said. "Hoover thinks John is a bad guy."

"He knows he is," Ash corrected.

"Fine. Let's say someone grabbed McKayla and a good guy pulled out a gun. 'Let her go, or I'll shoot.' Would Hoover break the arm of the good guy because he was holding a gun and pointing it in McKayla's direction?" Lynx asked. "Perhaps he just knew that John is a trained fighter and has the skills to be lethal?"

Ash shook his head. "No, ma'am. Hoover is around latently lethal men all day, every day. He's in the field while we practice with our weapons. He can tell the difference between someone who will bring force to protect and those who will bring force to harm."

"That's the number three?" Lynx asked.

"Right, Hoover won't let a weapon be deployed against his protectees. Knife in the hand, fine. Knife swinging toward his protectees, attack. Gun in the hand with finger on the trigger guard, *might be* fine. If the finger moves to the trigger, one hundred percent that gets stopped."

"You said two bad guys so the other one is Misha?" Lynx asked. "That's an interesting interpretation. In the whole time that McKayla has been working undercover, according to the files I've read, she's found him to be just a normal guy. Well, as normal as you can be under the circumstances of his wealth, and his family of origin."

"Let me be clear about what I'm seeing. Of the two

men, John was the aggressive bad guy. The immediate threat. Hoover is always determined to get between the greatest threat and the person he's protecting." Ash pointed at the screen again. "Even with his harness on, Hoover forces McKayla to transfer her hand on the stability bar in order to get between John and McKayla. Hoover says John is the real threat."

"Son of a gun. Look at that," Lynx said. "McKayla had to change from a left-handed grip to a right-handed grip." She slicked her hand up her arm. "Ha! Hoover gave me goose bumps."

"Lynx, what were you saying about your dream and Dr. Jeffers?" Striker asked.

"I showed this video to Dr. Jeffers." Lynx focuses on Ash. "If you haven't come across Jeffers, he's one of the in-house Iniquus doctors." She twisted back toward Striker. "He watched the footage all the way through, not only observing Misha but also keeping an eye on the monitors. Kudos to McKayla for keeping them in focus almost the entire time. From White's notes, we know that Misha's medication was indeed an antiarrhythmic drug. That medication can indeed leave a guy with an inability to get an erection and give him headaches as he said. His doctor may well have told him that there was the possibility of something very bad going on if he were to have sex and might have said no to the little blue pills. None of that is in dispute."

Lynx picked up a fob and scrolled forward stopping at a frame, then zooming in until they were looking at the top of Misha's hospital gown.

"This was the piece that had caught my eye when I

first saw it. To me it looks odd. Having worked as a volunteer with EMS and having been in the hospital my fair share of the time, I'm saying that it looks odd from my personal experience. It's as if he draped that gown just so when he pulled the neckline down. Like he wanted McKayla to be able to see the bandage just peeking out of there. While this might have served his purposes with McKayla, it served my purpose, too. And that's to say that he lied to McKayla. My words, not Dr. Jeffers' words. Dr. Jeffers is careful never to use a definitive. Everything is 'in my experience' or 'I've never heard of such an event' it's the doctor speak that keeps them from getting sued for malpractice."

"What did Jeffers see?" Ash asked.

"Misha said his heart rate was too fast, so he needed to have surgery," Lynx started.

"He looks pretty healthy for someone who just had open heart surgery," Gator said.

"Dr. Jeffers said there really aren't a lot of emergency reasons to have open heart surgery because if he's followed by a doctor any interventions would be a known, and they'd be planned in advance. Jeffers said surgery for fast heartbeat isn't a thing. He also says that four by four dressing for a heart surgery isn't a thing."

"There is blood on it, though," Blaze pointed out.

"I went back to look at the video of McKayla pulling Misha into the club. There was blood on his shirt in that same area. I would speculate that debris cut him and that was sewn up. Jeffers said that the numbers on his monitors are normal. And that at Misha's age, which is young medically speaking, they should have just sent him home."

"So, he's lying about the surgery?" Striker asked.

"Not by definition. Operation is the term used in British English to say surgery. Surgery in American English includes repair. So if the doctor sewed a wound, he did have surgery. My guess?" Lynx said. "He's milking the explosion. It's his ticket to stay home from the Seychelles and the emotional screw to get his significant other to do him a favor."

"But he could have gotten on that plane," Striker said.

"From what Dr. Jeffers could see, Misha was probably fine to fly."

"He was fine, but they kept him in the hospital?" Gator asked. "Seems like a stretch."

"I asked Dr. Jeffers about that as well. He said that if Misha had talked to his doctor and told his doctor he didn't want to leave for a certain amount of time that the doctor could have made it clear that he wanted to keep his patient hospitalized for monitoring, or what have you. Do you want to hear a very interesting timing item?" Lynx asked.

Striker leaned in. "What's that?"

"Deep used a tracker that McKayla has on each of Misha's cars to follow Misha leaving the hospital twenty minutes after McKayla's plane took off." Lynx popped her brows. "And he didn't go back to his house. He went to a restaurant for lunch, then he went to the phone shop. Misha thinks that he lost his phone during the explosion, but McKayla scooped it up and has it at her penthouse."

"Could one of his staff have been using the car?" Jack asked.

Deep leaned into the picture. "I've got a London

contact who was able to get me CCTV verification. It was Misha, all right."

"To what end?" Striker asked. "Why take the phone?"

Lynx said, "McKayla told me that Misha never lets that phone out of his sight, and she's never been able to get into it to look around. She thought there might be some asset pressure points in the call and text histories. So, she took the opportunity."

"She knows the code?" Gator asked. "Bet White is thrilled."

"Wait. Can bad guy John get into her penthouse and grab the phone back?" Deep asked.

"We changed all the security codes. No one is getting into that penthouse." Striker stroked his thumb along his chin. "So, I want to lead you back to where this all started, Lynx. You had a dream about Antisthenes. The quote was 'Pay attention to your enemies, for they are the first to discover your mistakes.' And my question for you, Lynx, is twofold. From your consultation with Dr. Jeffers, and the information that Ash picked up from Hoover's behavior, now we know of two bad guys, Misha and John. Question one, which one of these enemies is in play? Question two, what mistakes were made?"

32

McKAYLA PICKARD
победоносный, Indian Ocean

"This is the puppy!" Uncle Niko met her as she boarded.

"Hoover, isn't he lovely?" She leaned to the left to give Uncle Niko the usual three kisses.

"Ah-ah-ah. You know of the superstition, never greet on a threshold or in the doorway. I suppose this is true when boarding a yacht. Come further in, let me see you." His eyes went immediately to her belly.

McKayla hadn't weighed her clothing into the equation. She might have just discovered her positive pee test yesterday. No idea, none, how to handle this, except to distract. "Far enough on now for a greeting?"

"Yes, my dear." He looked her over. "Scabs. So many. It must have been a terrible ordeal for you."

After the left right left kissing head bob, McKayla stepped back and sighed. "This is just what my doctor asked me to do. After the explosion and the physical exertion and stress, I was told to relax near a beautiful vista."

"This I can accommodate." He offered her a courtly bow.

McKayla glanced around the milling guests. "Have Rajja and Nadir already arrived?"

"No. No, my dear. You are the last to board, all of the other guests are here. But four very sadly cannot join us. Had I known, I would have had sleeping space to invite others. This is a waste of cabins on our lovely voyage. But even so, I can't call anyone last minute, as the three might still join us along our route."

"Did they say why?" Mc Kayla pushed her windblown hair back. "I mean, I was talking to them last night at the botanical soiree. They told me they planned to come. Of course, Karl seemed to be in pain. Perhaps he didn't feel up to today's choppy seas."

"I wasn't told why they were held up. But they think they might make it later. They'll just get our coordinates from my captain and have a speed boat bring them out if they can join us before we're too far out or we have turned back."

"They have our itinerary, the plans for the trip?" she asked as she grabbed her hair in a fist and just held it there. McKayla needed to get to her cabin and put it in an updo.

"Yes, I had my captain give them the information." Uncle Niko's weathered face forced a smile. He lifted her hand and patted the back. "Don't you worry your pretty head. First, I'm sure they will try very hard to get here and be with us."

"You said four, though? Do I know the fourth?" Her

ears still weren't a hundred percent. McKayla had to strain as the wind whipped away Uncle Niko's words.

"Ivan Krokov, of course. His absence is a great tragedy."

"I'm sorry." McKayla blinked behind her sunglasses. "Did you say Ivan was supposed to come?"

"Yes. Shipping. We are here talking about shipping."

"It's just that…well, you know I was there with Misha and Ivan the day he died. I was told that he was going to Russia this week."

"Russia, no. He was coming here."

McKayla worked hard to keep her brow from knotting. This was just a no-consequences conversation. *Don't shut him down.* "Was Rachel invited?"

"Of course."

Maybe Ivan said he was going to Russia so Rachel wouldn't want to tag along. Who wouldn't want a trip to the Seychelles. She had been talking about escaping to Paris and getting out of London. "Did Misha know that Ivan was coming here?"

"Yes, of course." He swung his arm wide to encompass his guests that were milling around the seating area at the bow. A quick headcount told McKayla there were twelve including her and Uncle Niko. "Everyone here has something to do with shipping. They run the major shipping in the Black Sea. All of the biggest names in the industry from the countries that abut the Black Sea. The biggest names." He slapped his hands together and smiled. "We will be making plans. Not all ships are barred from exporting. Russia yes, others? No. It is good that we treat each other well. One never knows when the tides will turn." He laughed like he'd told the best joke.

"Not Karl and the others, though. They don't ship."

"No, but they…" He patted her hand like he might a cat.

Stroking and patting her.

Sometimes Misha would do that, too.

McKayla didn't like it.

"You know that Karl Davidson has much to do with oil and helium. Much to do with many things. And of course, Rajja and his family, oil. And Nadir, Nadir is not in oil but the three together have influence that is important to shipping or not shipping. They have been political gatekeepers, if you will."

"Oh?"

"Now, those three young men were not to be the most important people who are on this yacht. Do you know who is here?" Uncle Niko dragged McKayla along, and she kept a tight grip on her stability harness. "Here. Here, let me introduce you to some women so you have someone to speak with."

Women, of course. What man from the world of shipping would want to speak with a woman? McKayla let that slide on by. She would try to speak with everyone.

"This here is Elzara. She is a fashion designer," Uncle Niko said, as they stood in front of a middle-aged woman with her hair in a severe knot at the base of her head and a daunting amount of smokey eye makeup. "You can speak with her about pretty dresses together. Yes?"

Elzara patted the cushion beside hers. After McKayla

and Hoover were settled, she reached over and felt the fabric in McKayla's skirt. "This is quite lovely," she said.

"Comfy," McKayla agreed.

"Who is designer?"

"Why you are." McKayla smiled. "I love your collection. I like my fabric to be like butter. I can breathe in it."

"You don't like Giovani's corsets and leather this season?" Elzara asked.

"Bit confining for me. Now if I dated a bore, then it would hold me upright and pinch me awake. Luckily, I have a lovely, interesting man at home." McKayla smiled at Uncle Niko.

He nodded as if satisfied and pivoted toward the bar.

McKayla squeezed the designer's arm. "I'll catch up with you in just a bit. I need to find my stateroom and get my hair out of my face. Once we're under way, I'm going to bug one of the crew to take me on a tour." When McKayla shifted her hips, Hoover stood to support her.

McKayla's inner announcer chimed in. *McKayla Pickard is supported by the K9 of her dreams. The hunky love of her life, and an ex-SEAL team of friends are just over the horizon. But her ears are still ringing from the explosion, and she has been humming since she left the hospital. These assaults on her system throw her off kilter. She feels adrift.*

33

JOHNNA WHITE
Strike Force War Room, Washington, D.C.

"HOW'S SHE DOING?" White asked as she moved through the Strike Force War Room and over to the computer where Lynx and Deep were working. "What's McKayla doing now?"

"She's asleep," Deep said. "It's zero two thirty-eight hours in the Seychelles."

"The last guests went to bed an hour ago," Lynx added.

White looked at Lynx's mug. "Anything like tea available?"

"Do you need something to eat?" Deep asked.

"No. No. I just grabbed takeout on my way over."

"At the coffee station, help yourself," Deep said.

White wandered over and picked out a mug and a bag of mint tea. "Is McKayla still wearing her contacts?" She leaned over the water station with the hot and cold spigots and filled the mug. The scent of mint hit her nose with the rising steam and revived her.

"Her team instructed McKayla that they are thirty-day wear and not to take them out."

"Good. Good." She pulled a chair with her as she rounded behind Lynx and Deep. "Let me see?"

Lynx flipped the screen to show a black room with the light glow to the right. Lynx pointed. "That's her cabin. The light is her bathroom. We got to watch Hoover use the head. Pretty impressive. You're looking at the last frame we have from her. Right now, we have this." The screen was completely blank.

"She's sleeping," Deep said. "Her vital statistics from her watch agree."

"I never sleep better than on a boat floating on calm waters, the sound, the rocking. Just lovely." White scratched her neck. "And the information she's sent back?"

"Gold," Lynx said.

"We have a face, at least the first name or nickname." Deep tapped the computer and pointed toward a picture wallpaper of faces and name labels. "We have a voice sample from everyone on board, including the crew."

"She's taken us on a tour of every inch of that boat." Lynx grinned. "I've never heard anyone coo over an engine like that."

"Have they said anything interesting yet?" White inhaled the scent of steamy mint then blew across the surface to cool it for a sip.

"The conversations are in Russian. I have a printout," Deep said. "They've been translated by AI. They need to be processed by our language experts before we can trust what's being said."

"Neither Deep nor I have the Russian language under our belts," Lynx said, looking over to the side of the room where her Dobermans were gnawing on bones, comfy on their dog beds.

"When McKayla went to her room, she tried to give us an English rundown of everything she saw and heard. I can print that off for you if you'd like. They're at anchor tonight. Here." Deep turned and pointed to a map screen on the wall to his left. "They're in red. Strike Force is purple twenty-four nautical miles out, which is the limit of their onboard radar. There are fishing vessels dotting this area. I can bring them up if you'd like."

"I don't need them right now, thanks." White pointed a chin at one of the computers in the row. "What's that one doing?"

Deep grinned like a proud papa. "It's making a 3D image of the boat. Once it's done, we can take it apart and look at each section separately and place people along a timeline. There are five levels. The lowest one is for staff, laundry, storage, engine room. The main deck has a galley and dining room, security guard's stateroom, bar, lounge, library. There's a diving platform, the place to get on their ocean toys, SCUBA equipment, things like that. The upper deck has outdoor dining, another bar, outdoor lounge, hot tub, pool, gym. That's the basics. The top looks like it's for sunbathing."

White pulled her brows together and thrust her face forward as the pixels were added line by line like a 3D printer. "This is from the images that McKayla sent in from the contacts?"

"Exactly. Want to know something even cooler?" Deep asked.

White turned with a smile. "Yes."

"With the 3D goggles we're sending out with our teams now, Strike Force can virtually navigate the interior as if they were there."

"Wait. Let me get this straight." White leaned back to focus on Deep. "Instead of building plywood mockups of buildings to use to walk through, teams can train the space virtually?"

"Both means of pacing a target have their pros and cons," Deep said. "One of the pros of having virtual reality goggles when we have specific information about a target area is that our operators can practice with moving around the furnishings and the decorations that are in each space."

White pinched her lip as she absorbed the information. "Name a con."

"You can't practice stairs, breaching doors, things like that. But in the virtual world, when a team bursts through a door there are elements that can be a hazard. With the virtual images, they know where all the shiny surfaces are. All the stools they'd need to leap over."

"That is totally cool." She rolled the mug between her palms, absorbing the warmth into her hands. She'd finished up a game of tennis with a power-hitter before grabbing a bite to eat and coming to Iniquus for a check in, the radiant heat felt *so* good. "I love your toys here at Iniquus."

"It helps us do our job with surgical precision." Deep turned his attention to Lynx.

She had her eyes glued to the image emerging on the 3D screen. "What is that thing?"

Deep froze the screen and zoomed in on an image. He squinted at it then shook his head. "I have no clue. I'm putting it through the system." His fingers moved over his keyboard.

White and Lynx waited silently.

"Nada." He shook his head.

White stood and leaned toward the screen, sloshing her tea and shaking the hot liquid off her hand. With the last layers being laid on the screen, her heart pounded against her ribs. "Oh, wow."

"That doesn't sound good." Deep shot a glance toward Lynx.

"Do you remember last year there was a couple caught for espionage," White asked.

"They put top secret naval information into a half-eaten peanut butter sandwich?" Lynx asked.

"That's the part that was allowed to be public. Prior to that, we speculated that they had stolen and distributed the plans for this very weapon. Looks like it anyway."

"Who got hold of those plans?" Deep asked.

"We don't know. Private individual instead of government as far as we could assess. And if I'm right—" White plopped into her seat. "I need you to forward that on to my office immediately and let my superior, John Black, take a look to see if he can corroborate."

Deep tapped at the computer.

White sent a heads-up message via text.

"Are you going to tell us?" Lynx asked.

"Let's give it a minute. Need to know. And if this isn't what I think it is, then there's no need for you to know."

It didn't take a minute. White got a text back: **Microwave anti-drone weaponry. How do you have this picture?**

She held up the text for them to read.

"Oh." Lynx exhaled.

Deep pulled his brow together. "Do you think they're afraid that someone has a drone overhead?"

"Could well be," Lynx said. "They're out on the water, one has to assume to get away from any kind of electronic connections during their shipping conversations. In the transcripts we read that Niko went over the rules—no sat phones allowed. No cell phones out—no photos, recordings, or video."

"It could be that Niko has this technology on board because so many Russian vessels have been hit by those drones at the mouth of the Bosphorus Strait through Turkey. He didn't pass through there. He moved his yacht out of the area just before the Russians began their incursion."

"If someone put a drone overhead," Deep said, "they might just need to microwave it?"

"That'll show 'em," Lynx said. "White, did the CIA put a drone in the sky?"

"No, but I had one available if McKayla had issues with her contact lens information getting through to a satellite because of cloud coverage," White said. "Seeing this? We'd need to check specks and see if we could get it above the microwave range. Luckily, right now, all systems are go, no need to even consider drone overwatch."

Deep froze, cocking his head toward the computer dedicated to watching McKayla.

"What?" Lynx asked.

"Did you hear that clunk?"

"No," Lynx mouthed so as not to be making noise.

Deep played with the computer. The audio showed a disturbance.

"I can't hear anything, Deep," Lynx whispered.

"No way to wake McKayla up?" White asked.

"No. None," Deep said, his focus on that audio readout.

"We need to fix that, like make the watches buzz in morse code," White said.

"We'd have to make sure someone who wore it knew—"

There was a low rumble coming from the computer.

"What is that?" White held her chin in concentration.

"That," Lynx said, "is Hoover warning a predator away."

34

McKayla Pickard

победоносный, Indian Ocean

McKayla flashed awake.

Hoover stood over the top of her chest, rumbling a warning.

She flipped on the light. "Whoever is watching me, something's up," she said to the air.

When McKayla said, "Check. Check," in the parking lot prior to boarding, Headquarters had said they had a good reception. There was no way to verify that the connection held since the time she'd gotten on the yacht, and they motored out of cellphone range. McKayla could very well be talking to the wind.

"This grizzly bear here is in go-mode." She'd heard this same rumble and seen the same posture at the gym back in London before Hoover was viciously ripping the weapon from Striker's hand.

And that meant something bad was about to happen.

No sirens were sounding. It wasn't a fire.

Strike Force was just over the horizon, she reminded herself.

McKayla could leap into the water with Hoover and a floaty, and swim to her seven o'clock. Or better yet, she'd seen the water scooters on the bottom deck. She could leap on one of those with Hoover over her lap and take off.

Interesting that her whole system was focused on getting off this vessel.

Before she went jumping ship, better that she figured out what caught Hoover's attention.

Last night, as the sliver of new moon rose, they'd anchored.

The security guard was left standing first watch.

McKayla checked her super-duper spy watch. That was three hours ago. They had switched to next-on-duty already.

McKayla didn't know this crew. Hadn't built up trust in their integrity.

Yana—the young woman who helped in the kitchen and made sure that the guests had snacks on demand—had given McKayla a very thorough tour of the yacht earlier. On the tour, McKayla said she was nervous about being on the boat as a cover for the exhaustive list of questions she was asking.

Yana had explained that the crew each took two hours of the night watch. The security guard had the first one, while folks were still awake. Then they switched out every two hours. Yana had the last watch from four to six. She liked that best; she didn't have her night interrupted in the middle. After Yana served breakfast and cleaned up, Yana said she got those two hours of sleep back as a break time. She would drink her coffee and read.

"Nice," McKayla had said. "That sounds lovely. So, the kitchen crew is watching the radar?"

"This isn't a military vessel." She'd looked perplexed. "We watch that the anchor isn't dragging, check the horizon for encroaching boats. We don't want to be hit. We would see their lights in the binoculars."

McKayla had been given that duty on a boat before.

At that time, she was told that even though it was required that someone, wearing a life vest, paced around, keeping an eye on things, in actuality, most people simply set a watch alarm and checked every hour if they weren't in a traffic lane. Things, after all, didn't happen fast out on the water after dark.

McKayla had found, on the night of her watch, that the rocking of the boat, a blanket of stars and a balmy night, it was easy to fall asleep standing up, leaning on the rail.

A scream went up.

"Do you hear the scream?" McKayla asked the air. She had to get ready. Preparation was key. What needed to happen?

First, she had to pee before she peed down her leg, nerves.

She sat on the toilet while she drank a glass of water. She'd learned that risk back in the desert. Lack of air will kill you first. Lack of fresh water in your system will kill you next.

While she pulled on her gym clothes and tennis shoes, she ordered Hoover to use the toilet. It was just to give him something to do other than growl. But he complied like a rock star.

Since McKayla didn't know what she was preparing for, she thought that layers were a good bet.

She drew on a sweatshirt and a waterproof jacket.

Dragged her hair into a ponytail.

It all happened in a flash.

McKayla had been part of so many missions where she got the call to go, and she was required to be prepped and ready, standing by the vehicle in two minutes tops. Through training, her brain processed and moved.

As Hoover jumped down from the toilet. McKayla put his food in the bowl. He sucked up the contents as she strapped his stability vest into place.

Bang, the door flew open. Two men with baseball caps and bandanas tied around their nose and mouth were in her doorway. Both with rifles. Fingers laid along the trigger guards. One crouching below the other, stacked.

These men looked like pirates in their ragged, sweat stained clothing.

Professionally trained, they might well be here to take hostages and seize the boat like a pirate would, but no way were they typical pirates.

Everything about them screamed militarily trained.

Adrenaline did what wicked adrenaline did, slowed time, hyper-focused her senses, crashed her heart into her sternum.

But with experience, adrenaline could be harnessed, used.

Unlike the other passengers on this ship, McKayla had years of experience reining in her survival instinct. She just couldn't let these men know that she was any different than the dress designer or the kitchen staffer.

"Hoover, stability." McKayla reminded Hoover of his role.

Ash had told her that Hoover had the best spy craft he'd ever seen in man or beast.

McKayla hoped that was true, or Hoover would be shot. Of that, McKayla was a hundred percent certain.

In Russian, the guy said, "You come, dog stay here."

McKayla gripped the handle tight. She couldn't allow that to happen for oh so many reasons.

She let her body shiver from the adrenaline. Let the hormone warble her voice as she touched her ear. She wasn't sure if she should play the language card or not, so in simple Russian she said. "Ear damage. I use the dog to walk and to help me when I can't hear."

The dog helped when she couldn't hear? Did that make sense?

Probably not. Oh well.

The guy at the top of the stack twisted his head left and right as he assessed Hoover's harness.

Hoover wagged his tail, and McKayla would swear he was trying to smile at the guy, *yup just some dumb pooch, man, no worries.*

McKayla burst out laughing. She slapped her free hand over her mouth and looked at the riflemen and said, "Nerves."

Somehow, that seemed to win her some points.

Top guy waved them out and pointed toward the stern.

There was another rifle guy in the corridor who directed her in front of him with a jerk of his head.

Hoover kept waving his tail in the air like they were headed to the dog park. And had McKayla not seen for herself what a vicious and courageous attack dog he was, she'd never believe he was a weapon that could help save her.

She arrived in the open seating area where the lights were bright. The other passengers cowered under the glowering faces of two more assailants.

That made five that she'd seen.

Both guests and crew sat with their hands on their heads, dressed in various levels of attire.

Overheating, McKayla pulled off her jacket and sweat-shirt, using the move to cast her contacts around in the hopes that Iniquus could gather some data. Like, now there was a high-dollar, high-speed electric boat tied to the diving deck. And on the seats were night vision goggles.

They'd come in from behind, silently with no lights.

Unless you were watching radar, it would be missed.

Iniquus would have their computers monitoring the radar, but that would only be within the circumference of Strike Forces capabilities.

Were they close enough to see?

Yeah, that was some high-dollar equipment for a group of poverty-stricken pirates.

That was a non-starter. This was a planned assault by someone with mega bucks.

Did White understand what was going on?

Did McKayla's comms work?

Did her team know their vessel was under assault?

Make-believe pirates—okay *that* wasn't on McKayla's BINGO card.

35

ASHER GIDEON

Fair Winds Yacht, The Indian Ocean

"AS A BROAD BRUSH, this is what we know of the area," White said as the video feed showed her standing in front of a map of the East Coast of Africa. "The waters off of northern Mozambique," she used her laser to indicate an area, "is a hotspot for insurrectionists. The government of Mozambique hasn't made inroads in suppressing the situation. This area here," she made another circle, "is the Mozambique Channel. The channel is eighteen hundred kilometers in length. Thirty percent of global tanker traffic moves through this area. Very important to shipping. Especially important to gas reserves."

Striker posted his hands on his hips. "Is Langley suggesting that the yacht has been taken over by insurgents?"

"The clothing, the accent of their Portuguese, and the

Russian they speak, leads us to believe that the men are from Mozambique. Their tactics and their supplies lead us to speculate that they were trained professionally elsewhere and that they are seasoned in the battle zone. We have information about a group of men from Mozambique who fought with Isis in Syria. There are no photos available of those men. Their clothing suggests that this is a group of mercenaries trying to make everyone believe they are pirates from the coast. Now, is this a shipping question? A gas question?"

"It doesn't matter to us, we don't need to know their motive, we just need to get in there and take control of that vessel tonight," Striker said. "Otherwise, based on their speed and direction of travel, tomorrow, they will reach Mozambique."

"Any thoughts on that electrical boat, White?" Jack asked. "Seems if they were only interested in taking the occupants hostage, they could pile them into the boat and shoot for shore. That particular model runs at a hundred miles an hour. Is there something interesting about that yacht we need to know?"

White exhaled as she brought her fist to her forehead and rubbed her thumb between her eyes. "As far as the insurgents in Mozambique go? I'm not sure. It could be that they need to pass Madagascar, and Russian satellite images might be monitoring them since the Kremlin's beloved Chupov Nikodim Tarasovich—or as we affectionately know him, Uncle Niko—is on board. They might want this to seem like a change in plans, a pleasant trip until they are past those naval ships."

"Speaking of naval ships, the United States has assets

in the area," Striker said. "We can request a SEAL team. The military can bring them in via helicopter."

"Not going to happen." White's face showed no emotion. "We need to know what's happening and why it's happening. If the US military shows up it becomes part of the news cycle. This all goes deep underground. Right now, when you all save the hostages, then it's just McKayla's A-Team security on the ball. None of the layers are the wiser. We can continue to gather intelligence and try to thwart whatever is happening. Which, I will remind you, is what Iniquus was hired to facilitate. Your close protection stint is your cover."

"We're pulling off everyone who doesn't have a gun?" Striker asked.

"No." White moved over to a chair and sat in front of the camera. "We're only interested in freeing McKayla. No one else is paying the bills. We can make sure that the captain and crew are in good enough shape to get the ship to a safe marina. McKayla comes off."

"Why leave them?" Jack asked.

White paused as she gathered her thoughts, lifting her mug, and sipping her tea. "A few reasons, first of all," she put her mug down, "we don't have the authority to insist that those people come away with us. I don't want to be responsible for them if we did pull them off and something went FUBAR. Even if it was a perfect extraction, the U.S. would end up on the front page of any papers over anything that might go wrong. Yeah," White waived her hands through the air, "I see your faces, no man left behind, Iniquus's golden reputation. I'm not saying leave people to be maimed or die. Give them a route home without your being involved. And that's the important part, the going home piece is important. I want to see what happens next. We'll be watching the players. We are here to understand what's going on. Period."

"Does McKayla look culpable if she's the only one that's saved?" Ash asked.

"When McKayla is asked, she says her team rescued her. Who is her team—per her contract, she's not allowed to identify them. End of story."

"That's a lot to pull off with four guys," Lynx said.

Striker said, "Tidal Force is in Madagascar."

White quirked a brow. "My understanding is that—and correct me if this information is wrong—Tidal Force is training with Madagascar's military, working on warming up relationships between our two countries. The location of their northern port was of vital importance in WWII, and the U.S. sees that as there are shifts in geopolitics. China, and recently Russia—because of sanctions—are looking to increase their influence. Uncle Sam doesn't want to cede the fourth largest island in the world over to our adversaries. They have a spectrum of equipment to show what they can do to intercept boats and take control."

"I know that they're operating in the north, ma'am," Striker said. "And that they do have helicopter and assault craft."

"Do we know the effects of the microwave weaponry on helicopters?" Lynx asked. "If it can take down a drone, can it take down a heli?"

"No idea, I'd assume we'd have to keep a helicopter out of radar range. I can check that with Langley. I have no familiarity with the weapon other than what it looked like as a prototype."

"The radar on the Russian yacht can sweep seventy-four nautical miles," Deep said. "That's not gonna work."

"Tidal Force has Spiro with them, he's a retired Night Stalker who's flying their heli on this evolution," Striker said. "We put it in the sweet spot in the in-between. Above marine radar below air radar. We come in the last seventy-two miles like that. We jump out in SCUBA gear. Spiro flies back out of radar range to hover and drop the tactical boat—our electrical boat can run at a hundred miles an hour just like theirs can. Tidal Force can be positioned forty-five minutes away."

"That's a long damn time if things get hairy," Blaze said.

"We each bring an extra mask and rebreather for McKayla. I'll bring a sled for Hoover. You all go deep," Ash said. "I'll go long, using one of the water scooters."

"And Tidal Force can swoop in and scoop us up," Gator said. "They drop us in Madagascar, and we regroup."

"I'm reaching out to Command with the basic information," Deep said. "See if we can get a thumbs up to continue the plan."

"What's the weather look like tonight?" White asked.

"New moon," Lynx said.

"Helpful."

"Otherwise, clear," Lynx said. "The winds will be strong. Water's going to be choppy."

Jack had a map out. "Our helicopter only has about a thousand miles of range. It'll need a good amount of hover time. Last thing we want is to be bobbing around on a boat with an electric motor that's out of juice, waiting for the pirates to pick up a very high-value package with ten or so ex-special forces operators and a billionaire."

"McKayla would hand over her wealth," Ash said.

Blaze quirked his brow. "But they'd keep hold of us. America would have to pay through the nose to keep our men from being handed over to some terrorist group that would get all kinds of cred and therefore recruitment if they did neck chop videos to put up on the Darknet."

Striker was drumming his fingers on the table. A sure sign that he wanted the chitchat to end. He wanted the team to be planning and practicing. Time was of the essence. The op was tonight. "We need Tidal Force to bring us a package of guns with silencers and bullets when they come to pick us up."

"Here's the deal," White said. "You're on International waters. But we can't have any friendly fire casualties. Also, the CIA would like the pirates alive."

"Hostage lives and safety come first." Striker was unequivocal. "I don't see how we capture a band of pirates for you to take to your black site. But we'll do our best to keep at least one alive."

White swiveled in her chair and looked at the screen with the pirates' images. With her laser, she circled the one they thought was the head guy. "I want him if possible."

"Is that all?" Striker asked.

The computer pinged. "Command says to proceed in the planning stage," Deep said. "Tidal Force is on standby in Madagascar. They're preparing for a marine assault with helicopter and combat boat. They have their full team of seven to back us up."

"Copy," Striker said. "Deep, I need you to send me the 3D model, so we can take a better look."

"Wilco," Deep said. "Incoming."

The computer on the Fair Winds pinged. Striker pulled up the file and looked it over. "Good. Okay, we're going to get to work here. We'll fill you in. While our attention is in the planning stage, Deep, I need you and Lynx to be with McKayla's comms. Look for anything—visual or audio— that might change our course of action. Out."

The computer went black.

"Ash." Striker turned to him. "While we start our initial plans, I want you to go back and review the tapes of Hoover's behavior on deck. What is he telling you? Most importantly, look at the bad guys I need to know who is in charge. And who *wants* to be in charge. Assess the folks on board as McKayla turns her head, do any of them need medical interventions? How are they being treated by the tangos? Food and water? Bathroom breaks? Anyone secured? Anyone harmed?"

"On it."

The nine weeks that Ash had known McKayla over in Afghanistan, they were outside of the wire every single day. Gun fights, roadside explosions, he'd worried for his safety, for his brothers' safety, but most of all for McKayla's safety. Rape was an act of anger and there were so many men who were furious that a woman was in a place of authority over them.

Palpable grievance from the local men, afraid that McKayla's independence might give their wives the idea that they too could be sovereign over their own lives, palpable grievance by her fellow soldiers that they were horny and there was no relief other than a quick jerk-off to help calm their nerves enough to sleep.

In the presence of both friend and enemy, McKayla was never in a place where she could let her hair down.

And Ash had been constantly vigilant.

He'd seen mama polar bears in the backcountry, he'd seen their level of awareness and ferocity, and while it seemed stupid to call himself a mama bear, that was as close as he could come to the sensation that bloomed in Ash's chest when he thought that McKayla was endangered.

Every sense sharpened.

His muscles strained to be used.

He was like Hoover, willing to use teeth and claw, to rip and mangle, wild and ferocious.

And when those sensations rose like a tidal wave in his system, Ash knew to wait until his system got squared away.

Quickly, he culled out the uselessness of savagery. His training clicked into place.

Lethal focus.

Deadly precision.

The best way to keep McKayla safe was to do his damned job.

It was only July, but Ash had come full circle. He had started the year in Russian disputed territory getting people out of the city before the Kremlin's bombs rained down on them. Then, he'd headed for training in the islands, lending support after a hurricane swept the island. There, he'd squared off with would-be pirates.

And now? Russian war and pirates together.

Life was crazy. *This* was crazy. That anyone would hurt a hair on McKayla's head made him *crazy*.

One bright spot, no matter who had taken over that vessel, they thought they had time and space.

They thought the hard part was over.

They had no idea what was coming for them.

36

McKayla Pickard
победоносный, Indian Ocean

The sun, reflecting off the water, burned McKayla's eyes.

The hostages lay on the floor outside. The lounge furniture was somewhere else. The guards locked the doors and guarded them from the outside.

Fortunately, the passengers had a cover from the July sunshine that beat down on the boat and made the water shimmer.

The pirates allowed a woman to sit in the hot tub. Two in the pool. One on a lounge with a book. New women rotated into these positions on a timer. The only thing that McKayla could guess was that pirates were afraid of eyes in the sky and were doing the minimum to make it look like people were on board and all was peaceful.

If that were a true scenario the pirates were playing out, McKayla guessed they wanted the watching eyes to assume that the men were in meetings, perhaps in the dining room.

Yeah, it seemed a little bizarre, but so did this full set up with the fake pirates.

She wondered if the other passengers bought into the pirate charade. That the bad guys were keeping it up over time gave McKayla a little bit of hope.

They were performing for someone, she speculated. Maybe all of them. Wouldn't that be lucky?

But in the end, at least one person had to live to tell of the performance, or the assault team wouldn't be pulling this farce.

McKayla was glad they left her alone in the extra shade of the bar. Perhaps they didn't want Hoover up and moving. Maybe they felt pity for her disability. Maybe it was luck of the draw.

Time crawled slowly and uncomfortably on its belly under stretches of barbed wire.

Yup, all she had to do out here was to observe.

Mutter her observations under her breath.

And speculate.

McKayla decided to chance rebuke and reached into the bar's fridge and pulled out a bottle of water that she poured into a tumbler, placing it in front of Hoover.

He slurped it up and looked around to ask for more. And she poured the rest of the bottle out for him.

Hoover had been golden. Head on a swivel just like his dad. But biding his time.

Still, McKayla kept him positioned between her outstretched legs, a hand on the vest handle to remind him he was playing his undercover doggo spy role.

They had begun taking the hostages one at a time to the loo.

Uncle Niko came back out the door, hands on his head, rifle to his back.

"Here, Uncle Niko," she said.

After he made his ungainly way down to sit beside McKayla, they pointed the rifle at Yana.

She stood, put her hands on her head and went inside.

The guy on the outside locked the doors again.

"A back rest, this is a much better spot," Uncle Niko said. "And a lot less sun. Still the puppy is over warm."

McKayla scrubbed her fingers into the furry butt.

Hoover yawned and dropped his chin onto McKayla's knee, and McKayla took that as a sign that things were calm for the moment.

"Uncle," McKayla said under her breath, "you know I was in the Army. You know that I worked with the special forces. In order for me to try to think of a way out of here, I need to know what's going on."

"I have no idea."

"I believe you do." She kept her chin down, hair in her face, stroking Hoover to hide the fact that she was breaking the rules and talking. "Here are some of my observations. The boat they have is what, maybe three hundred thousand dollars?" She angled to see his reaction. "Twenty million rubles?"

Uncle Niko's face darkened.

"These aren't pirates. These are people playing the role of pirates. This is very well funded."

Uncle Niko swallowed audibly.

"All I can think is that Karl, Rajja, and Nadir didn't get

on the boat. And they didn't get on the boat after they got very upset last night when they found out that Ivan was killed in the explosion."

Uncle Niko started to suck in a lungful of air but seemed to get stuck halfway through and he hovered there, not breathing.

"You can trust me. Tell me what is happening, so I can plot a way for us to survive this."

"These young men," Uncle Niko shook his head, "and Ivan—Ivan was part of the plan."

McKayla didn't press. She'd learned in her work with the Army that one gets the most information when a story is unfolded by the witness rather than by answering questions.

"Misha, I needed him here. He is friends with all four and would know best how to negotiate with them. I needed Misha to help me convince the four, well three now, that they must stop their plotting."

The story wheel came to an abrupt stop. Time to get it rolling again. "What would they be plotting that has anything to do with you?" McKayla asked.

"Us, I gathered all of the top shippers from around the Black Sea to speak to them and ask them to stop with their drone strikes. You remember there was a blockade that halted all shipping in Qatar a while back? That was them."

"I remember that it started an international helium crisis."

"They planned that to happen. They grew their wealth substantially on that ploy. Now they are playing games in the Black Sea."

"Because of the war?"

"The war is a vehicle to an end. They wish to stop global shipping of fuel and food. You hear how these men speak amongst themselves in Portuguese? This hostile takeover of my yacht has to do with the Mozambique Channel and fuel along with the Black Sea and food. You mark my words. What makes the world work? Food and fuel. They wish to stop the grain from leaving the Black Sea, they wish to stop the petroleum products from allowing the farmers the ability to farm at a volume that would feed the people."

"To what end? They have more money than they could possibly spend."

"Yes, well, you have been rich long enough to know that it brings no satisfaction. They always think, maybe a little more money, and I'll finally be happy. I believe Karl, Rajja, and Nadir have realized that money will never bring them contentment, so they are trying a different goal."

"Which is?"

"Power. Control. They were absolutely giddy over the pain they caused in Qatar. It's like the people who cut themselves to feel pain in the hopes that they can feel something. Only these three will cut others, watch their pain, and feel powerful. At least then they will feel something. These are men who are angry that they feel empty."

"And shipping is their knife of choice?"

"And I have, unfortunately, sharpened that blade. I thought that Misha's friendship would soothe these men. But Ivan is no more. And Misha sent you in his stead. And you, my dear, have no emotional sway over these men."

"Even if Misha had come, I don't think it would have made a difference." McKayla hoped that her watch was functioning clearly, and White was getting all this. "I'm trying to form a picture. This is what I have in my mind, you tell me, Uncle Niko, if you think this is right. The three pretended that they would come on the cruising party. They knew that they would not. They told you they would join you later in a fast boat, so you gave them the path we were scheduled to take."

"Yes. So it seems."

"They did not lie. They came, or their representatives came in the fast boat. I am a billionaire. They can ask for my wealth as ransom. But your guests represent the biggest shippers on the Black Sea. Holding them means they can force the families not to ship. They might say something like, 'If you ship, we torture your loved one.' Something like that?"

"It would work."

"Why don't they just build penis shaped rockets and launch themselves into outer space? Maybe that would give them some satisfaction."

"Yawn. It's been done. What they're looking for now is land. They want all the land they can lay their hands on. If it has gold and diamonds, like in South Africa, bonus. If it has helium, like in Tanzania, even better. But what they want is to control things that are necessary to modern life. With no helium, no computer chips, no MRI machines. That's powerful leverage. Gold and Diamonds, meh. But land with lithium for car batteries and silicon for solar panels? Vast deserts where solar farms can produce electricity? Yes, owning and controlling the land. Look at Saudi Arabia, they already lease the water in Arizona and are draining the aquifers. Do you think Arizona can exist without water? Do you think that Rajja isn't paying attention?"

"Oh," was the only thing that McKayla could think to say.

"Winter is coming. Heat and food in these parts of the world. A potential crisis to be exploited."

"It's already being exploited. Billionaires are growing their riches around the world. But when you have ten billion, what's another ten billion? It's just a race of one upmanship, right? Money is power."

"This is old school," Uncle Niko said. "Money is not power anymore. Power is power. And power is an addiction as you see in my country right now. When you have everything when you want it, how you want, just by opening your mouth, boredom sets in. Boredom is the great misery of wealth. Nothing to conquer. Nothing to feel joyful over. The huge rock offered up as an engagement ring—they could buy that for themselves. So those with that much wealth become more deviant, looking for a sense of forbidden."

McKayla frowned deeply as she squished her fingers through Hoover's fur. "When money is boring, then taking control becomes sport." She looked out over the glittering waters. "I am so depressed right now."

37

ASHER GIDEON

The Indian Ocean off the Coast of Madagascar

THE HELICOPTER HOVERED over the water as low as it could go without setting off the Russian yacht's radar systems.

The Iniquus team should look like a pod of dolphins if they were picked up at all as they moved toward the Russian yacht.

Plunging into the waters with their supply bags and underwater scooters, the Iniquus men pawed their way to the surface to count heads and regroup.

Dragging their face masks into place, they let their weighted belts pull them under in a curtain of bubbles.

The hooks that would allow the team to attach slender rope ladders to the yacht's railing, were fastened to the scooters. This configuration allowed the team to stick together as they powered the final two miles to the yacht in the dark of night.

They'd be following compass readings and distance meters to get in place.

Ash was coldly determined.

He pulled his emotions out of the equation. As his scooter dragged him through the dark waters, he reviewed each step of the plan they had developed off of the only intelligence they had available—a 3D AI design of the yacht, and McKayla's narration of what she saw around her.

The last thing they heard from McKayla was that they were given food and water. Hoover was a star. No one was injured or abused, and the lights were being turned off as they passed Madagascar in the dark of night.

"If any of this has gotten through to you, then you know tonight is the only night for a successful raid. The assault team hasn't raised their stress levels. They seem to be going through the steps as just performative at this point. They weren't congratulating themselves yet, but plainly, they think they are free and clear to fulfill their plan. Anyway, I'm hoping you know about us. I hope you're coming. Please be safe."

How many times had his team trained this?

How many times had they performed this rescue?

Ash was just glad this had been his SEAL team; they would work in concert, Gator fitting in seamlessly.

Striker slowed his scooter, then brought it to a stop. They were signaling with taps and squeezes. They were blind in the ink of night.

Feeling along the yacht, they came to a stop under the bow. The shape of the vessel made this area impossible to see. Shooting them here would require a trick shot through the hull.

Jack pressed suction cups with D rings that extended an arm away from the boat. These would hold their equipment in place with enough distance that their tanks wouldn't knock against the hull and call attention to their presence.

They inflated a shelf that was then suction cupped into place. Reaching for their dry bags, cuffed to their ankles, the men dragged their equipment out of the water and placed them along the shelf for easy access.

Slowly, so that there was no tell-tale splash, off came their SCUBA gear and fins. These went into net bags and were hung on the extended hooks. Water shoes, combat gloves, guns, and knives were checked and placed on their bodies.

They dropped the magnetic comms devices into their ears.

They wrapped throat mics around their necks. These contact microphones absorbed vibrations from the speaker's throat and translated them into words for the team. They could speak to each other noiselessly.

Striker signaled a comms check.

And with a thumbs up all around, the night vision goggles were strapped into place.

Tonight's ability to process form was dependent on the light of the smallest sliver of moon, but a galaxy of glitter rounding over them like a bowl would give them added clarity.

"Striker to Tidal Actual," he mouthed.

"Tidal Actual, copy loud and clear."

"Strike is in position. We will be boarding in three mics." Striker used the abbreviation for minutes.

"Three mics, copy. In five mics, Tidal will advance the boat and helicopter to your location. Time starts now."

This meant that if the helicopter or the combat boat were spotted on the radar, Strike Force would already be boarded.

Striker and Blaze were headed to the bridge to capture control of the craft.

Jack and Ash swam aft. They would make first contact.

The last of McKayla's video feed, before the dark made viewing impossible, said there were two guards. One that stood in front of the doors. One that stood in the center of the hostages.

Ash, from portside, would have the best angle to take out the central tango.

They would time their shots to take the guards down simultaneously.

The silencers and subsonic bullets would cut the noise to the barest minimum.

Slow and steady, Ash slid his hook up, slicing into the night air. The hook was rubberized to muffle the noise as it fixed onto the railing.

It was hard as hell to maneuver as he kicked his feet and bobbled in the ocean waves.

If anyone messed up with a clang or bang, those tango rifles could aim down from above and take the team out.

Even with the heli and fast boat heading in, the tangos' electric craft was just as fast and could shoot away with the hostages in the blink of an eye, to be lost in the vast expanse of the Indian Ocean.

Ash was sweating. His heart pounded as he set his hook.

Slowly, slowly, he climbed the ladder as it swayed. Each time it dragged him toward the hull, Ash reached out to silently stop his body.

His head rounded the railing.

Hoover was looking right at him.

Ash pulled his rifle around and mouthed. "Ash in position."

McKayla opened her eyes. Her hand snaked toward Hoover's butt, up over his back, up the length of the handle. So slow that the guard continued to stare off the back of the boat into the void.

"Striker in position."

She depressed the button, releasing the handle and collapsed her arm at the elbow, snail-like.

"Striker. Boarded. McKayla counted five heads. I'm looking at a grouping of seven. It looks like they're gathering night vision binoculars and are being dispersed."

"Jack in position. I have no eyes on my target. Repeat, no eyes on my target."

"Ash. Target in scope."

"Gator. In position, enemy in my scope."

"Striker. Minimum of seven. Follow the plan."

McKayla pulled the handle across her abdomen and held.

There was a crackle in the translator apparatus that Ash had in one ear. The Portuguese voice coming from the walkie-talkie attached to the leather strap around the tango's torso was pressed back behind the voice veneer of the AI translation.

Voice one: "Two high speed vehicles will intersect with our trajectory in a calculated forty-five minutes. One by air. One by sea."

Voice two: "Cut the engines. Let them fly on by. We have enough fuel and supplies to wait until tomorrow night to proceed if need be."

Voice three: "Do you think they know about us? Do you think they're hunting the yacht?"

Voice two: "How could they possibly? It's probably a night maneuver by the Madagascar Navy we are just now crossing their northern-most point."

There was a moment of silence.

"Striker. All right, gentlemen, here we go. On the count of three, Ash and Gator take your target, and then the others board. I am at the bow's eleven o'clock. And. Three. Two."

As Striker said, "One," the door to the main salon crashed open, the sudden light through Ash's night vision blinded him. He popped the gear off his eyes and blinked blindly in front of him.

There was a pop and screams from the passengers as they shifted and heaved in front of him.

Ash blinked his eyes again then dragged the goggles back in place, so he could get a bead on his target, but Hoover was launching through the air. His jaw clamped down on the trigger arm of the tango.

Ash raised his sights and double tapped the tango who had just come onto the scene.

As Ash threw his leg over the railing, McKayla dragged the bar apart, wrapped herself into position, and unrolled, clocking the tango across the temple.

He dropped.

"Hoover. Release. McKayla find cover."

McKayla glanced around. There was no cover to be had on the yacht.

"McKayla, to me!" Ash yelled over the commotion. "To me!"

McKayla bent and grabbed the rifle that the tango had dropped. She lifted it over her head then slammed it into the man's skull.

Hoover released the unconscious tango's arm. He jumped up to catch the hem of McKayla's jacket. Then, Hoover dragged her to Ash.

"You okay?" he asked breathlessly as he made his way to the interior, her hand on his back just like they did it over a decade ago.

"I'll be okay when there are no more bad guys, and I have my feet on dry land."

38

McKayla Pickard.

The Sleeping Lotus Hotel, Madagascar

McKayla answered Ash's knock, holding the door wide as he brought in her luggage from Uncle Niko's yacht.

He walked into the cheap room that smelled of mold and plastic. The furnishings in the room were made of pressed wood. The fabrics were cheap and rough. Ash looked around. "Not exactly to your standard." He set the suitcase down.

This was the first time she'd seen him since the helicopter loaded her on. Iniquus had returned in the pirate's electric fast boat. The rest of the passengers were still on the yacht, the captain taking them back to the Seychelles to report the crimes. Dead bodies and all.

The CIA took control of the three fake pirates that were still alive before Strike Force left international waters.

They stared at each other. Just stood there and stared.

Finally, McKayla got herself together enough to say, "You're fired."

Ash released Hoover's lead. "Oh?" He turned and shut the door, throwing the lock.

"I sent an email to your company letting them know that having finished my stay in the Seychelles, I no longer feel a K9 operator is required. I terminated the contract, effective thirty minutes ago."

"I see." He tipped his head.

"So now, I need you to take me to bed."

With one step Ash was wrapped around McKayla, holding her ear to his throbbing heart. Crushing her to him, his fingers laced into the long strands of her dark hair. He dragged his hands down to tip her face so he could kiss her.

It was nothing like the heated anger over his absence like in London.

It was just an intense pressure as if she wanted to meld with him and become one, so they never had to live a lie or apart again.

When he lowered his forehead to rest against McKayla's, she backed until she felt the mattress behind her knees. She dragged open the bodice of her wrap around dress, then tugged his shirt over his head until she could feel his muscles under her palms. She could feel the warmth of his skin. She leaned in and breathed in the hot salt of his sweat.

Ash's hands slid up under the skirt of her dress, and he pulled her tight.

His cock hard against her belly.

She leaned back until gravity drew her to the mattress.

Ash climbed on. Pulling his knees under him, reaching under her arms, he moved her up the bed until she could lay comfortably.

McKayla splayed her knees cradling Ash between her thighs.

He brushed her hair back and then framed her face with his hands. "McKayla, I was so focused on getting you home, I was just in operator mode. But it's all hitting me now, like a sledgehammer."

She nodded.

"I could have lost you."

She shook her head. Emotions were choking her. To think that she might not ever have seen his precious face again.

"McKayla—"

"You're shaking."

"I'm telling you, the thought of someone hurting you terrifies me."

"Thank you for caring." She wrapped her legs around his waist, crossing her ankles behind his back and curling up to kiss him. "Thank you for coming for me." With another kiss, she laid her head back on the pillow. "I was calm the whole time. I knew you'd keep me safe. I sincerely trusted you. Just like that terrible day in Afghanistan. The weight of the plaster was pressing me down. I couldn't move. And I just told myself, 'Slow your breathing, Giddy's coming.' It was a blanket of peace. And then, there you were."

"I want to be, McKayla. I always want to be."

"Thank you." She smiled. What a beautiful-souled

man. What an amazing feeling to know someone cared like this.

"No, McKayla, I want to officially be there." His face had a fierceness to it. "Always."

She didn't understand. She waited.

"There's a lot to figure out about how this could work, but one thing I know is that I want you to be my wife. I want to marry you and love you. I want you in my arms until I'm an old, withered guy, shuffling along with my cane."

"That's adrenaline talking."

"It's not. It's *not*. I said this, just not as clearly, when we were in London."

"You're serious right now."

Hoover jumped on the bed and stuck his nose forward, joining the huddle.

"I am more serious about this than anything in my life. And Hoover agrees with me."

"He told you that?"

Ash turned his head to talk to Hoover. "Hoover, should McKayla marry me?" When he raised his brows, Hoover gave a high-pitched bark.

"Ah, he did," McKayla didn't think she'd ever be able to wipe that smile off her face. She was in bliss. "Well, if Hoover thinks it's a good idea, then I guess it's a good idea."

"That's a yes?"

Okay, the smile didn't last long. "It's a yes. A *private* yes. Just between us, until I can figure out how to keep you safe from my reputation."

"I HEARD YOU FIRED ASH," Lynx said quietly while the rest of the team gathered at their respective computers for the video conference. "Congratulations. I wish you two every happiness."

"Thank you, but you know what, Lynx? I'm still humming." McKayla slicked a hand down her left arm then repeated it on the other side.

"Interesting."

"You never did hypnotize me the way you promised when I told you something from the explosion was bothering me. Everything was happening so fast," she quickly added. "That wasn't a rebuke. But you know, even after all of this, I'm still caught on the day of the explosion. And now that this happened... Would you be willing?"

"Of course." She flipped to the whole group. "Guys, let's postpone just a bit. I'm going to hypnotize, McKayla."

"You can do that over the computer?" White asked.

"Yes, but privately. I'll tape it in case McKayla retrieves a useful memory, and I'll ask her permission to share. That privacy aspect is imperative to someone's feeling comfortable enough to divulge the subconscious."

"That's safe?" Ash asked.

"You're there with her. She'll be fine."

Once Lynx talked to McKayla about the process, and Ash was comfortable with his role, Lynx slowly moved McKayla into an altered state where she was more likely to see things that her conscious mind was too uncomfortable or too busy to process.

"McKayla, let's start with the helicopter on the way to the hospital and work our way backward. Tell me when you're on the helicopter."

"I'm sitting next to the pilot. Misha is in the back. He has a paramedic with him. He's awake but not talking or focusing."

"Let's look at the monitors in the helicopter. Can you read them?"

"Not from my angle but I can hear the paramedic talking to his partner. He's saying Misha's vital signs are steady and looking good."

"What else did they say?"

"Why is he acting nonresponsive? They said things. Stroke. Blast damage to his organs. Shock." She made a face.

"What was that memory?" Lynx asked.

"The paramedic said he hoped it wasn't blast lung or blast abdomen as the mortality rate is high. Not out loud like that. They hid it behind military speak. But in the hospital, John said that Rachel had primary blast lung and blast abdomen and it was serious but she should be fine. I don't know who was telling Misha that either one was fine. Perhaps he heard the truth but couldn't absorb it since he had been standing beside them. Survivors guilt?"

"Focusing on Misha," Lynx used a neutral tone, "all of those things that could go wrong. But none of that turned out to be accurate. What happened to Misha?"

"He had a small piece of metal in his chest. I remember that. It was right where he had his bandage. When I dragged him in, his body didn't have the deadweight feel of people I had dragged in the field. He was conscious. I thought he was faking his injuries, and I was pissed he was letting me drag him and hurt myself so he could play dead."

"Good. Now let's go back further. Let's go to the point where your group walked out the door. Start with the things that you noticed as you passed through the doorway. Ivan, his wife, and her friend were going to a concert." Lynx positioned McKayla's focus.

"We all walked outside, and Misha asked, "Where are you parked?"

"Good."

"Ivan pointed. You can see all of this in the CCV footage." McKayla sounded agitated.

"Yes," Lynx said, her voice hadn't changed from its neutral tone. "We have the camera's point of view. We don't have it from your point of view. And we don't know what thing is wanting attention."

"Okay, Misha said, 'the women are in heels, that's a long way for them. Why don't you get the car? And I'll stay here with them while my man pulls round."

"What did Ivan do?"

"Looked at him like he'd never seen Misha before."

"Why?"

"Misha isn't gallant. He's a chauvinist. He thought about men's comfort and women needed to suck it up and go along. Ivan was the same. Most of Misha's friends were the same. That Misha was treating the women with concern was out of character."

"What did Ivan do next?"

"He gives a kind of curt nod then pulls his fob from his pocket and starts for his car."

"Good. Where are you?"

"We are all on the porch, the one I dragged Misha up in the newsclip."

"What is happening next?"

"The women walk down the stairs to stand on the walk and wait. Misha is looking off to the side, he looks like he is trying to find someone by the brick wall. He steps off the steps and is looking. Not in an obvious way. His eyes are scanning. He is touching his nose. He takes a step backward toward the stairs."

"Is he looking at something or someone?" Lynx asked.

"There is a man behind the brick wall. The wall is maybe four feet high. The man salutes Misha."

"What does the man at the wall do next?"

"He has his phone in his hand and is looking at Ivan. Then ducks out of sight."

"Do you know the man standing behind the brick wall?"

"Yes, that's John. He's part of my London security team."

"What happens next?"

"There is a flash of light. My body throws me into the clubhouse. Oh shit. Bring me up. Bring me up. Bring me up, now."

Lynx didn't try to coerce her to stay under. Her voice never left its neutrality, her words a slow drumbeat. "I'm going to bring you up now. You are deeply under at the number ten. With your next inhale you come up a little further to nine. You become aware that you have a body. Eight. You can feel the temperature of the air. Seven. You know you are lying on a surface and can feel your body pressing down. Six. Wiggle your feet and toes. Five. Shift your shoulders and arms. Four. Touch your tongue to your teeth and feel how solid they are in your mouth. Three. Another deep breath and blink your eyes open. Two. You are here and now. Fully back in your body. One. Take a moment to shift your attention to the room. And when you're ready, slowly sit up again.

Ash arrived, glass in hand, and McKayla took a sip of the water.

McKayla lay there blinking, Ash sat beside her, taking the glass to set on the table, then lacing his fingers into hers.

After a moment Lynx asked, "Better? Ready?"

"That was a set up. That whole thing was a set up. Misha had insisted that we go to that club for tea. No one wanted to. No one. He was bizarrely adamant about it. It was supposed to be Ivan and Misha, but his wife reminded Ivan of their tickets, and so he called to say he was bringing along Rachel and her friend. Then Misha insisted I go too, so he didn't have to listen to the hens cackling. From what I learned on the yacht, do you think Misha knew what Ivan, Karl, Rajja and Nadir were planning?"

"They'd have to be very careful, wouldn't they?" Lynx asked. "With their war blazing, and London already furious about Scripal and his daughter being poisoned with a nerve agent in London. They couldn't have the usual falls or poisonings."

"The gas was an ancient system that just couldn't hold up, is a good cover. In the summer months they just used it for cooking."

"How would you do that, Ash?"

"It would take a little extra work but drill a hole into the pavement at the right place, put an explosive unit in, stand back, and detonate it with a phone, seems pretty straight forward."

"Funny, but by mentioning the women's heels and keeping them back might have saved their lives," McKayla said. "And mine. He told me to wait on the porch for his driver."

"He wanted to explode his driver?" Lynx asked.

"I don't think so. *I* texted the driver. I thought the look on Misha's face was that he was upset that I would do that. I'm a woman and it was his driver." McKayla frowned. "I guess, he's dead because of that text. He sits with the engine running. If he was on the other side of the building, he would have put the car in gear and rounded into the blast zone. Misha wouldn't have known where the car was, and even still he'd need to keep up the charade. His mission was in play."

"What are you thinking? Lynx asked.

"I spent an entire year with him, and I never ever would have guessed that he would do that. Never. I guess I was seeing the posture he was taking for polite London society. I guess he never dropped his costume, so I would see the true him. And yet, now knowing that he allowed his friend to be killed, one assumes for self-preservation, it makes perfect sense that he'd send me out on that boat to interact with his family. To put me at risk."

"Next steps?" Ash asked.

"I can go to London and confront him," McKayla said. "And I can threaten him. I have his phone in my penthouse."

39

JOHNNA WHITE
Iniquus, Washington, D.C.

"WHILE I APPRECIATE THE MEMORIES," White said after she watched the hypnotism session, "they won't hold up in the court of law."

"Let's look at it frame by frame. I had already worked through a lot of what she said. For me it was an affirmation. For example, look here. As the light flashed, McKayla dove for the door. She was up on the porch. We had been focused on her. But look at Misha, as McKayla dives, Misha falls to the ground, and covers his head. Then the blast concussion. Then McKayla finds him that way."

"Split second," White said. "Granted, Russian men had compulsory military service."

"Do we know what he did for the military?"

White smirked. "McKayla's notes say Misha served as

a valet of sorts for a general, one of Papa Popyrin's friends. He wasn't out training in battlefield skills."

"He sees the light and drops," Deep said. "He'd be waiting for it."

"Zooming in. As McKayla is trying to get him to safety, he pops his eyes open twice. And he grits his teeth as they move up the stairs."

"Interesting." White watched carefully. "How did you get the zoomed video so clear?"

"Our AI systems," Deep said.

"Now, going back. Before the door opened and Misha et al exited. There's the person that I labelled in my notes as the gardener with a weeder by the fence. When the group comes out, he lays the weeder down and watches the group."

"Misha is pushing McKayla back and wagging his finger at her. Interesting," White said.

"He goes to the bottom of the stairs. He's facing Ivan. Ivan has his fob out. Ivan walks to his car."

"Frame by frame. Light."

"On the right," Deep said. "McKayla's diving."

"Misha's dropping to the ground. But look," White pointed, "the women are still upright. Ivan is still fine."

"Now comes the shake of the camera," Lynx said moving the frame forward. "When it stops, Ivan is gone. The women are on the ground like Misha."

"Okay." White put her hands on her lap and sat up squarely, a little shocked that she'd been given this information. She had been so sure that Lynx would take it to her buddies in the FBI or NSA.

"White," Lynx said, "you need to personally take this

back to Langley, ASAP. This case is *highly* sensitive. I think we're done playing here. This needs to get bumped up to the highest levels of British and American security."

"I see. Well, Iniquus and the CIA do indeed work differently." As White said that, she felt Lynx's gaze bore into her.

Yes, Lynx was the ethical one who lived up to not just the letter of her agreements but the spirit of the agreement, as well. "Look, I'm sorry about your situation with promises made by my department and promises that went unkept, I—"

"I'm at work," Lynx cut her off with a biting tone. "I don't do personal at work."

"Yes, but I wanted you to know that I—" White felt her face flame red.

"Look, I know you know about my situation. But knowing about something and having power to do something about it are two different things. If it makes you feel any better, you're not on my shit list. I think of it this way, if I were a soldier and was being treated like crap, I'd still have a duty to perform. Assume that's how I'm framing things when I'm on a mission working with the CIA. A successful mission and the safe return of my team and McKayla are my only interest here."

40

McKayla Pickard.
Penthouse, London

"I just got off the phone with Uncle." Misha pushed past her into the salon. He turned and stared at her. "You're safe."

"Of course, I am. I hired ex-Navy SEALs to keep me whole and healthy." She moved toward the sofa and sat; her arms spread wide across the back to discourage him from joining her.

Misha sat on the occasional chair in front of her.

"You put me in danger, Misha. The press wants a tell all. I *will* tell all. I know, for example, that John and you colluded to kill Ivan, and your driver was also killed in the explosion. I not only watched it happen myself. But I looked through your phone."

Misha's face turned purple.

"When I tell all, you will be investigated for two

murders and all of those people who were hurt. Their families will sue you penniless. You will rot in prison."

"Don't do that, McKayla." He jostled to sit on the edge of his seat. "What do you want from me?

"The truth. It seems a small thing compared to what you've put me through."

"Ivan got drunk one night. Boastful. Angry. He told me he didn't like to be in his position. He said that Rajja and Nadir came to solidify their final plans." He put his fists to his chest. "I am the good guy here. They were colluding. They wanted to starve people all over the continent of Africa and in India. Not just during the war but after, too. Food and fuel as tools of power. I hinted at what he said the next day, he said he had no recollection past our dessert."

"Do you know the details of the plan?" McKayla asked.

"Only that they would discuss it in the Seychelles. His job was to get me on the yacht for the meeting. That was his task. They thought if I was on that boat that all would go to plan. I stopped Ivan from going, and I made sure that I could not go and have anything to do with this. I didn't mean for him to die. I meant for him to be injured as Rachel was."

"But you sent me." She crossed her arms tightly over her chest.

"No man would bring you into the conversation, McKayla. No man would cause you harm while you were pregnant."

She leaned forward, jutting out over her knees. "So that whole pregnancy thing was to keep me safe?"

"Something big and public took place. I have a very good excuse. I did my best to make sure that I did not become a target of Russian wrath in case this was a directive from the Kremlin. I did this by sending you. Selfish? Yes, of course, you know I'm a selfish man. And the pregnancy, the grandchild of my father, would add safety."

She fell back into the cushions. "Until it didn't."

"I could not have predicted that my friends would do this. I never knew the whole scheme. It's over, McKayla, just be glad it's over."

"It's over, all right," McKayla said as the London police swarmed into the room.

EPILOGUE

THREE YEARS LATER

HIGH ON THE TOP OF A WEST VIRGINIA MOUNTAIN, McKayla heard the rotors of the helicopter landing. Felt the rattle of the windows.

She smiled into her hot cocoa where a marshmallow melted.

Any minute now.

And soon enough, the door flung open and the snow spiraled in. Ash sent her a grin as he stomped his boots. "Mrs. Gideon."

"Mr. Gideon."

"Do we have enough wood? It looks like the snow's going to be heavy tonight."

McKayla glanced toward the wood stove. "Plenty."

Ash toe-heeled his boots off to dry by the door, then came over and kissed her, laying a newspaper on her lap as he went over to shuck his coat. "Not one. Not two. But three stories of interest today."

"Yeah?"

The front page had a picture of Karl Davidson being

sentenced to life in prison on murder-for-hire charges. "Well, I guess they got Al Capone for tax evasion. What does it matter how he's stopped as long as he's stopped."

"Agreed." Ash moved over to poke the fire.

"Where's the next one?" McKayla asked after scanning the article.

"World News."

She flipped through. "Oh, wow." Her eyes slid over the story. "Misha Popyrov was traded to Russia for two British journalists who had been held on false charges in the penal colonies for over five years. And as the exchange took place, he had a heart attack and died in a Moscow hospital."

She blinked and shook her head. Her entire system was like a tight wire that got snipped then dangled lifelessly. She shook herself and the sensation disappeared. "Not sure how I feel about that. That kind of throws me. Certainly, it was good that the Brits got handed over before it happened." She looked up. "I'm afraid to ask. Number three?"

"Local news," Ash poked the fire sending up a shower of sparks.

The Greensborough High school, sponsored by McKayla Pickard over the last five years, has moved students from a forty percent dropout rate to a two percent dropout rate.

All of the students in last year's graduating class were accepted to college or trade schools that will be fully funded by the crypto-disruptive billionaire with her

Butterfly Initiative, where Pickard strives to give people the skills and support they need to be the change for hope and kindness.

One of the students who has moved on to university has just won an international award for developing a means to use low frequency sound waves to fight fires.

. . .

McKayla shook her head. "Low frequency sound waves to fight fires. Wow." She reached for Ash's hand.

"That's what you wanted, right? To change the world for the better?"

"*This* is what I want, the top of a mountain in a snowstorm, and a peaceful family."

Hoover lifted his head, looking toward the back of the cabin.

McKayla moved to stand up.

"No. No. No." Ash put his hands on McKayla's shoulders, so she'd stay seated. "You've had Brooke all to yourself for two whole days now. It's my turn."

As he went back into the nursery and scooped up his daughter, her eyes bright, a smile of recognition quivering on her lips, all Ash felt was bliss.

He was the luckiest man in the whole damned world.

While this is

THE END

of Hero's Instinct…

Readers, I hope you enjoyed getting to know McKayla, Ash, and Hoover. If you had fun reading Hero's Instinct, I'd appreciate it if you'd help others enjoy it too.

Recommend it: Just a few words to your friends, your book groups, and your social networks would be wonderful.

Review it: Please tell your fellow readers what you liked about my book by reviewing Hero's Instinct.

Discuss it! – I have a SPOILERS group on Facebook. (**Fiona Quinn's SPOILER group**)

If you're reading the Iniquus World in chronological order, the next book is: STRIKER

If you want to learn more about Karl Davidson and Strike Force's mission read: InstiGATOR

If you're curious about Lynx and the debacle with the CIA that develops in book four of the Lynx series, the first book is WEAKEST LYNX. The Lynx series should be read in order. If you are new to Iniquus and want to start at the very beginning, turn the page for an excerpt from book one in the Iniquus chronology, WEAKEST LYNX.

Ready? Let's go! Turn the page!

A LOOK INSIDE

WEAKEST LYNX (BOOK ONE LYNX SERIES)

1

THE BLACK BMW POWERED STRAIGHT TOWARD ME. Heart pounding, I stomped my brake pedal flush to the floorboard. My chest slammed into the seat belt, snapping my head forward. There wasn't time to blast the horn, but the scream from my tires was deafening.

I gasped in a breath as the BMW idiot threw me a nonchalant wave—his right hand off the wheel—with his left hand pressed to his ear, still chatting on his cell phone. Diplomatic license plates. *Figures.*

Yeah, I didn't really need an extra shot of adrenaline—like a caffeine IV running straight to my artery—I was already amped.

"Focus, Lexi," I whispered under my breath, pressing down on the gas. "Follow the plan. Give the letter to Dave. Let him figure this out." I sent a quick glance down to my purse where a corner of the cream-colored envelope jutted out, then veered my Camry back into the noonday DC gridlock, weaving past the graffitied storefronts. I recognized that the near-miss with the BMW guy probably wasn't his fault. I couldn't remember the last ten minutes of drive time.

I watched my review mirror as a bike messenger laced between the moving cars on his mission to get the parcel in his bag to the right guy at the right time. Once he handed over his package, he'd be done—lucky him. Even though I was handing my letter off to Dave, the truth that wouldn't be my endpoint. I wasn't clear about what an endpoint would even look like. Safe. It might look like I was safe, that I had my feet back under me. But that thought seemed like it was far out on the horizon, and right now, I was just looking for something to grab on to, to keep me afloat.

When I finally parked in front of Dave Murphy's mid-century brick row house, I sat for a minute, trying to regain my composure. I'd pushed this whole mess to the back burner for as long as I could but after last night's nightmare... Well, better to get a detective's opinion. Dave had handled enough crackpots over his time with the DCPD that he'd have a better grasp of the threat level. Right now, even with all my training, I was scared out of my mind.

I glanced down at my hands. The tremor in them sent the afternoon sunlight dancing off my brand-new engagement and wedding rings. I felt like an imposter wearing them—like a little girl dressed up in her mother's clothes. *I'm too young to be dealing with all this crap,* I thought as I shoved my keys into my purse. I pulled my hair into a quick ponytail and stepped out into the February cold. Casting anxious glances up and down the street, I jogged up the stairs to bang on Dave's front door.

The screen squeaked open almost immediately as if

he'd been standing there waiting for my knock. "Hey, Baby Girl," he said, stepping out of the way to let me in. Dave had been calling me Baby Girl since I was born because my parents couldn't decide on my name, and that was how I was listed on my hospital ankle tag.

"Glad I found you at home." I walked in and plopped down on the blue gingham couch. It had been here since I could remember. The fabric was threadbare, and juice stained by his five-year-old twins. On a cop's salary, fine furnishings ranked low in priority. Right now—edgy and confused—I appreciated the comfort of familiarity.

Dave shifted into detective mode—hands on hips, eyes scanning me. "Long time, no see."

"Where are Cathy and the kids?" I asked.

"They've got dentist appointments. Did you come to tell us your news?" He lifted his chin to indicate my left hand and settled at the other end of the couch, swiveling until we were face to face.

"Uhm, no." I twisted my rings, suddenly feeling drained and bereft. What wouldn't I give to have my husband Angel here? The corners of my mouth tugged down. I willed myself to stay focused on the reason for the visit. My immediate safety had to take priority over my grief.

Dave raised a questioning brow, waiting for me to continue.

"Angel and I got married Wednesday. I'm Lexi Sobado now." My voice hitched, and tears pressed against my lids. I lowered my lashes, so Dave wouldn't see. But his eyes had locked onto mine, and he never missed much.

"Married? At your age? No introduction? No wedding

invitation? Why isn't he here with you now?" Dave angled his head to the side and crossed his arms over his middle-aged paunch. "I'd like to meet the guy," he all but snarled.

Dave probably thought I'd come here because my husband screwed things up already. I pulled the pillow from behind my back and hugged it to me like a shield. "I'm sorry. I should have let you and Cathy know what was going on—I was caught up, and I just..." I stopped to clear my throat. "Angel and I got married at the court-house, and no one came with us. Not even Abuela Rosa."

"Angel Sobado. He's kin to Rosa, then?"

I gave the slightest tip of a nod. "Angel is her great-nephew. I couldn't bring him with me today because he deployed with the Rangers to the Middle East Thursday. That's why everything happened so fast. He was leaving." The last word stuck in my throat and choked me.

Dave leaned forward to rest his elbows on his knees. Lacing his fingers, he tapped his thumbs together. "Huh. That's a helluva short honeymoon. Married Wednesday. Gone Thursday." Dave's tone had dropped an octave and gained a fringe of fatherly concern.

His compassion gave me permission to break down. But those Angel-emotions were mine. Private. Right now, I needed to hold myself in check long enough to get through my mission of handing off the letter. I shifted my feet back and forth over the rug as I glared at my purse.

"Might even explain the expression on your face," Dave said, narrowing his eyes. He slouched against the arm of the overstuffed couch.

Stalling wasn't going to make this any easier. I reached a hesitant hand into my bag, pulled out a plastic Zip-loc holding the envelope, and held it up for Dave. "The expression is because of this," I said.

Dave took the bag. After a brief glance, he hefted himself to his feet. Over at his desk, he pulled on a pair of Nitrile gloves, then carefully removed the letter.

DEAREST INDIA ALEXIS,

O my Luve's like the melodie
That's sweetly play'd in tune!
As fair thou art, my bonnie lass,
So deep in love, am I:
And I will love thee still, my dear,
Till a' your bones are white and dry:
Till a' your veins gang dry, my dear,
And your skin melt with the sun;
I will luve thee until your heart is still my dear
When the sands of your life shall no more run.
And fare thee weel, my only Luve,
And fare thee weel a while!
And I will come again, my Luve, so I can watch
you die.

DAVE READ the words aloud then stared at me hard; his brows pulled in tight enough that the skin on his forehead accordioned. "What the—"

"Someone shoved the poem under the door to my room, and it's scaring the bejeezus out of me." I gripped the pillow tighter.

Dave peered over the top of his reading glasses. "Last night? This morning?"

"Wednesday morning." I braced when I said it, knowing it would tick Dave off that I didn't bring this to him immediately. Ever since my dad died, his buddies had stepped in and tried to take over the fathering job, even though I'd be turning twenty in a few days.

True to my expectations, Dave was red-faced and bellowing. "*Wednesday?* You waited two whole days to tell me you've gotten a friggin death threat?"

Yup, this was exactly the response Dad would have given me.

Dave jumped up, pacing across the room. Obviously, he didn't think this was someone's idea of a joke. Fear tightened my chest at his confirmation. I had hoped he'd say, "No worries—someone is having fun pranking you," and then I could go on about my life without the major case of heebie-jeebies that tingled my skin and made me want to run and hide.

"It was our wedding day." I worked to modulate my voice to sound soft and reasonable. "I only had a few short hours before Angel had to take off. So yeah, I decided to focus on us instead of this." I motioned toward the paper in his hand.

Dave took in a deep breath, making his nostrils flare. "Okay." I could almost see his brain shifting gears. "When you first picked up the letter, did you get any vibes?"

"You mean, ESP-wise?"

He nodded stiffly; his eyes hard on me.

Vibes. That wasn't the word I would have chosen to explain my sensations. "I didn't hear anything. It was more like an oily substance oozing over me." I tucked my nose into the soft cloth of the pillow and breathed in the scent of cinnamon fabric freshener. "I vomited." My voice dropped to a whisper. "It felt like evil and craziness, and I can still smell that stench." A shiver raced down my spine.

Dave's lips sealed tightly; he was probably trying to hold back a litany of expletives. Finally, he asked, "That's all?"

"Yes."

"Did any of your neighbors notice anyone unusual lurking around? Did you check with management and run through the security tapes?"

"Dave, didn't you hear? My apartment building burned to the ground three weeks ago. I assumed you knew. It was on the news."

Dave's eyebrows shot straight up.

"I've been living in a motel the Red Cross rented out for all the families displaced by the fire. But to answer your question, no, nobody saw anything, and there were no cameras trained on my motel corridor." I curled my lips in to keep them from trembling. I was used to holding my emotions in check. I trained myself to present a sweet exterior, a costume of sorts, but right now, I was filled to overflowing, and my mask kept slipping out of place.

"Shit." Dave ran a hand over his face. "I had no idea. I'm letting your parents down. Apartment burned, married, husband gone, and now a death threat." His eyes narrowed on me. "Do you think that about covers all of your surprises for me today?"

I paused for a beat. "Yeah, Dave, I think that's it for today." Okay, even if he was like family, the way Dave was talking pissed me off. I was frightened. I wanted a hug and his reassurance. What I was getting was... Dave's brand of love. He wouldn't be this red-faced and agitated if he wasn't worried about me. Tears prickled behind my eyelids, blurring my vision.

"Hey, now. Stop. We'll get to the bottom of this. Did you already let Spyder McGraw know what's going on?"

I wiped my nose with the back of my wrist. "Spyder's still off-grid. I have no idea when he'll get home."

"Were you assigned a different partner while he's gone?"

"No, sir. I only ever worked for Spyder—he sort of wanted to keep me a secret." I still couldn't believe Mom had sat Dave down and told him all about my apprentice-ship with Spyder McGraw. Under Spyder's tutelage, I was following my dream of becoming an Intelligence Officer, learning to out-think and out-maneuver the bad guys trying to hurt American interests. And like anyone heading toward a life in the intelligence community, my skills needed to go under the radar. Now that my mom had died, only four people—Spyder, the Millers, and Dave—knew that side of my life. I would prefer Dave didn't know.

"Still, did you consider bringing this to Spyder's commander? Iniquus would probably give him a heads up. Get a message to him."

"Iniquus is my last resort. Sure, Spyder told me to talk to them if I ever found myself in trouble." I sucked in a deep breath of air. "Bottom line? He never wanted them to know I worked for him, well, for them. Safety in anonymity and all that." My fingers kneaded the stuffing in the pillow. "Besides, I guess I was hoping this would all just go away."

Dave's eyes were hard on me. "You know better. Once some psycho's caught you on his radar, you're stuck there until someone wins."

"Okay, so I make sure it's me who wins."

"Exactly right." He considered me for a minute before he asked, "You've kept up with your martial arts training?"

"I have a sparring partner who's pretty good. We rent time at a Do Jang twice a week."

Dave lowered his head to read over the poem again. He put the letter and envelope back in the Zip-loc and placed it on his mantle. Pulling off his gloves with a snap, he looked down at them. "I hate these things. They give me a rash. Look, I'm going to take this down to the station and open a file. If you get anything else, I want you to bring it to me right away. Understood?"

"Yes, sir."

"This is the only poem, letter, communication of any kind you've gotten?"

I nodded. For the first time since I walked into Dave's house, I became aware of sounds other than our conversation and the thrumming blood behind my eardrums. A football game played on TV. I glanced over as the announcer yelled some gibberish about a first down, then moved my gaze back to Dave. "You must have taken graveyard shift last night," I said.

He picked up a remote, zapped off the TV, and sent me a raised eyebrow.

"It doesn't take a psychic. You look like an unmade bed."

Dave ran a hand over his dark hair, thick on the sides, sparse on top. He hadn't used a comb today or bothered to shave. He was hanging-out-at-home comfy in jeans and beat-to-hell tennis shoes. It looked like the only thing I was interrupting was the game re-run.

"Double homicide. Turned into a long night up to my ankles in sewage."

"Yum." I tried on a smile, but it was plastic and contrived.

Dave narrowed his eyes. "We need to move you. Pronto. It's priority one. You need to be someplace secure where I can keep better tabs on you."

"I've been looking since the fire, but I haven't found anything."

"Would you consider buying?" he asked.

"Yes, actually—I'm looking for a low-cost fixer-upper I can work on to help me get through this year without Angel." I followed Dave into the hallway. "Diversion, and all that."

"How about here, in my neighborhood? I could keep a better eye on you—and you won't be showing up at my door with a suitcase full of surprises." He grabbed his coat from the

closet and shrugged it on. "I'm taking you over to meet my neighbor. She has the other half of her duplex on the market." He looked over his shoulder at me. "You shouldn't be running around without a jacket." He handed me an oversized wool parka that smelled like raking leaves. He kicked a Tonka truck out of the way, and we moved out the front door.

On the front porch, I slid into the shadows and took in

the length of the road—no cars, no barking dogs, everything quiet.

Dave glanced back. "Coast is clear."

I tucked the coat hood up over my ponytail. Screened by Dave's broad back, I started across the street. Down the road, a car motor revved. I reached under my shirt and pulled out my gun.

Enjoying the read?

FIND WEAKEST LYNX IN EBOOK, PAPERBACK AND NOW HARDCOVER.

THE WORLD of INIQUUS

Chronological Order

Ubicumque, Quoties. Quidquid

Weakest Lynx (Lynx Series)

Missing Lynx (Lynx Series)

Chain Lynx (Lynx Series)

Cuff Lynx (Lynx Series)

WASP (Uncommon Enemies)

In Too DEEP (Strike Force)

Relic (Uncommon Enemies)

Mine (Kate Hamilton Mystery)

Jack Be Quick (Strike Force)

Deadlock (Uncommon Enemies)

Instigator (Strike Force)

Yours (Kate Hamilton Mystery)

Gulf Lynx (Lynx Series)

Open Secret (FBI Joint Task Force)

Thorn (Uncommon Enemies)

Ours (Kate Hamilton Mysteries)

Cold Red (FBI Joint Task Force)

Even Odds (FBI Joint Task Force)

Survival Instinct - (Cerberus Tactical K9 Team Alpha)

Protective Instinct - (Cerberus Tactical K9 Team Alpha)

Defender's Instinct - (Cerberus Tactical K9 Team Alpha)

Danger Signs - (Delta Force Echo)

Hyper Lynx - (Lynx Series)

Danger Zone - (Delta Force Echo)

Danger Close - (Delta Force Echo)

Fear the REAPER – (Strike Force)

Warrior's Instinct - (Cerberus Tactical K9 Team Bravo)

Rescue Instinct - (Cerberus Tactical K9 Team Bravo)

Heroes Instinct - (Cerberus Tactical K9 Team Bravo)

Striker (Strike Force) 2023

Marriage Lynx (Lynx Series) 2023

Blaze Ahead (Strike Force) 2023

Coming soon, more great stories from the ex-special forces security team members who live, work, and love in a tightly knit family.

ACKNOWLEDGMENTS

My great appreciation

To my publicist Margaret Daly

To my cover artist, Melody Simmons

To my editor Kathleen Payne

To my Beta Force, who are always honest and kind at the same time. M. Carlon, E. Hilder, P King, K.L.B. Napolitano, and K. Schup. Thank you, ladies!

To my Street Force, who support me and my writing with such enthusiasm and kindness.

To the real-world K9 professionals who serve and protect us.

Virginia K9 search and rescue teams for their work in our community, their dedication, and professionalism. Every time I search and train with you, I'm inspired.

To all the wonderful professionals whom I called on to get the details right—

Please note: This is a work of fiction, and while I always try my best to get all the details correct, there are times when it serves the story to go slightly to the left or right of perfection. Please understand that any mistakes or discrepancies are my authorial decision making alone and sit squarely on my shoulders.

Thank you to my family.

I send my love to my husband, T. I love all of our adventures together—and for this book, Alaska with whales and bears—they, and you, feed my creativity and enjoyment of life.

And of course, thank *YOU* for reading my stories. I'm smiling joyfully as I type this. I so appreciate you!

ABOUT THE AUTHOR

Fiona Quinn is a six-time USA Today bestselling author, a Kindle Scout winner, Amazon Top 40, and an Amazon All-Star.

Quinn writes suspense in her Iniquus World of books, including Lynx, Strike Force, Uncommon Enemies, Kate Hamilton Mysteries, FBI Joint Task Force, Cerberus Tactical K9 Series Alpha and Bravo, and Delta Force Echo series.

She writes urban fantasy as Fiona Angelica Quinn for her Elemental Witches Series.

And, just for fun, she writes the Badge Bunny Booze Mystery Collection with her dear friend, Tina Glasneck, as Quinn Glasneck.

Quinn is rooted in the Old Dominion, where she lives with her husband. There, she pops chocolates, devours books, and taps continuously on her laptop.

Visit www.FionaQuinnBooks.com

COPYRIGHT

CPSIA information can be obtained
at www.ICGtesting.com
Printed in the USA
BVHW080946230323
661008BV00006B/110